W. Wallace

Other books in the Chance series:

WILD CHANCE

Whitewater Awakening *by Ron Gamer*

Adventure Publications, Inc.
CAMBRIDGE, MINNESOTA

dedication

To Madeleine, for all you do.

This book is a work of fiction. Although the Canadian wilderness is a popular destination for fly-in fishing trips, the spider-looking lake referred to in the text; along with all characters and institutions, public or private, are inventions of the author's imagination. Any resemblance to people, living or deceased is purely coincidental and unintended.

Cover and book design by Jonathan Norberg

Cover illustration by Julie Martinez

Copyright 2005 by Ron Gamer
Published by
Adventure Publications, Inc.
820 Cleveland Street South
Cambridge, MN 55008
1-800-678-7006
www.adventurepublications.net
Printed in the U.S.A.
ISBN-10: 1-59193-128-2
ISBN-13: 978-1-59193-128-7

Chapter One

C H A P T E R   O N E

Under a sky scrubbed spotless by an overnight shower, Minnesota's Boundary Waters awoke to a clean blue ceiling. If the latest forecast could be believed, more days of delightful weather were on tap.

Far out on a scenic lake, ripples trapped sunbeams, lighting strings of pearls. The two teens perched on an old wooden pier paid no attention to the display. Instead, each had eyes trained toward the distant shore, hoping to be the first to spot an incoming aircraft.

The boys had awakened long before sunup—filled to the brim with hard-to-hide eagerness. This was the big day. After weeks of anticipation, their first fly-in fishing trip was about to begin.

Following a final review of the packing list, and after enduring hugs and safety suggestions, the two had been car-pooled to the seaplane base. Now, restlessly waiting for their ride to arrive, they passed empty time with playful bantering; usually at the expense of the other.

"So tell me, Trav, which one of us is gonna ride shotgun? Or should we flip a coin for it?" Seth Springwood inquired of his pal, Travis Larsen.

Slouched against a canvas carryall, the gangly youth considered the question. "Hmm," he murmured, turning his head lazily and squinting at his friend. "I think Bob's got a new policy about where we can sit."

"Oh, is that right? My guess is that it's a rule you just now invented. What...with those tall stilts of yours, I bet ya think you ought to park in the co-pilot's seat," Seth retorted with a wide smirk.

"Naw, you're wrong 'bout that. It's got nothing to do with long legs. Bob told me that Canadian Customs have become real picky about people crossing over the border. He said that they're not allowing in many short dudes these days. So the way I see it, you're gonna have to sit on a pillow in the back. Who knows? Maybe you'll get lucky and they won't even ask you to get out."

Travis paused, hoping for a reaction. When none came, he added, "Hey bud, don't feel bad. The fellow's just trying to do you a favor."

"Thanks a lot. You're such a kind and caring friend. I don't know what I'd do without you. But hey, at least the legs on my jeans reach my shoes. Not like those high-water pants you're sporting."

"What? You talking 'bout this?" Travis quipped; pointing to the wide patch of pasty skin displayed between a sneaker and the bottom of a pant leg.

Pushing upright, the long-limbed teen got to his feet and stretched. Then like a model showing off the latest in fashion wear, he put his hands on his hips and swirled in a circle.

"Just try hard not to turn green. Jealousy is never attractive, especially on a face like yours. Besides, these are one of a kind. I even had to order 'em special. They're called wading pants. All I have to do is slip off my shoes and jump in."

7

Seth swung his shaggy raven-haired head from side to side. "Jeez! I swear, Trav. How d'ya do it? You come up with an answer for everything."

"Better brain power...hey, would ya stop yapping for a sec? I think I hear an airplane. Over that way," Travis said, tipping the bill of his Twins cap toward the south-west. "I bet that's him. He said he'd be here between eight and nine."

Ignoring the request, Seth blurted, "Say Trav; are you as revved-up about this trip as I am? I didn't get much sleep last night."

"Yeah...me neither. What with the two close calls the past year, I'm surprised my folks let me go. Mom reminded me that trouble often comes in bundles." Travis said, remaining tight-lipped about his own sleep-disturbing thoughts.

What was it that his mother had said before he and Seth had departed on a simple canoe trip last October? He badgered his brain for a few seconds before the answer came. "Trouble," she'd advised, "can be like buying bananas. It often comes in bunches."

His mother had been on the mark. For certain the simple portage trip they'd begun from their beachfront homes on Poplar Lake had been a disaster—right from the get-go. They'd experienced everything from food-stealing bears to being trapped by the storm of the century. He and Seth had been lucky to escape with their lives.

Then there had been the winter snowstorm ordeal. Somehow he'd plucked up the courage to venture out on a solo overnight fishing trek. The weather had been ideal when he'd left home. There had been a string of warm days, gentle clear nights; so absolutely perfect for proving he had nothing to fear from Mother Nature but his own negative thinking.

Right! Almost from the very beginning he'd been plagued with problems. If it hadn't been for Seth never giving up on hope and striking out on his own to help in the search, he'd be nothing now but bleached bones. Travis shuddered silently at that mind's eye photo.

But something positive had come out of his close encounters with death. When faced by a serious problem, and if time permitted, he'd learned that keeping his wits and making a plan was the best way to come up with a solution.

A second observation had been stored away; something he found hard to put into words. Before the two awful ordeals, he'd been a real worry-wart—always looking at the dark side of what might possibly happen.

Ever since early childhood, Seth and he had been so different in the way they viewed the future. Or at least that had been what Travis believed to be the case. But being stranded by the windstorm calamity and trapped in a blizzard had made the teen look at things from the other side of the mountain.

He realized that his friend's swaggering, 'take-no-prisoners' personality was only a blustery blanket to hide beneath. It was no doubt the reason Seth was so shy when he had to speak up in a group setting. Travis realized his macho acting pal had fears and concerns identical to his own.

The difference being that Seth usually kept negative thoughts under wraps—he didn't put them into words. Instead, he plunged ahead as if he didn't have a care in the world.

* * *

"There it is! I see it!" Seth yelled, directing his gaze far over the water. "That's gotta be Bob's plane. The old guy's right on schedule."

Travis focused where Seth was pointing. Sure enough, off in the distance—but growing larger by the second—was the bee-shaped silhouette of a flying machine.

Moments later a red-trimmed floatplane banked into the light breeze. Then, like a big bird clutching tight to a pair of silver eggs, the aircraft splashed down and pointed its beak toward shore.

Travis and Seth's first surprise of the day came as the plane taxied to the dock. Anxiously awaiting Bob's arrival, the boys were surprised to see a passenger already occupying the right front seat.

The plane's pontoon gently bumped the dock, and the passenger door popped open. A willowy girl with a head of closely cropped jet-black hair stepped carefully onto a float, and then jumped to the pier.

She was dressed in faded jeans and an oversized gray sweatshirt, and made no attempt at eye contact. Instead, she stood quietly with her back to the boys, clutching a pair of tie-off ropes that snuggled a pontoon to the dock.

The pilot, Robert "Bob" Ritzer, an old family friend of the Larsens', introduced her as Jessie, his grand niece. "She's from Minneapolis and is just your age." Apparently she had a special place in her uncle's heart. He clapped a hand on her shoulder and said, "Couldn't love her more if she was my own flesh and blood."

Seth and Travis had listened without saying a word. Jessie. What kind of name was that for a girl? A nickname for Jessica? Travis thought grumpily, giving her a slight nod of the cap covering his untrimmed sand-colored hair. But more importantly, he wondered, why was she butting in on their trip and riding shotgun in the first place? This was to have been their special time—a unique gift for upcoming birthdays. Just the two of them, along with Bob, flying to a remote wilderness lake, enjoying a few days of camping, fishing, and bragging about the big one that got away. One thing was for sure, Travis determined after catching Jessie's eye: she didn't appear happy to be here.

The only bit of good news was that they'd be detouring to a wilderness fishing lodge to drop her off. There she was to spend the remainder of summer vacation working as cabin girl, dishwasher, and all-around resort 'gopher.'

* * *

Several hours later the view out a side window looked a good deal different than it had at takeoff. At the time the single-engine Cessna departed Devil Track, the sky had been color-crayon blue—not a clue of a cloud as far as an eye could reach. The first leg of the journey had been silky smooth—almost as if the floatplane was tethered to an iron rail.

After a quick stop to refuel, clear customs and secure angling permits at a remote outpost, wispy-white cotton-balls began dotting the horizon. For a time they added a pleasant variety to the otherwise endless vista of forest and water. But now more than an hour into the second half of flight, and as if preparing to do battle, the clouds were closing ranks.

The two boys slouched on the rear seat noticed the change, but said not a word. Neither wanted to hint that it might be wise to do a one-eighty and return to the fueling post. A turnabout would only delay the upcoming adventure.

What was there to worry about, anyway? Travis contemplated. Their lives were in capable hands. Bob had logged hundreds of hours, maybe thousands, in this very same airplane. The man wouldn't take any unnecessary chances; especially with three young, future-filled passengers on board.

And so what if they flew into foul weather? Possible

landing sites were too numerous to count. The green carpet below was dappled with water—lakes of all sizes and shapes—most large enough to accept a small seaplane. There were limitless bays and inlets willing to provide protection until storm clouds passed by.

It was only after a long series of roller-coaster dips and dives that the pilot's voice piped through the headsets. With a tone of grave concern, he said, "Kids, I don't know about this. We might have to change plans. Air's gettin' pretty darn bumpy. And those clouds ahead look to be spoiling for a real brouhaha. See those fat dark bottoms and rising white tops? Those, my young friends, are your textbook cumulonimbus...thunderboomers in the making."

After a moment of silence, he added, "We're gonna have to change our heading. I can't risk flying into a squall. 'Specially the way we're loaded. That canoe tied to the struts could pose a problem. It might not fare so well if the wind starts to really gust."

No sooner had the words echoed through the earphones, when a brilliant flash filled the windscreen.

"That settles it!" the pilot snorted. "We're gonna change course. Best you all keep quiet. I'll try contacting air control...maybe get directions to steer around this stuff."

Travis and Seth hunkered in the back, listening, as the man worked the radio, hoping to get a call-back to his broadcast. This flight wasn't quite what they'd imagined when they'd been teasing each other earlier, waiting for their ride to arrive.

The airman's gravelly voice broke into the boys' thoughts. "Kids, I can't seem to reach anyone. We're probably not high enough to receive a call-back. So before splashing down on one of those lakes below, I'll make a circling climb to gain some altitude. The higher we are, the farther we can broadcast."

"I'll announce our intentions on several frequencies," he added after a brief pause. "Could be that some jet-liner will hear the transmission. They can pass the message along to air control; let the controllers know we're delaying our flight plan. We don't need a search and rescue mission getting geared up while we're waiting out a bit of bad weather."

Bob made several minor control changes and then pushed the throttle full forward. After several seconds, he put the plane into a climbing turn toward an opening between a pair of broccoli-shaped clouds.

Unseen gusts continued buffeting the tiny airplane as the prop chopped the air for altitude; the engine maxed, straining hard to defy the law of gravity. Outside the passenger windows, dark cloud bellies filled the view in every direction. Hunkered in the rear, the boys' thoughts began rounding the corner from mild concern to real worry.

Was it happening again? Travis considered this question while staring through the scratched and pitted Plexiglas—reflecting on past experiences. Was his mother right? Did trouble come in bunches? Travis's mental musings were suddenly interrupted by the pilot. "Okay folks, sit still and keep mum."

The passengers sat silent, listening, as Bob radioed his intentions—that they were planning to set down for a few hours to wait out the weather. He switched to an alternate frequency and began repeating the message when his words were cut off in mid-sentence.

Without a hint of warning, blinding light enveloped the aircraft, accompanied by an eardrum-piercing screech. Then the headsets went dead, acting only as muffs against the unified racket of the engine and the wind rushing past the wings. Seconds later the acrid odor of burnt wiring, paired with the clamor coming from the exhaust, quickly filled the interior with the unpleasant union of stench and noise.

Tucked deep in the back seat, the boys looked at each other through saucer-sized eyes. Meantime up front, the pilot was busy feeling circuit breakers on the instrument panel, checking how many might have popped from the unexpected voltage surge. To his right, huddled in the other front seat, Jessie sat with her head down and eyes shut tight, clenching her hands in a tight double-fisted prayer-like position.

"What the heck was that all about?" Seth hollered over the engine clatter.

"Lightning strike!" a frantic yell came from the front. "We must have been struck by cloud-to-cloud static. Whatever it was, we've got problems. I need to change course right now. Need to get away from these clouds. If and when we find a patch of blue, we'll pick a lake and put down. We'll check the damage once we're tied up."

Bob tipped the wings in a gentle turn, leveled off, and then eased back on the power. Once the aircraft had stabilized in a slow descent, he began checking gauges. What he found was a mailbag full of bad news.

"All the electrical instruments are out!" Bob shouted. "Even our GPS." Travis felt a lurch in his stomach. Getting their trip underway again after they set down would be more difficult without the recently installed GPS unit—an up-to-date Global Positioning System— that Bob had been using to track progress across the vast roadless area below.

For the next quarter hour no one peeped out so much as a sigh. Scruffy dark billows continued rushing by the cockpit windows, racing past as if they had a date with a pre-planned rain event. Eventually, to everyone's relief, the aircraft descended low enough that the pregnant-bellied vapors were above the flight path.

"This isn't working!" Bob said loud enough for all to hear. "I don't see any blue sky. Help me choose a lake to land on. Try to find a big one with a bay where we can tie up out of the wind."

The boys trained their eyes on the green-fuzzed haze of the forest a few thousand feet below. Although countless lakes speckled the landscape, neither saw one that best-suited their immediate needs.

Finally, far off to the west, Seth spotted the shiny glimmer coming from a larger body of water. "Over there! To your left," he yelled. "Looks like a big one with a few islands."

"I see it. Let's have a better look," Bob hollered in reply. With a gentle touch, he nudged the nose to the left. After a moment the Cessna's propeller aligned with the lake and he steered straight ahead.

A few minutes later the aircraft made a wide, descending arc over a uniquely formed gathering of water. Peering nervously out the side window, the odd-shaped waterway reminded Travis of a giant spider. The bulk of the lake, the body, was made up of a large, open middle. Near one end, two egg-shaped islands poked up and out like eyes staring into space. Spreading out for miles in different directions—and looking much like gangly spider legs—much narrower, tree lined channels curled away from the fat middle.

Bob circled twice before deciding where he wanted to park. "No electric for the flaps," he said as much to himself as to the uneasy teenagers. "We're going to need a longer stretch than usual. Have to keep the air speed up. Make sure we don't stall."

First flying with the wind until they were well beyond the forested shoreline, Bob swung the plane back toward the lake. Next he lowered the engine's power setting. Fully loaded, and without flaps for additional lift, the aircraft began to bleed altitude faster than usual.

What had just moments before been a mat of muted greens now took on shape and substance. It appeared to the rear passengers that the forest couldn't wait for introductions and was rushing up to meet them.

Seth could make out hundreds of individual trees zipping by under the pontoons; some tall, some short, but none that he wanted to get to know personally. Travis had much the same sensation: That they were descending too fast, and were already too low to reach the water. Jessie was gripping the edges of her seat very hard, preparing for the bang of wood on metal.

But Bob knew precisely what he was doing. When it seemed the pontoons couldn't drop another foot—that the limbs and branches racing by under the floats were about to reach up and pluck the noisy bird out of the air—he pushed in the power and leveled off the aircraft. Then, just as they cleared the tree line, he pulled the throttle to the idle position, pulled gently back on the yoke, and began muttering to himself.

"Easy does it. Easy does it," he kept repeating; all the while gingerly tugging at the control wheel, holding the cowl of the Cessna slightly above the horizon.

Seconds later the step-bottomed floats kissed white-crested waves as soft and easy as any landing the man had ever made. With only the slightest hint of indecision, the aircraft stopped performing as a flying machine and became a boat.

The pontoons skimmed across the choppy waters of the unfamiliar lake—pushing out a plume of spray—tossing droplets of water up and over the side windows. As the Cessna slowed, the floats settled into the water and began forming furrows as if it were a double-bladed plow.

Chapter Two

C H A P T E R   T W O

"I'm afraid the news isn't good. Even the battery is toast. When the weather clears, we'll have to hand-prop the engine. There's no other way to start it," Bob reported glumly, extra wrinkles of concern creasing his already well-weathered brow.

He had selected the tie-up area while making the second pass over the unusual looking lake. One of the bays was well over a mile long. It would provide plenty of room for takeoff when clouds cleared, providing the wind was favorable. But more importantly, near the end of the watery arm, as the spruce- and cedar-filled shorelines drew close together, the bay made a twisting turn, forming a small harbor.

Once into the cove, Bob had taxied toward a slab of gently sloping granite. His thought was that the flat rock would serve as a natural rock pier. Then just as the pontoons were about to strike stone, he'd killed the engine, threw the door open, and lowered himself to the float.

Nimble as someone half his age, he'd jumped into the water and stopped the seaplane's progress before the floats hit the granite. With the aid of several ropes, and

17

pieces of driftwood for dent protectors, the aircraft was tied-off to nearby trees.

It only took moments for the man to find the lightening strike. He'd quickly discovered an area of what looked like burnt paint on a section of the tail, likewise for the finish on the propeller.

"I'll bet that the static charge flashed straight through the frame—sizzling wire along the way. Took out the entire electrical system. Only the engine wiring is still okay, probably because the sparkplug wires are designed to take that high voltage," Bob told the teens.

A deep reverberating rumble captured the group's attention. The young people were standing at opposite ends of the seaplane. The boys chatted nervously near the tail, joking around a thing of the past. Jessie was far off to the front, standing silent; arms folded.

"Gather up!" Bob commanded in his gravelly baritone. "I think it'd be wise to unload the camping supplies. Then we need to tug the plane farther down the bay.

"Over there," he said, pointing toward a marshy section of shore near the end of the cove. "It's probably best if we pull the pontoons partway up on that swamp grass. Then we'll tie 'em to a couple of sturdy trees."

"I really expect that this weather will pass by in an hour or two, maybe less. But if it doesn't, I think the safe thing for now is to act as if we're staying the night. As long as the pontoons are resting sideways, we can empty the cargo hold in minutes," Bob said in a businesslike manner.

"One of you fellows hop up on the float and open the baggage door," he directed, ignoring the look on his niece's face. "The other one can wade in the water and pass the bags to Jessie and me. We'll pile everything over by the edge of the woods," he said, nodding to where spindly birch, spruce, and cedar sprouted from cracks and splinters in the block of granite.

Seth did as told, jumping up on the pontoon and unlatching the baggage door. Then the burly teen reached in and began lowering the first of four duffel sacks. He passed a blue bag to Travis, who in turn passed it to their pilot.

"What about fishing poles?" Seth asked after the duffels had been removed.

"Sure, grab those too. You fellows can cast from shore while we wait out the weather. Who knows...."

The man's words were cut short by a sharp flash. Striking directly across the waterway, the lightening bolt had shattered the tip off a tall pine. For a moment all were too startled to do anything but stare at the smoldering tree top. Jessie stood petrified in place—eyes wide and face pale.

"Hurry up!" Bob yelled to Seth. "We're about to be hit by a squall. We need to get the plane tied off, pronto!"

Seth pitched the fishing rods out the cargo door. Somehow Travis was able to catch all three without doing damage. Passing the poles to Bob, Travis asked, "Anything else we need to pull out?"

"Ahh," the man muttered, thinking aloud. "Probably my flight bag and the cooler tucked in the rear. I'll need to study the charts to find out just where we are. But that can wait 'til after we're tied down. We're out of time. We've got to get the plane to the end of the lake and secure it before winds drop from that thunder-boomer."

"How are we gonna do that?" Seth asked, jumping from the pontoon. "We sure can't pull it with the Wenonah," he said, pointing to the skinny canoe strapped tight along the far float.

"You'll have to walk in the water and tow it," was Bob's quick reply. "Jessie, untie that line and give the end to Seth. Travis, unhitch the other rope and hold it snug. Seth, go ahead and grab the loose end of Jessie's cord. Tie it to the cleat on the far float. The three of you can wade in the water and pull. I'll stay along the shore and make certain the wing doesn't smack a tree. Got it?"

Jessie untied the cord closest to her, then stooped to remove her shoes.

"Leave 'em on!" Bob warned. "Some of those rocks are sharp and you'll need your shoes to protect you."

"But they're new!" Jessie protested. "They'll be ruined!"

Bob barked out a stern command. "Jess, get in and help! You can always buy a new pair of shoes!" He knew they were running out of time.

Grimacing, Jessie stepped gingerly into the lake and gasped as the icy water flooded into her shoes. But once she had the rope in her hands and began to tug, the boys were surprised that the plane pulled much easier. Jessie was stronger than either would have guessed.

To the ever-closer applauding of thunder, the teens sloshed and stumbled toward the marshy end of the bay; a gigantic red and white pull toy bobbing behind them.

They were within yards of their goal when a deluge fell from the sky, drenching the towing crew in seconds. Torrents of rain—buckets of rain—obscured the forest only a few dozen yards away.

Seconds later a sudden wind turned the rain sideways, snatched the aircraft with the force of a dozen hands, yanked the tow crew off their feet, and plunged them face first into chilly water.

Upon being jerked into the lake, Seth had quickly regained his footing. He tried planting his feet. But even as Travis and Jessie, both coughing lake water, added their weight to the line, he knew it was no good. They had no choice but to release the rope, or like puppets on a string, be dragged into deeper water. The trio watched helplessly as their link to civilization was whisked away into a murky haze.

It only got worse. Just as they reached the marshy beachfront, a terrific roar rose above the din of thunder and rain. With the howl of a jet engine on takeoff, a whirlwind dropped toward earth. The miniature tornado couldn't have made a more direct hit. Precise as a guided missile, the tiny twister targeted the edge of the cove.

"Get down!" Seth shouted. "Grab onto something!"

The teens plopped face first onto the swampy shore, grasped handfuls of weedy grass, and then held on for their lives.

Bob hadn't fared any better. When the first of the heavy gusts struck, dunking the teens and threatening to push the aircraft out into the bay, he'd frantically plunged after it. But once the water became waist deep, the man realized his efforts were hopeless.

The 'pride and joy' he'd polished and buffed for more than twenty years was about to become a memory. He'd barely sloshed back to land when the funnel passed overhead. Reaching shore, he'd flopped flat, clutched tight to a tree, and prayed his charges had done the same.

This fierce little thunderstorm was a classic summer squall. As quickly as it had chased in, the rain and wind departed, racing away to do damage elsewhere. Left in its wake, four soaked-to-the-skin souls lay quaking with fright and dismay.

After a long fear filled moment, Bob rose on wobbly legs and hollered down the shore. "Everyone okay?"

"Yo!" Seth bellowed as he rose to his knees and then

stood. "We're all here. I don't think anybody's hurt. Are you?" he asked, turning toward the others still snuggled in the reeds.

Jessie and Travis rolled over and sat up. Sitting on soggy bottoms in wet weeds, their rain soaked heads scarcely topped the vegetation.

"I'm okay. What 'bout you, Jessie?" Travis asked, swiping a clump of swamp grass off his forehead.

"Terrific. Never been better," she mumbled shakily while wringing out the bottom half of her sweatshirt. Travis noticed that tears, not rain water, streamed down her cheeks, glistening in brilliant sunlight that had magically reappeared.

"Thank God!" Bob exclaimed as he sloshed closer. "Are you sure you're all okay? No cuts or bruises?"

"We're fine, Bob. But I guess we can't say the same for your Cessna," Travis said morosely, pointing across the cove opposite the granite pier. "Looks like our ride didn't fare so well."

All turned to look. Across the bay, bobbling gently on the now sun dappled surface, were a pair of aluminum floats. The angry water spout might have been under-sized, but it had been big enough to flip an aircraft—bottom-side up.

Chapter Three

C H A P T E R   T H R E E

There was no pleasant way to put it—they were stranded. The first task now was to return to the wedge of bedrock and see if the camping equipment had been blown away.

The duffels were where they'd been dropped, resting undisturbed on the wide slab of granite. Other than several stunted trees being tipped, roots and all, and a few leaves and broken branches, the site looked much as it had before the squall blew through.

Without uttering a word, Jessie plopped onto her luggage bag. Frowning, she took off her shoes and started wringing out her socks.

"What first?" Travis asked, knowing they had to work to do. "Reach the plane or set up camp?"

After glancing at his watch, Bob said, "Well, let's see. It's almost two now. Being the end of June, the sun won't set 'til ten or so. That gives us at least eight hours of good light. Which one of you is the strongest swimmer?"

"Why? What's that got to do with anything?" Seth asked, pulling his duffel closer to the trees.

"Because I'm thinking one of you will have to hike

around the bay, and then swim out to the plane. You'll need to find the tow line. We'll want to pull the floats as close to shore as we can. There's stuff in the cockpit and cargo space we could use."

"Like what?" Travis asked. "Don't we have everything we need right here? It shouldn't take long for search flights to find us."

"Yeah...maybe—maybe not. But unless you catch a fish or two, we're gonna get mighty hungry come sunrise. Remember, the cooler's still in the cockpit. The same thing's true for the flight bag with all the maps," Bob said, rubbing his chin in thought.

Hearing the mention of fish, and without looking up, Jessie muttered, "I don't eat anything that comes from animals. I only eat food that comes from plants."

Travis and Seth eyed each other with brows raised as if to say 'what color is the sky in this girl's world?' Her Uncle Bob tried a bit of tact.

In a gentle voice, he said, "Well, my dear, I don't think you'll starve. There's a box of powdered food packets in the cooler, bundles of freeze-dried veggies. We should have it out before dark. But, if you do get hungry before then, maybe you can find some berries. I don't think the blueberries are ready, but you might get lucky and find some partially ripe raspberries."

"I'm not going into those woods. I'd be lost in a minute. I'd rather go hungry."

Exhaling a soft sigh, and with a slight nod of his crinkly, gray-haired head, Bob gave up. "Okay, but if you change your mind, just walk along the lakefront. As long as you see water, you won't get confused."

"Right," Travis smiled, attempting a touch of humor. "Just remember to keep whistling. It'll give the bears and wolves time to scamper out of your way."

The girl's dark eyes opened wide. "Bears! Wolves! Forget it! I'm staying put. Sleeping out with wild animals wasn't part of my contract."

Bob gripped his niece's shoulder and said sternly, "Jessie, get your act together. No bears or wolves are going to bother you. The boys are just joshin'. Now then, we've got work to do. You can help by opening the duffels and pulling out the tent sacks."

Bob released his hold and then nodded toward the water. "Look down the lake. More rain clouds are on their way. If you want your things to stay dry, we'll need the tents up before round two arrives."

As if to validate his statement, a distant thunderclap grumbled in agreement.

Turning to the boys, Bob asked, "Have you decided which one of you is gonna be doin' the diving? With that second squall line bearin' down, I think it'd be wise of us to salvage all we can right away."

Travis studied the sky and then looked at his buddy.

"We're both good swimmers. But Seth is stronger when it comes to lifting things. Why don't you two hike to the plane? I'll stay here and get the tents up. It shouldn't take long. I've certainly had lots of practice."

"Jessie, are you all right with that?" Bob asked. "If not, you can come along with Seth and me."

"Oh...whatever. As long as someone stays here, I'll be okay," she mumbled toward the ground.

* * *

Trekking the lakefront ate more time than Seth would have guessed. Although the pontoons were bobbing just across the bay, less than a quarter mile distant, the trip around was nearly a mile of hard travel. It had taken a half-hour of wading, slogging, and crawling over windfalls before the pair reached the site.

There'd been plenty of opportunity to discuss what should be attempted first. At the top of the list was cutting the canoe loose. They could use it to paddle the remaining gear to camp, and then later, to fish from.

They arrived none to soon. The second round of rain was approaching; announcing its arrival with flashes of lightening and rolls of thunder. Without a moment's delay, Seth splashed headlong into the lake. Several dozen swift strokes later he arrived at the overturned aircraft.

Pulling himself up on at the end of an upside down pontoon, the youth went to work on the boat bindings. The razor-edged blade of his survival tool sliced the half-dozen nylon straps with no more effort that cutting through toasted bread.

The difficulty came when it was time to push the canoe to the surface. Built-in air pockets forced the skinny boat to rise tight to the metal float.

Again and again, in lung-testing bursts, Seth dove under; each time tugging the canoe closer to the surface. Nearing exhaustion, and with muscles cramping from frigid water, the teen finally wiggled the Wenonah free.

By the time the canoe was completely liberated, his energy was spent, at least until he caught his wind. But chilled to the bone, and only after a very brief rest, Seth began dog-paddling, gulping air, pushing the half-submerged watercraft toward shore.

Moments later, with Bob's help, Seth beached the canoe. Once the gunnels were above lake level, they began rocking the canoe back and forth.

Each time they tipped the canoe, more water sloshed out, making it easier to pull the craft farther on land. Finally they'd emptied enough to roll the canoe over and pour the liquid back to where it belonged.

"What next?" Seth wheezed, once the canoe was empty. "Think I should try to get the rope? You realize, don't you, that it won't be long enough. And I don't think we can pull the plane much closer. It's not more than eight or nine feet deep out there. The tail's gonna drag bottom."

"What I think," Bob said, "is you should try to unhitch that second rope from the far side. If we hitch the two lines together, it just might just reach."

A brilliant bolt of lightening lit the sky. The instantaneous earsplitting crack that followed left both open-mouthed.

After the clap echoed away, Bob had a change of heart. "Seth, I don't want you going back in the water. Not until these clouds pass. Those metal floats will act like lightning rods. If they attract even the smallest charge, you'll be fried like crispy chicken. As much as we'll need the flight bag and cooler, they're not worth risking your life over. Let's tote the canoe further inland and then find a low spot to hunker down. You can do the diving later."

The Wenonah had just been tucked into the woods when the cloudburst struck—huffing in with rain, wind, and pea-sized hail. Through the haze-filled downpour, Bob and Seth huddled under a cedar, hoping the outburst would be short lived.

The pontoons, urged on by the latest wind spurt, starting moving up and down, and then in the foggy mist of the wind-chopped surface, disappeared from view.

* * *

Travis had three tents up and ready to tie down in a matter of minutes. Because the girl had been on the way to a lodge, the only thing she brought along in the way of camping gear was a sleeping bag, a thin satiny affair better suited for slumber parties than outdoor use. Without a shelter of her own, Travis concluded, she'd just have to double up with her uncle.

Once Jessie had pulled the bright-colored tent sacks into daylight, she'd returned to her perch on her carryall. There she sat, drying her now semi-damp clothing in the soon-to-be disappearing sun rays.

"Do you want to help me set up the tents?" Travis asked, trying to make conversation.

"I don't have a clue what you're doing. From what Uncle Bob told me, you're the hotshot woodsman. You shouldn't need my help."

While it was true that Travis didn't need help getting the tents set up, he thought it would be a good way to get Jessie to settle in a bit more. Travis had never met someone who was so uncomfortable in the woods. Before too long, he had the tree tents propped open and ready to be placed.

"Where would you rather be, out here on the rock or in the woods?" he asked, ready to secure Bob's two-person enclosure.

"What difference does it make? We're only gonna be here one night, right?" Jessie muttered.

Travis shook his head in frustration. He'd fix the tent on the flat rock alongside the wood-line.

"Jeez! What's with all these flies biting at my ankles?" The girl complained moments later.

Travis couldn't help but smirk. If she thinks the flies are bad, he mulled, wait until sunset. No doubt mosquitoes would be thicker than sprinkles on a doughnut.

Keeping that thought locked tight, he said instead, "That's why I asked where you wanted the tent. Do you want it out here on the rock where it'll catch a breeze, or in the woods? It's your call."

Jessie was slow to reply. After an awkward silence, she said, "What do I know? I don't know a thing about camping. Truth be told, I'm not even sure why I'm here."

Travis was tying down the bigger tent when the lightning bolt cracked across the cove. As he'd labored he'd been curious about Bob and Seth's progress. He'd even stopped to watch when the two had emptied the canoe.

But with the squall line closing, there wasn't much time to complete his tasks. He went back to work, scurrying to get tents tied down before being drenched.

He had just tied off Seth's shelter, and was about to do his own, when a look over his shoulder said the contest was ending. He was about to lose. A torrent of water was dashing down the lake, racing toward the campsite.

"Come on!" Travis yelled to Jessie. "We've gotta get everything inside before it starts pouring!"

Without a moment's delay, the teen dragged his well used shelter a few feet into forest. Quickly tying the corners to saplings, he sprinted back to the opening.

The lightning strike had jolted Jess to life. Travis was pleased to see her bustling Bob's duffel to the larger tent. Once there, she unzipped the door, crawled inside, and pulled the bag in behind her. She emerged a second later and did the same with her fabric carryall.

Except this time she remained inside.

Chapter Four

C H A P T E R   F O U R

Four sodden campers stood close to the flames, attempting to dry damp clothing. Following the second round of wind, rain, and hail, Travis had ventured into the woods. He returned a short time later loaded down with an armful of dead wood. Fire starting was his specialty. Within minutes he had a hot fire burning.

The sky refused to clear after the second squall moved on. Thick wooly clouds continued rolling above the horizon. Afternoon light remained dull and dreary, the lake face reflecting a gunmetal gray. The temperature also made a harsh alteration, from warm and muggy to brisk and blustery. Cool enough that most biting insects had gone into hiding.

Bob and Seth had condensed the trip to camp by using the canoe. Seth had conveniently taped a pair of paddles to the thwarts. The Wenonah was a new lightweight Kevlar model borrowed from his supervisor, friend, and outdoor tutor, Rollie Kane.

Rollie and his wife Kate were the elderly owners of a lakeside retreat nestled along the Gunflint Trail. The Springwoods had moved into one of the resort cottages several seasons earlier. In trade for rent and utilities,

Seth, his sister Sarah, and their mother helped manage the rustic lodge.

The three life vests Seth had taken on loan were another matter. The orange flotation aids had been tucked in the back of the cargo bay. Seth pictured them floating in the overturned aircraft somewhere in the open part of the lake. The curve in the bay blocked their view, so they weren't certain where the plane had ended up.

Despite an on-again, off-again mist, Bob instructed his sodden charges to listen up. They had plans to make and items to inventory. As they huddled together, waiting for the elder to begin, Travis was troubled by the color of Bob's face.

Travis couldn't remember not knowing the man. In the years before retirement, Mr. Ritzer worked with Travis's father on scores of wildlife projects. Travis found it hard to believe that Bob was well into his seventies. That he was really that old didn't seem possible.

The alert, easygoing chap often acted and moved more like a youngster than most adults. Bob was always helpful, full of life, and quick to praise. So when did he grow old? Travis pondered, sneaking another look at the man's skin tone.

It wasn't that Bob was pale. He was too tanned and weathered for that to happen. Rather, Travis noted, the man's complexion had taken on a sallow shade, as if there was a yellowish light under his leathery skin.

Bob started talking, pulling Travis back to earth. "Okay. Here's what we're gonna do. I know you kids didn't leave home without sneaking along a few snacks. To be expected. Tell you the truth, so did I. But right now we need to collect everything edible and put it in one pile. Let's take a look at what we have to eat."

Minutes later, a small mound of munchies rested on the

rock. The heap included a several Snickers, a sealed foil containing a half dozen breakfast bars, a bag of oatmeal cookies, and a package of beef-jerky sticks.

"Jessie, I don't think everything's here." Bob said when they had again gathered about the blaze. "I know full well your dad sent a big bag of Tootsie Pops to help you lose your habit."

"Jeez! What is this, a detention center? He sent them along for me!"

"Listen up little lady! This is a serious situation, not some TV reality show. We can't expect Canadian Search and Rescue to be on this right away. Don't you remember my broadcast? I said we were setting down and waiting out the weather. So it could be quite some time before anyone realizes we're even missing."

He hesitated, getting a handle on his emotions. When he spoke again, it was in a calmer tone. "When they do start looking, they won't even know where to begin. It might be days, or it could take a week or more before we're spotted. In the meantime, I want you to empty your duffel of anything edible...now."

Reluctant as a mule leaving a warm barn on a cold day, the girl crawled inside Bob's tent. When she emerged her hands were filled with treats: Tootsie Pops, a bag of colorfully wrapped chocolate kisses, a sack of Chips Ahoy, and a jumbo-sized package of fruity gum.

"Here!" she said, dropping the sugar-loaded hoard onto the pile. "That's everything. Are you happy?"

"Thank you," Bob replied, offering a small smile. "That's more like it. Tell you what, Jess. You can be in charge of this stash. Put it all into one of the tent sacks and tuck it in our shelter. If we come up short on fish or berries, we'll dip into it. Right now the safest thing to do is squirrel everything away for emergency use. That sound 'bout right to you fellows?"

Seeing both boys nod in agreement, Bob moved on. Because the day had become blustery, he declared it too chancy to paddle about in the canoe, especially without life jackets. Gathering food was the next priority.

Travis and Seth had packed along small tackle boxes. The plan was for the boys to amble along the cove's beach, casting lures in hopes of hooking a meal. Fish of any size would receive a warm welcome in camp. And while the boys plied the waters, Bob and Jess would search for berries. They would regroup at the campsite in a couple hours.

* * *

"What's your take on Jessie? Is she weird or what?" Seth inquired of Travis once the twosomes had split and gone their separate ways.

The boys were slogging the forested lakefront, heading for the swampy end of the bay. Travis reckoned they'd have better luck near the weed-line as it'd provide cover for fish to hide.

"Well, she's different, that's for sure. Definitely not a happy camper. But what I don't get, if she doesn't like the outdoors, why was she headed for a fishing lodge in the first place? Seems to me that'd be the last place she'd wanna be," Travis said, dodging an overhanging limb.

Seth chewed on the remark for a few wet steps before responding. "Did you catch the bit about signing a contract? What's that all about? She shouldn't have had to sign anything to work as a waitress or dishwasher. And then there was Bob's remark about the Tootsie Pops. I don't know Trav, it doesn't add up."

"Well, I can tell you this much. Even before all our troubles, she seemed out of it. She's got something stewing on her back burner. Whatever. It's none of our business. Our concern right now is to catch a few fish."

There's an old saying bait casters spout when fish refuse to bite; 'you oughta have been here yesterday.' That axiom held true for the pair of hopeful anglers. They'd snagged weeds, branches, and an occasional rock, but only a single small pike had been harvested before time ran out.

* * *

"One little jack! That's all you caught? Heck, I'd figured you fellows would come back with at a least limit," Bob snorted as the fishermen trudged in with only a skinny northern impaled on a stick.

"Later, Bob. Just before dark. We'll probably catch some big ones then," Travis retorted, plopping close to the rekindled fire. Wearing waterlogged shoes and soaked jeans, the youth was shivering.

"So, how'd you do? Find any berries?" Seth asked, standing with his back to the blaze.

"Not many. A few not-quite-ripe raspberries, but we really didn't wander very far. Jessie's skittish about going into the woods. You fellows have to remember she's a city kid. This is all new to her. She must be terrified."

"So where is she now?" Seth asked, dropping the pike and plopping next to his buddy.

"Jessie's in the tent. Said she wasn't feeling well. I told her to puff up my mattress pad and crawl into her bag. But that's okay. I wanted to talk to the two of you in private anyway," Bob said softly, ambling closer.

"I'm going to be up front. I'm not doing all that well, myself. I got light-headed when Jess and I were hiking the woods; enough so that I thought I was going faint. I don't want to worry you none, but I think until we get located, you two rascals will have to carry most the load. I've got a throbbing headache. Probably shouldn't push my luck."

An alarm went off in Travis's brain. The earlier observation had been accurate. Studying Bob's facial features doubled the youth's concern. The man looked older now than he had just hours earlier.

After making eye contact with Seth, Travis stood, forced a smile, and reassured his old friend. "No problem. With it being the middle of summer, our biggest hassle will come from flies and mosquitoes."

"And don't worry. We'll catch plenty of fish. Right, Seth? As a matter of fact, I'll clean this scrawny jack and cook it right now. Then afterwards, while we go land some real keepers, you can take a nap."

Once the fish was cleaned, Travis threw out a suggestion. "Tell ya what," he said, "Since that fish is so skinny and loaded with little bones, let's make chowder."

"Ever do it that way? You always fried those little sunnies you caught when we were stranded last fall," Seth said.

"Yeah, I have. That's the way I did that trout fillet last winter. What you do is use a pot instead of a pan. Fill it about two thirds full of water, then drop in the fish. Let the water boil and steam away. Once that's happening, take a stick or a fork and break the meat into tiny pieces."

Seth retrieved a small pot from the cook set and then walked to the lake's edge. "What about all the little Y-bones?" he asked, scooping up a pot-full of water. "Won't they be a problem?"

"Not if we strain the soup through a cloth. Heck, even Jessie can have some. If you boil the water long enough, everything just dissolves. We'll tell her it's a broth mix we brought from home."

Later, when the soup was ready, Travis toted a steaming

cupful to Bob's tent. "Jessie. We heated up some broth. Would you like a cup?"

The reply seeped through fabric in a small voice. "No. Go ahead. Have it yourself. I'm really not hungry."

"Are you sure? There's enough for all of us."

"Yeah, I am. I'll just hang out in here for a while."

Travis shrugged and trudged back to the fire. "Says she doesn't want any," he reported.

Seth took a sip from his cup, swallowed, and nodded his approval. "It's her loss, boss. This stuff isn't half bad. 'Course it could be that it tastes so good 'cause I'm half-starved." He took a second swallow and then asked Bob for the time.

Bob pulled up his sleeve and looked at his watch. "Almost seven-thirty. You two still have plenty of light to catch something big enough to fry. Travis, if you don't mind, I'm going to lie down in your tent. Maybe after a tad of rest I'll feel good enough to try some fishing myself."

"Good idea," Travis answered, hoping the warble in his voice didn't give away his worry. "Seth, let's work the shore in the other direction. Maybe we'll get lucky enough to catch a few fish and spot the plane...both."

"Okay, let's get to it," Seth said, setting his cup on the rock and picking up his rod. He was soon treading along the shoreline, ready to do battle with anything that would bite.

A short while later both fishermen waded to an automobile-sized boulder rising out of the water. They'd use the mammoth rock as a casting platform; hoping lures would be better able to reach feeding fish.

"So what's going on with Bob? Or didn't you notice?" Seth asked while retrieving his bait.

"Notice? Jeez, how could I help but notice? He looks awful. I don't know, maybe all the stress got to him," Travis replied, jerking his rod tip as he cranked the reel.

"Trav! I got one! A good one!" Seth interrupted, holding his pole high. "How much did we bet on the first keeper? Five bucks, right?"

As Travis predicted, fishing improved before sunset, although it'd be too cloudy to witness that event. A depressing blanket still drooped over the lake, darkening the day. The boys tramped into campsite shortly before dusk and despite the murky awning overhead, a lingering occurrence this far north.

They were feeling good about their success. Seth had pulled in several walleyes; including one that went well over three pounds. Travis had managed to hook on to a medium-sized pike and a two-pound lake trout. There would be enough fillets for several servings.

All the angling had been done from the big rock. From that location neither had been able to spot the pontoons. But they'd talked it over and weren't worried about locating the aircraft. Early the next morning, when the wind was down, they'd investigate with the canoe. They felt confident they'd be able to salvage the food container and other items shortly after sunrise.

It was eerily quiet when they returned to camp. Apparently Bob and Jess were sleeping. Seeing no real reason to disturb either, the boys went about their business, talking only now and then in hushed tones.

Each had grown up on the shores of Poplar Lake. Both were equally skilled at cleaning fish. Within minutes of their return, eight fillets were soaking in a pot, ready for someone to take on the role of chef.

While Seth filleted the final walleye, Travis ventured after more firewood. Without sunshine, and with a biting wind blowing off the lake, the air held a definite chill. Before calling it a day, they needed fire to dry socks and shoes.

"So what d'ya think? Should we wake 'em up?" Seth asked, tending to the pan of fish.

Before rekindling the blaze, he had positioned flat stones into a crude circle. After Travis had the fire burning, they'd waited for flames to subside before placing the pan on the rocks. They knew the secret for cooking fish properly was to have patience. Heating the thin pieces too rapidly only caused the outside to char. Meanwhile the inside remained raw and uncooked.

"Jeez, I don't know. From the dull look of Bob's eyes, I think we should just let the man sleep. Only thing is, it'll be dark soon and he's in my tent."

"Well, if we aren't going to wake them, you might as well double-up with me. We can turn my mattress pad sideways and open up my sleeping bag to use as a blanket. I know it's chilly, but it's not nearly as cold as last October. Tired as I am, I shouldn't have trouble falling asleep."

Chapter Five

C H A P T E R   F I V E

Settling in, and after whispering a few words about the devastating set of events, both youths had fallen fast asleep. A few hours later Travis awoke just as a loon's haunting laugh faded in the distance.

Dreary light was already oozing through the thin tent fabric. A measly four or five hours after slipping below the horizon, the sun was already rising again, ready to reign over a new day. Not fully awake, Travis couldn't decide if he should try nodding off or get up.

One thing was certain, muscles and joints disapproved the sleeping situation.

During the night he'd rolled off the pad they were supposedly sharing. And because the nylon tent floor made a lousy mattress, he'd spent most of that short night dozing on rock. After a painful stretch of arms and legs, aching limbs said it was already past time to get moving.

The teen had turned in fully clothed, so when he crawled outside he was already dressed. To his surprise, he wasn't the first one awake. Jessie was squatting near the lake's edge, staring over flat water.

The second thing Travis noted was a blue-gray swirl of

rising smoke. For a brief moment he thought she had a fire burning. That notion was short lived. He watched silently as Jessie's hand rose to her face. The arm movement was followed by a second skyward curl haloing over the girl's head.

A puzzle piece tumbled into place. The Tootsie Pops, he recognized, had to be substitutes for cigarettes. Without making a sound, Travis reversed directions. He had no reason to spy. Besides, there was no rush get up. He'd could wait a few minutes and then come out again, making enough noise to be noticed.

Once inside, Travis nudged his slumbering pal, and in a hoarse whisper said, "Seth, you awake?"

"Hmm...I am now. It can't be time to get up already? We just went to bed."

"Yeah, it almost is. It's startin' to get light. The sun will be up soon. The wind's down and the water's smooth as glass. I think we ought to hop in the canoe and go look for the plane."

"Yeah...okay, I suppose. Give me a minute," Seth said in a voice raspy with sleep.

Remembering why he'd returned, Travis mouthed, "Oh, I almost forgot. Jessie's up. She's at the lake, sucking on a cigarette. Can you believe it? I thought you oughta know so you don't go puttin' your foot in your mouth."

"Huh? Whatever," Seth grunted, pulling the top of the sleeping bag tight to his chin. "You go ahead. I'll be up in a few minutes."

Travis hacked a couple of coughs, and then stumbled outside. He needn't have bothered making a racket. The girl was gone, vanished like the smoke she'd been puffing minutes earlier. For a time, Travis stood tall, rocking back and forth, thinking. Satisfied he could hobble without hurt, he shuffled to the shoreline.

During the night the clouds had cleared, and a few stars still glittered overhead. A crisp pre-dawn chill filled the air; cold enough that splotches of foggy vapor lay in long strips above the lake surface. Sucking in a deep breath, Travis tasted tobacco smoke mingling with the musty scent of leaves rotting on the forest floor behind camp.

A scan in both directions revealed nothing new—only woods and water. In the dim light he could discern the dark shapes of trees along the lakefront and soft wavelets lapping gently on beach rocks.

Jess must have walked into the woods for privacy or snuck back into Bob's tent, Travis determined. Curious as to which, he stood quiet, listening for any clue of her whereabouts.

From somewhere deep in the woods a raven's raucous caw announced that the day was open for business. Moments later the rifle-like report of a beaver's tail smacked from the far end of the cove.

The young outdoorsman knew the large water rodents made that sound only when startled. Something, or somebody, had to have frightened the animal or wouldn't have splashed the alarm.

Travis turned to study the hazy wall of trees and brush encircling the bay. And then he saw her, the gray sweat-shirt barely silhouetted against murky forest shadows.

Why was she there? And what was she doing?

Travis was so focused in thought that he failed to hear his friend approach. When tapped on the shoulder, he jumped in shock, nearly falling into lake.

"Jeez, Trav, I didn't mean to give ya heart attack. So, what are you gawking at?"

"Check it out for yourself," Travis muttered, indicating the end of the cove. "Go figure, will ya? Our reluctant camping companion is wandering around down there. But I haven't got a clue what she's doing. Is she looking for something?"

"Yeah, I see her. That's the spot where we hunkered down. It looks like she's wading. Maybe she dropped something."

"Speaking of looking for things, we better get cracking before the wind comes up. You ready to work?" Travis goaded, gazing at canoe resting near the wood-line.

Soon the slick craft was cutting water; the only sound was that of paddles rippling the placid surface. And although the sun hadn't yet pushed all the way over the earth's edge, it announced its presence with long shafts of yellow light; casting a golden hue on the window-paned lake face.

The boys stroked without speaking until they were a good distance from camp.

"Trav, don't you think it's odd that Bob's still in bed? Cripes, he turned in long before dark. That's, what, a nine- or ten-hour nap?"

Travis rested his paddle across the gunnels, considering the weight of Seth's query. "Somethin' like that. Too long, I should think. I'm starting to get worried."

He picked up the paddle before adding, "One thing for sure, he wasn't himself after the storm. But then, who can blame him? Gosh, with his plane trashed and the four of us stranded who the heck knows where? I have to tell ya though; I've never seen him so worn out. He's looking like an old man."

For a time they went on quietly, each lost in thought. Full light was only minutes away. From the nearby forest a chorus of bird whistles and chirps rejoiced at the sun's return, celebrating a glorious start to a new day.

Seth broke into the warbling festivity. "I'm telling ya,

Trav, that Jessie sure is a strange one. What's the funny word we learned in English class? The term used to describe opposites? Wasn't it like 'oxen-moron' or somethin' like that?"

"The word is oxymoron, you dimwit. Cripes, Seth, don't you remember? Mrs. Crawley made us do a whole list of 'em. They're terms like hot water heater or jumbo shrimp. Or the one my dad thinks is so funny...government intelligence. You know, words that when you think about them, don't make sense being put together. But what's that got to do with Jess?"

"Well for one thing, smoking. She says she doesn't eat meat. Like meat's gonna pollute her insides. Then she turns around and puffs on cigarettes. Aren't those things kinda like opposites? One's good, the other bad?"

"Sorta, I guess. But I don't know if you'd call that an oxymoron. I don't know enough about her yet to say. I don't know. I think she's had some trouble."

"Yeah, you're probably right. Who knows where she's comin' from. But one thing's certain; she isn't the friendliest kid in the woods."

"Hey! I hate to be the one to tell you, but you aren't always Mr. Cheerful yourself. And don't forget, she's Bob's niece. So for now, let's just cut her some slack."

The boys had been keeping the canoe close to the curved shoreline. A few hundred yards ahead lay the large body of open water. Surprisingly, they had yet to catch sight of their flipped-over transportation.

"What d'ya think? Right or left?" Seth asked as the canoe entered the big lake.

"I don't know. Which way was the wind blowing last night?"

"Well, let's see. When we were fishing, weren't the waves going away from us? That'd be that direction,"

Seth said, using the blade of his paddle to point across several miles of open water.

Travis gnawed on that for a moment before making a proposal. "Why don't we beach the canoe and one of us can climb a tree. When the sun's full up, spotting the floats should be easy. I'd think they'd act like a couple big mirrors."

The boys targeted a medium-sized pine growing near the lake's edge. It'd make a perfect lookout roost as its limbs were spaced like rungs of a ladder. After receiving a boost to reach the first branch, Travis had scurried skyward with the ease of a bear cub.

The teen was hanging tight to a sturdy bough, viewing a spectacular sunrise, when Seth yelled up for a report. "D'ya see it?" He'd hollered from his much safer seat on the weathered trunk of a fallen tree.

"Not yet. Sure wish I had a pair of binoculars. You know, the lake didn't look this big from the air. It's gotta be three or four miles over to the other end. Sure wouldn't want to get caught crossing if a wind starts blowin'."

"I hear you. We better shake a leg. But don't ya see anything?"

"Well, duh! I see lots of things, but not the airplane," Travis yelled down, his eyes scanning the surface for anything out of the ordinary. "Hold on! Look to the right, 'bout halfway across. I can't tell if that's a big boulder sticking its head out of the water or the pontoons," Travis bellowed, not certain what he was looking at.

The color seemed right, a buffed gray. But the object looked low in the water; not riding high like the pontoons should appear. But, because it was the only thing he could see, they chose to check it out.

As often happens, a breeze rose along with the morning

sun. Shortly into the paddle, a fresh draft began fanning at the boys' backs. Fifteen minutes later the Wenonah pulled alongside a pair of half-sunken pontoons.

"What gives? Why are they so low?" Travis asked, reaching out with the paddle to snag a tie-up rope.

Seth steadied the canoe by placing his paddle tip on the aluminum float. "Some of the air chambers must be leaking. If I remember right, they have flaps on the top side, holes to stick in a hose and pump out water that might have seeped in. They must be working in reverse. And if all the rivets aren't super tight, air escapes, water trickles in. Every time the pontoons bob up and down, they're probably taking on more of the lake."

"Well, we're here, so what's next? You think you can dive deep enough to get in the cockpit? You know, don't you, the water's gonna be awfully cold. It felt like ice yesterday and that was near the shallow end of a bay where the sun had a chance to warm it up."

"All I can do is give it a try. What should I go for first— Bob's bag or the cooler?"

"I'd say the flight bag. It was on the floor, tucked under the front seats. You should be able to reach it through either door. The cooler's way in back. It won't be easy gettin' at it."

With Travis steadying the canoe, Seth transferred his weight to the float and climbed aboard. Then he raced to remove tennis shoes, windbreaker and sweatshirt before stripping off his jeans. Next, after rolling everything in a ball, he dropped the bundle into the canoe and prepared himself for the plunge.

He hadn't as much as put a toe in the water but was already shivering. "Tell me again how I qualified for this job," Seth stammered through chattering teeth. "It seems to me that it's your turn to take a bath. I had mine yesterday, cutting the canoe loose."

"And I appreciate the effort," Travis replied, knowing full well there was no way he could tolerate diving down into the tiny cabin. He dreaded tight closed spaces. It would take a life or death state of affairs before he could force himself into such a tiny space.

So he avoided the question by making a joke. "You know, don't you, that you're my hero. So go ahead. Impress me."

Seth plunked down on the pontoon and stuck a foot in the water. "Cripes, Trav! I've had root beer floats that weren't this cold. I don't know 'bout this. One dive and it might be all over. I'll be too chilled to make a second try."

In a burst of determination, the youth slid off the pontoon, gulped a big breath of air, and sunk out of sight. Travis started counting off the seconds; worried that his friend may be right. That the water was too cold, that it would cramp muscles and sap strength.

Even with brilliant early morning sunshine, visibility was limited. Unlike many Canadian lakes that are clear as expensive crystal, much of the liquid draining into this waterway flowed from spruce and tamarack bogs. That meant the water took on a brown-tinted stain, often helpful for catching fish, but miserable for deep-water diving, especially without a mask or tank.

Seth had no trouble opening the cockpit door. However, with the plane being upside down, little light seeped into the cabin, and locating the flight bag cost several seconds of lung testing anxiety. The satchel was almost where Travis had said it would be, aside from the fact it had slipped under the seat.

Seth snatched a handle loop with one hand while clutching tightly to the doorframe with the other. He gave a quick tug, expecting the bag to come willingly. It moved several inches and then came to an abrupt halt. The second strap had become looped around a seat lever. Seth was forced to make a split second choice. Try to break it loose or head topside?

Frigid water was already causing muscles to quiver and ache. Yet this might be the only chance they'd get to salvage the map container. Decision made, Seth grabbed the bag with both hands and then tugged with all his strength. Success. The strap tore free.

Travis had counted into the forties when a dark head of hair popped up between the pontoons. With one hand on a cross support, Seth flipped the carrying case up on the float. Shivering, he climbed up after it.

"Pretty chilly down there, huh?" Travis gushed with relief. "Good work. Are you gonna try for the cooler?"

"Forget it! Not this morning, anyway. Once you get a foot or two below the surface it's just too damn cold. It was all I could do to grab that," Seth said, nodding toward the satchel. "Maybe this afternoon or tomorrow I can try again, unless you'd like to take a turn."

"Naw, I can get by on fish for a while. Hey, at least you were able to get the flight bag. Bob should be able to figure out just where the heck we are."

Sitting up, Seth swung his feet into the canoe, and then lowered the bag and himself into the boat. "Speaking of location, let's head for camp. I need to get my muscles moving."

* * *

Rising from a foggy state, Bob had awakened to the plop of the canoe being plunked into the water. He'd heard the boy's whispers as the teens prepared to depart. And he even recognized the faint splash of paddles fading off into the distance.

The man wanted to get up; or at very least, call out to the kids. But he couldn't. Something was wrong, terribly wrong. Muscles and limbs refused to follow orders. Sometime during the night part of his body became missing-in-action, including his ability to yell for help.

The man lay petrified in panicked fright, trying to make sense of his situation. Although his head was fuzzy, his brain seemed to be functioning. He recognized familiar sounds; the cawing of a crow, birds trilling in the woods, a loon squawking for its mate; even the splash of a fish jumping far out on the bay. And he understood where he was—in a tent—on a flow of ancient rock—in the middle of the wilderness—stranded by a windstorm.

So why couldn't he move? What had happened? Slowly, like unwanted water in a cellar, the answer slowly oozed into his skull. He realized what the symptoms were pointing to—a stroke. A sour stench filled his nose. The reek cemented his thinking. He had obviously fouled himself. Genetic history had hunted him down. Like his father, he'd become a prisoner in his own body.

There wasn't a thing he could do but lie and wait. The young people would have to make the terrible finding on their own. The old man closed his eyes, attempted to breathe deep, and tried to picture pleasant things from the past. And then, without really meaning to, he fell into a coma-like slumber.

* * *

Shortly after the boys paddled away, Jessie trudged gloomily back into camp. Her quest to find a special charm bracelet proved fruitless.

She hadn't said a word about losing it, but the glittery trinket was her most valued possession. It had been a gift from her birth mother, her real mother. At the time of giving, the shiny ornament was appreciated, but not nearly so cherished as it was now. It was the last gift her mother gave anyone. The woman's sudden illness and untimely death had drilled a hole in Jessie's heart no one had yet been able to fill.

Uncle Bob seemed to be the only one who was trying. While others had continually ragged on her to improve her attitude, study harder in school, or make some friends, Uncle Bob never mentioned any of those things. Instead, he conversed with her as a grownup; never judgmental. Deep down in that place she never let anyone in, she felt like a scared little kid. When she'd climbed into Bob's floatplane for the long flight, her bucket of fear had filled to the top and spilled over. Now, more than ever, she felt as if she'd been pushed off a cliff.

Good, she thought after arriving at camp chilled to the bone. The canoe was missing. That meant the scouts were out searching for the supplies. She'd have time to change into something dry, start a fire, and then talk to her uncle in private.

Later, maybe she'd even try to talk to the boys. After all, they couldn't help being so square they could be gift wrapped and be put under a Christmas tree. One had to consider where they lived, about a zillion miles from the real world.

Fire-starting was not one of her hidden talents. The wood was damp, the pieces too large. The flame on her lighter had weakened considerably before she finally gave up in frustration. But by then the sun had climbed high enough to dispense some warmth of its own.

It was probably best to wake her uncle. She sauntered over to Travis's little faded green shelter, and then paused to listen. Except for the rustle of leaves as a freshening breeze fanned through tree tops, and an occasional bird tweet, there was only silence.

"Uncle Bob? Are you awake?"

No reply.

She tried again, using a louder voice. "Uncle Bob, are you in there?"

An animal-like grunting came from inside the tent, sending a shiver of panic down her spine. Jess jumped back in fright, half afraid a bear or similar wild creature lurked within the tiny domed-shaped tent. It took a moment before the impossibility dawned on her. The door was closed. Even she knew that animals don't do zippers.

"Uncle Bob, it's not funny. Stop teasing. I need to talk to you."

More guttural musings came from within—low and long—half-formed vowel sounds.

Her uncle understood how frightened she was of the woods. He wouldn't make fun of her like this. It had to be one of the boys playing a prank, hoping to scare her half to death. Uncle Bob had probably gone off in the canoe, leaving the tall kid behind. After all, this was his tent. Resentment boiled up, replacing her panic with rage.

"Oh, you think you're such a big shot, don't you? You probably think I'm about to wet my pants out here 'cause I'm not used to the woods. I was gonna say sorry for acting like a snot, but forget it. Far as I'm concerned, you can go pee up a rope."

She stood with fists clenched to her sides. But just then more sound came from within, a long word she recognized, one only her uncle would know—a nickname she'd endured since she'd been a little girl.

In a long, low, throaty whisper, the moan repeated itself. "Jaz-zi-belle...it's ssmee, Uncl' Bob."

In a blink of an eye, Jessie leapt to tent, undid the door, and pushed inside, only to be greeted by a stench that doubled her anxiety.

Her uncle lay on his side, unmoving. His eyes rheumy, bloodshot, wet as if he'd been crying. One side of his mouth was turned down in a grimace. Saliva drooled out onto his lips and cheek. An arm rested on top the sleeping bag, the hand curled inward like a claw.

"Uncle Bob, what happened? What's the matter?" Jessie exhaled in one long breath. "Are you sick? Did you have an accident?"

The man struggled to answer. He fixed his dim gaze on his niece, sucked in a bit of air, and tried to talk. "Str-...stroke. I...must have...had a stroke," he mumbled, the words a mangled slur.

After another gulp, he strained, "I'm so...so sorry. I never...meant for...this to...to happen."

Hesitating a moment to push down her alarm, to get over the shock, Jess searched for words of comfort. On the edge of tears, she managed a reply. "It's going to be all right, Uncle Bob. Soon as we're found, they'll fly you to a hospital. You're going to be all right. You're going to be all right. I know you are."

"I'm...I'm not so sure, Jaz-zi" he whispered, closing his eyes, breathing in shallow bursts. "I'm not...so...sure. I think I just want to...rest."

"Sure, Uncle Bob. Get some sleep. You'll feel better when you wake up," Jess croaked. But her words went unanswered. Uncle Bob had already fallen back to sleep.

Chapter Six

C H A P T E R   S I X

The boys were stroking toward a welcoming plume of gray smoke when Seth observed, "Looks like Bob's already up and at 'em. Sure hope he's 'bout to fry up the fillets. I'm hungrier than a bear crawling out of its winter den."

"Even if he hasn't started the cookin', at least the fire's going. It shouldn't take long to heat up a few fish. Maybe we can send Jess to the woods for some breakfast berries," Travis joked, taking notice his belly was also asking to be filled.

With a final flurry of effort, they beached the canoe and then portaged it to its resting perch. With the exception of the small blaze snapping out a greeting, the campsite appeared vacant.

"What d'ya think? You figure they're already out huntin' for berries?" Seth asked after making a quick scan of the area.

"Don't know," Travis mumbled. "The cook set's nested just the way I left it last night. They would've needed a cup or a pan so the berries wouldn't get squished."

"Whatever. But I'm not gonna sit around and wait. Let's

start without 'em," Seth said, removing the rock holding down the lid on the pot of leftover fillets.

Jessie came into view as Travis was about to dismantle the cook set. Clad in clean jeans and a hooded sweatshirt, she came trudging from the woods, burdened with an armload of broken branches. Upon spotting the boys, she let the load tumble, and then sprinted toward the fire.

"Where have you guys been? My uncle's really sick. One of you is gonna have to go for help," she wheezed in a sudden gush of words.

"What d'ya mean he's sick? Does he have the flu or somethin'?" Seth asked. Staring wide-eyed at her, he couldn't help but notice she'd been crying. Below a pair of red-rimmed eyes, her cheeks were streaked with tear tracks.

Travis made a similar observation. And though his heart seemed to have leapt to his throat, he fought to remain cool and collected. "Calm down and tell us what's wrong," he said in a squeak that revealed his anxiety.

Jess wrapped her arms around her middle, took a deep breath, and then studied her damp shoes. When she spoke, the words tumbled out in a tiny voice. "Well, when I came back into camp, the canoe was gone. I figured you two were either fishing or trying to get the stuff from the airplane. I wanted to talk to my uncle in private, so I walked over to your tent," she said, looking up.

"I called his name, but didn't get a reply. So I tried again, thinking he was sleeping. That's when I really got scared. At first, when he finally answered, it sounded like an animal. Then after a minute or so, I thought it might be one of you guys teasing me."

She paused, deciding how to best describe her uncle's problem. Seth leapt into the lull. "Did you look in on him? Maybe he's just having fun with you? He's probably trying to prove there's nothing to be 'fraid of."

Jessie's head swiveled, red eyes glaring. "Look Mr. Smarty-pants, I might not know much about the woods, but I'm not stupid. Of course I checked on him. He's had a stroke. He can hardly talk. That's why you have to go get help. Right now! He needs to get to a hospital."

Travis's pulse began racing like a runaway freight train. Cripes! What more could go wrong? His mom had hit the nail on the head. Trouble did often come in bunches—really big bunches. He stood staring at his tent, uncertain what to say.

"How do you know it was stroke? You have some nurse's training or somethin'?" Seth asked. But before Jess had a chance to snap back, he added, "Sorry. You got me a little shook up here."

For a moment Jess remained voiceless—eyes glaring; anger, confusion, and fear contorting her fine facial features. When she did speak, the words were spit out one at a time. "I know because he told me so himself. He can't talk, but he can whisper...sort of. And, no, I don't have any training. But after my mom died, I spent time volunteering in a nursing home. I've seen other old people with these same symptoms. If you don't believe me, go look for yourself."

Travis stood silent, trying to digest this headline of bad news. For one thing, he sidetracked, another puzzle piece had just fallen into place. Jessie's mom was dead. That thought flashed by in a blink, replaced by panicked concern for Bob. Just how sick was he? Would the man even live long enough for help to arrive?

Death was not something new to either boy. Grandpa Larsen died unexpectedly from a heart attack when Travis was around nine. That had been the only time Travis witnessed his dad shedding tears.

Seth had experienced something even more devastating. Two years ago, the Springwoods received the dreaded middle-of-the-night phone call—news of a deadly auto accident. Seth's father had managed to avoid a collision with a drunk driver by steering his truck off the highway's narrow shoulder. Although his truck had only nicked several small trees, it burst into flames. Seth's father was engulfed in the inferno before he could even unfasten the seatbelt.

These past events tumbled about in Travis's skull as he stood with his back to the fire, trying to dike a flood of intensifying panic. Even though his face remained wooden, Seth was having similar feelings. That they were knee-deep in quicksand and help would be a long time coming.

"Seth, we better check on Bob. Maybe there's something we can do for him," Travis croaked after several moments of quiet.

Travis became aware of the stench before even he unzipped the door. Down on all fours, he twisted his face toward Jess, and then raised a hand to his nose.

She understood without having to be asked. "He soiled himself," she whispered. Then she added, "I think that's common with stroke victims."

Once the flap was undone, the boys braced themselves for the opening shock, each hoping Jess had exaggerated.

But she hadn't. If anything, Bob looked more pitiful than either had visualized.

The man lay on his side, his ashen face turned toward the door. With every ragged breath, drops of spittle bubbled from an open mouth. Mucous dribble lined his lips, an occasional rivulet trickling down his chin.

The reek of human waste and urine filled the small enclosure; forcing the boys to hold their breaths. After a few seconds, they had seen and smelled enough. Both clambered outside on hands and knees, gulping fresh air.

"Oh man! What now?" Seth gasped.

"What now? It's pretty obvious one of you is gonna have to go for help. The other will have to stay here with me. What choice do we have?" Jessie pleaded in yet another voice the boys hadn't heard before.

Travis searched for the right words. "Okay, we need to sit down and talk about this. But let's put a few of those sticks you gathered on the fire. There's no sense letting it die out."

When they were seated around the renewed blaze, Seth said, "I'd like to know something. Who got the fire going?"

Jessie's head jerked up. "What kind of a dumb question is that? I did. The first thing I did when I returned was to try to get one going. It wouldn't start. Then after finding Uncle Bob, I couldn't just sit around here and do nothing. I remembered watching you yesterday," she said, rotating toward Travis. "I remembered how you started it with tiny pieces of bark, and then stacked little twigs in a pile. So I did the same. It took off with the first flick of my lighter."

Jessie shrugged and then asked, "So, which one of you is gonna go for help?"

The boys eyed each other and then slowly shook their heads.

"Neither. Think about it. We have no idea where we are. Even if we knew where to look, the nearest fishing camp's probably dozens of miles from here, maybe more," Seth said, staring vacantly at the fire.

"Right," Travis added. "Seth and I had a similar situation last fall. We got caught in that terrible windstorm you might have seen on the news. Seth had a broken ankle. I left our campsite to get help. I knew where we were and what direction to go. But I almost didn't make it out alive." Travis stopped, recalling how narrowly he had missed becoming a big banner in the local paper.

"Anyway," he went on, "If we learned anything, it was to stay put. Let help come to you, not the other way around. Isn't that right, Seth?"

Seth picked up a small pebble and then flung it force-fully over the water. Even here, in the protected cove, a smart breeze was frothing the surface, forcing tiny whitecaps to lap along the shoreline. He was glad they had taken the canoe out at daybreak. The way the wind was blowing now, paddling the open part of the lake would now be a chancy undertaking.

"Well, almost always. It certainly applies in this circum-stance. We don't have a clue as to where we are. And if we did, we don't know which way to go. But we're gonna have to make a plan anyway."

"Yup," Travis agreed. "But Jess, how was it that you went in the woods by yourself? I thought you were scared of getting lost."

The girl shot Travis a quick glower. "I'm not brainless. Didn't you ever read that Hansel and Gretel fairy tale? I didn't go very far. No more than a few yards from the water. And when I did go into the woods, I dropped a piece of Kleenex every few feet to mark my way. All I had to do was follow the tissue trail out."

"Pretty clever," Seth praised. "But let's get back to busi-ness. What should we do first?"

"Probably tend to Bob. Clean him up and get some liq-uid into him. Two of us can work on that while the other one makes breakfast. Does that sound right to you?" Travis asked, looking straight at Jessie.

"You don't have to fix anything for me. I'll just munch some cookies or a candy bar. Then maybe later one of you can help me find some berries," she answered, returning again to the small voice.

"Tell you what, since you don't eat animal parts, how 'bout I make a fish broth like the rest of us had yesterday? It's tasty and doesn't have any real meat in it. You're gonna need more than a couple of cookies and a few berries," Travis offered.

Jessie mulled the offer over for a moment. "Well...as long as there aren't any lumps, I'll try a cup. Just make sure it's all liquid."

"It's a done deal. Soup it is. Seth, you want to be the cook or help with Bob?"

"You're the chef. Go ahead and fix somethin' to eat. I'll help Jessie. We'll have to get Bob out of his dirty clothes and then wash him up. Jess, are you okay with that? Are ya willing to work with me?"

Jessie sprang to her feet, ready to get going. "Of course I am. I've helped nurses clean patients lots of times. But I have to be honest. They were always women. When we get to changing his underwear, I can wait outside. I don't want you to be embarrassed."

Seth blushed, his dark cheeks filling with extra color. "I think we should try to move him into his own tent. It's bigger than the one he's in now."

"Travis, I'll let you know when we get him cleaned up. Then the three of us should be able to carry him in his sleeping bag. If you think it's safe to move him," he added, seeking the girl's approval.

"Yeah, it should be all right. It's not like he has broken bones. If he wakes up, he can probably even help. From the little I know, most strokes usually affect only one side of a person's body."

Their plan worked. Bob did wake up. And true to Jessie's guess, he was able to move enough to aid with the cleanup and clothes exchange. Seth had become embarrassed, but not because of the girl's presence.

It was his first experience dealing with an invalid. When it came time to change Bob's underwear, Jess quietly slipped out of the shelter. Using tissue and a pan of warmed lake water, Seth managed to get through the ordeal. Then, after he had slipped a fresh pair of briefs onto the man, he called for help.

"Travis, Jessie. We're ready to make the move to the other tent."

Bob suddenly stretched out his good arm and clutched Seth's shoulder. "No, Seth," the ailing man whispered in a gravelly slur. "I'd rather...be outside...maybe you can pr-...prop me up against the duf-...duffel bags. I'd like to sit and look at the lake."

"Sure, no problem," Seth answered, amazed at the strength of Bob's grip.

With two boys half-lifting, half-carrying, they were able to place Bob in a sitting position on a pair of bags. Once Travis had the fish chowder heated, Jessie took on the role of nursemaid. With the aid of the cooking spoon, she was able feed him a small cup of broth.

"Th-...thaank yoou, Ja-...Jaz-zi-girl," Bob garbled as Jess wiped his chin with a tissue. "This...this is some k-...kettle of fish I g-...got you into, huh?"

He took several ragged breaths, gripped her arm with his strong hand and went on. "Jessie, d-...don't you be fretting too much. Listen to the boys. They know the way of woods and water. K-...keep each other safe 'til help arrives. You're all g-...good kids."

* * *

The midday sun was a large happy lemon when three castaways gathered near the fire. Bob was resting.

Moments earlier, and with some effort, the trio had trundled the man into his shelter and sleeping bag.

"I'm surprised we haven't heard or seen a floatplane. This is the peak of fly-in season. I can't imagine a big lake like this not being used by outfitters," Seth volunteered.

"Ahhh...unless it's off limits to seaplanes. Who knows, maybe it's a tribal lake or part of a park? Maybe like the Boundary Waters Canoe Area. Maybe it's a lake where planes can't land or even fly low," Travis speculated.

Seth bounced to his feet and trotted to the canoe. With all the commotion, they'd neglected to look in the flight bag. He returned a moment later, plunked down, and opened up the top. Inside the case were dozens of water-soaked charts lined up like books on a shelf.

"There's a whole bunch of maps in here," he said. "How will we know which one to even look at?"

Jessie was quick to answer. "That should be simple. First find the one for northern Minnesota. Then look at the top edge. It should have some printing telling you which one comes next. We only flew a few hundred miles. I wouldn't think we'd flown off the second chart already. And if we did, use the one after that."

"How d'ya know about that?" Travis asked, impressed.

"Because Uncle Bob let me look at the maps before we picked you guys up. He wanted me to check to make sure we didn't wander over that no-fly area near where you live."

Seth nodded. Then he began gingerly pulling out maps. With care not to rip or cause tears, each was opened and placed in sunshine. Jess and Travis were kept busy finding rocks to hold corners from the catching wind.

Once the charts were open and drying, the threesome stood peering down with young eyes, hoping to be the first to spot their unusual looking lake. The blend of sun and wind quickly did its work. Within minutes the first map was dry enough to handle.

"This is the sectional for northern Minnesota," Seth said, holding up the color-coded sheet of paper. "And I think we're in luck. Bob used a marker to plot the flight path."

He laid the map flat on the slab. Jess and Travis knelt to get a better look at the red streak drawn across the multi-colored surface.

"Trav, see here," Seth said, pointing with a forefinger. "That's Devil Track Lake. And here, that line going north into Canada should be the first part of the flight."

Jessie didn't wait. She stood and started scanning the remaining documents. "Got it! This should be the next one. And you're right. There's a line on this one, too," she said, kneeling down for a better look.

Seth placed a pair of rocks on his map before moving over to join Jess. "Trav, do you know how to read these things? There are all kinds of circles, boxes, and numbers. What's that all about? And I don't see any roads. Do you?"

"Here," Travis said, putting a finger on a thin dark line squiggling its way over the green and blue background. "I think that's the highway from Kenora to Thunder Bay. Do you see where the Bob's red line cuts across it? We flew over that road after gassing up."

The boys were in for another small surprise. Jessie, despite her lack of knowledge about the wilderness, was an expert at map reading. It was one of the things she enjoyed doing in school. She could easily lose an hour or two poring over atlases, taking herself to far-off cities on imaginary sight-seeing trips.

Dropping to all fours, she traced the flight path with a finger. When she came to the edge of the paper, she removed the rocks and flipped the map over. Then she found the red line on the opposite side and continued tracking.

"Here's a lake marked with a circle. I'd bet that's where I was supposed to be dropped off," she said, placing her finger on a red oval enclosing a large splotch of blue.

"Yeah, I see it," Travis said, crowding close. "But I don't think we're anywhere near there now. Remember, once we ran into storm clouds, Bob changed direction. The question is—which way did we go?"

"Let's back-track the red line. Maybe there's a lake or two we'll recognize about the time he was on the radio," Seth suggested, inching closer for a better look.

Travis suddenly became aware that Jessie was between them, and that his shoulder was touching hers. Travis felt his face flush.

Pushing up, he blurted, "Umm...why don't you two keep looking? I'm gonna go check on Bob, see if he's still sleeping."

* * *

Jess made the find. She located a bug-shaped body of blue on the third chart; the map showing land west of their original goal. Just as it had when they viewed it from the air, the blue outline appeared to be one of the larger lakes in the area.

After making her discovery, she started carefully moving the maps in such way that their features connected. As she spread them out, Seth placed rocks to keep the charts from flapping.

"Okay. Let's have another look. There must be a town or fishing camp somewhere 'round here," Jessie said, "Someplace with a phone so we can call for a doctor."

Travis returned from checking on Bob. The man was

sleeping. The good news—it appeared that both his color and breathing had improved.

"So, what did ya find?" he asked, squatting next to Seth.

"Jessie thinks she found our lake. Now we're trying to locate a town or an outfitter's camp. For sure I don't see any roads. Except for way over there on the edge," he said indicating the far side of the map, "there's nothing much else but woods and water. The problem is that these charts are confusing. There are so many lines and boxes, all with a jumble of numbers."

Travis dropped flat to his stomach, his eyes only inches from the paper. After a moment he speculated, "It'd be my guess that they're common flight paths. And those boxes with numbers, they're probably the radio frequencies a pilot's supposed to use."

Jessie jumped up, an animated look brightening her face. "Oh! I completely forgot. There's a cell phone in my bag. We can call right from here." She whirled and started running toward the tent.

Travis shook his head, and then yelled after her. "Forget it, Jess. Cell phones don't even work where we live, much less way up here. You've gotta be close to a tower. Otherwise they're useless. We'd be better off sending up a smoke signal."

Jess stopped mid-stride, shoulders slumping in defeat. "I don't believe it! And you guys actually wanted to come here and camp out? You two must be goofy! Okay, just forget it. I'm out of ideas." She paused. "And I'd appreciate it if you two stayed put. I gotta go in the woods. No funny stuff."

Pulling a prank was the last thing on the boys' minds. Thinking of a way to help Bob was first on their to-do list—catching and gathering food was a close second. While Jessie was off seeking privacy, Travis and Seth discussed their situation.

When Jess returned, they got right to it.

"Jessie, there's just no way one of us is gonna go for help. The nearest outpost has to be miles away. So forget that idea." Seth intoned in a businesslike voice.

"What we have to do," Travis broke in, "is divide the chores."

"Remember what I said about sending up a smoke signal? I meant it. That'll be our best chance for attracting attention. We'll need to stock pile a bunch of wood, dead and alive. You ever use a pruning saw?"

"Use a what?" Jessie asked, wrinkles grooving her forehead. "Are there even prune trees around here?"

"A pruning saw. It's a little curved saw that folds in half. It's used to cut branches and shrubs," Seth snickered. But knowing there were no such things as prune trees, he was unable to keep from smiling.

"And yeah, we have one with us. Since you don't want to go too far from camp, Seth and I thought we'd try you find some berries. You must be starving. We had a couple of fillets for breakfast. That and beef stick a while ago. All you've had are a few cookies and a cup of broth," Travis said.

The screeching of sea gulls diverted their attention. The boys had tossed the fish guts several hundred feet down shore. A flock of the water birds had made the discovery. Like unruly children ready for recess, the scavengers pushed and poked, squawking and screaming, each wanting to be first in line.

"Wait a minute. Jess, you said you don't eat meat, but what about poached eggs? If we can find you some bird eggs will you eat some?" Seth asked, pleased with his inspiration.

She thought about that. "Maybe, if they're fresh and don't have things growing inside."

"Let's get back to the plan," Travis said, ignoring the noisy food-fight. "Since you were able to start the fire, why don't you spend the next hour or two bringing more wood into camp? Make a pile close to the burning spot. When you think you have enough last all day, get the fire blazing again."

"Right. Once it's burning hot, use the saw to cut live branches into smaller sections. If you hear anything that sounds like an airplane, start tossing on green wood. It'll make lots of smoke. Think you can handle that?" Seth asked.

Ignoring the boy's query, Jess tossed out a question of her own. "What about Uncle Bob? Shouldn't we be doing something for him?"

Travis pursed his lips in thought. "What would you suggest? He was sleeping when I looked in on him. And he did look a bit better. Some color has returned and he wasn't breathing so hard. You can check on him each time you bring in a load."

Jessie looked down as if inspecting her toes. After a long silence, she raised her chin and asked, "How far do you plan to go? I just thought it might be better if one of you stayed here."

Seth caught the clue. She wasn't just thinking about Bob. She was uptight about animals. "Look, if you're worried about critters coming into camp, forget it."

He nodded toward the nearby barrier of trees. "What I'm gonna tell you is the truth, so believe it. Every living thing in those woods is far more frightened of you, than you are of it. With the fire going, and all the human scent around camp, there's not a thing to worry about. About the only critter bold enough to come close would be a chipmunk."

"Exactly," Travis broke in. "There could be a few ground squirrels, birds, and maybe a skunk or two in the middle of the night. But that'd be after sunset. We'd be in our tents. And since we don't have any meat, or other real food for them to smell, I doubt that even skunks will be a problem."

A second group of gulls had gathered at the feeding frenzy. Despite the breeze breaking up the racket, raucous squawks filled the air.

Seth sensed that Jessie was troubled by the commotion. "They're just gulls, fighting over fish scraps. That happens all the time back home. Don't give the birds a second thought. They're loud but harmless."

Jessie gazed down the lake, considering what was said. "All right...I guess. If you're sure you won't be gone long. Just don't take all day, okay?"

Travis hadn't waited for a response. He'd busied himself selecting a pot for berry picking. Selecting the medium sized pot, he asked, "Which way we gonna go?"

"Let's check out the woods over there," Seth answered, pointing to the end of the cove.

"There's a creek running into the lake just past where we hunkered down. There could be a swamp opening or pond not too far in. Maybe we'll get lucky and find some cat tails or lily pads. We can pull them out by the roots. Didn't you say they're starchy vegetables?" Seth posed, looking at Travis.

"I think so," Travis replied. "Why don't you show Jess how the saw works so we can boogie?"

After a quick cutting lesson, and reminding Jess to throw wood on the fire if she heard an airplane, the boys trekked off.

Chapter Seven

C H A P T E R   S E V E N

"Man! I'm sure glad we remembered to put on bug spray!" Travis wheezed, waving a hand at the insect cloud swarming about his head. "Mosquitoes aren't so bad, but the no-see-'ems are torture!"

The explorers were sloshing ankle deep in the brook Seth had crossed on his way to free the canoe. The reasoning was that by following the waterway, they couldn't get lost.

Tangled trees and brush bordering the creek shut off any hint of a breeze. And without air movement, the heat and humidity was stifling. Rivulets of sweat dribbled from foreheads and cheeks. An occasional mosquito buzzed through the scent of bug spray to chance a free meal. Although the boys had been slogging against the current for twenty minutes, they had yet to find the source of running water.

"What d'ya think?" Seth asked, swatting a blood-seeking parasite drilling a hole in his hairline.

Travis stopped, bent, and scooped a pot full of water. He took a sip, removed his cap, and then poured the remainder over a mane of unkempt hair.

"I'm not sure. Maybe we should turn around."

"Yeah, I'd guess you'd wanna get back to the big lake, now that you washed off most the bug stink."

Travis balanced the pot on his head like a tin helmet before slipping a hand into a pocket. He pulled out a small container and then held it up for Seth to see. The plastic bottle held an ivory substance. Unscrewing the cap, Travis splattered a glob of the thick goop onto the palm of his hand.

"Not to worry. I brought some heavy duty lotion along. I didn't want to use it 'cause it's kinda greasy. But if there was ever a right time for it, it'd be now."

"Cut me a break! You mean you've had that stuff in your pocket and didn't say anything? Cripes, I'm about ready for a transfusion and you're hiding the cure. Some friend you are!"

"Here. Help yourself," Travis said, under-handing the bottle. "But don't use too much. It's potent stuff. Just put a little bit in your hand. Then smear it all over exposed skin, at least that what the directions say," Travis continued, rubbing his cheeks with an open palm.

"I know it stinks. But my dad says it the best repellent on the market," he added, catching the kettle as it tumbled from his head. "Okay. What say we follow the creek for another fifteen minutes or so? If we don't find the source by then, we'll head back."

Several twisty turns later, the boys were standing at the edge of a narrow lake. But it wasn't the picturesque pond that had them excited. Resting upside down on shore—its faded red bottom scratched and bruised from years of use—was an old Lund fishing boat.

"What the heck? How d'ya suppose this got here?" Seth pondered, plunking down on the fat end of the boat.

Travis tapped the aluminum bow with the pot, as if checking to make certain the boat was real.

"I suppose with all the lily pads, this would be a good lake to catch northern pike. Hey, you know what this means, don't you? It means that the big lake must be used for fly-in trips. I bet if we explore more of its bays, we'll find other boats stashed away."

Seth remained quiet, speculating Travis's remark. Then, without a word, he stood, bent, and clutched the edge of the boat in both hands. With a quick thrust, he hoisted the watercraft so it was resting on its side.

"We're in luck, Trav. There's even a pair of oars tucked in the bracing. We can do some exploring by water."

An hour later the voyagers were back where they'd begun. They'd circled the entire narrow lake. They'd discovered a few animal paths; no doubt made by moose, bear, or deer. A few beaver lodges stood near an open patch where the tree-chewers had dropped every aspen on the slope. But they had found no sign of human activity.

Coming upon the clearing, the boys beached the boat, hoping to find berries. They did. A copse of raspberries flourished in the sun-filled gap, and though not yet ripe, they gathered enough to fill the small pot.

"What now? Leave the boat where we found it or float it down the creek?" Seth posed, aware that the sun was casting longer shadows.

With a sudden thrust of a hand, he pointed to the sky. A bald eagle was surveying the lake, gliding soundlessly on wide wings. The raptor made a circling approach before coming to rest high on a pine bough overlooking the water's edge.

Travis was busy applying a second coating of repellent. He noted the big bird's presence with a nod of his cap and then said, "Take the boat with us. I know it's slower to row a boat than to paddle a canoe, but it'll be a whole lot safer. Besides, it's not like we'd be stealing it. Someone left it here to be used."

"Hey, don't be hogging all the goop!" Seth boomed, snatching the bottle from Travis's hand. He plopped a glob onto a palm, screwed the lid tight, and then tucked the container into a front pocket.

"I'm gonna guard this for you," he grinned, wiping his hands together and then rubbing his face and forearms. "Now, 'bout this boat? I think you're right. Even if we don't use it to travel around the big lake, it's easier to fish from a boat than a canoe. And, tall skinny friend of mine, I'm getting hungry. Do you really want to take time to pull lily pad roots?"

Travis chewed his lip, pondering. "Tell ya what. I'll wade in and pull up a half dozen or so. If Jess finds a use for them, we can always come back for more."

* * *

Jess was worried. The boys had been away far longer than expected. She tried to quell her rising anxiety by keeping busy gathering wood and checking on her uncle. The tall kid had been correct about the man's complexion. His color was almost normal. And his breathing was more relaxed, not nearly as labored as earlier in the day.

Having scavenged every scrap of fish, the gulls had departed. The only sound was that of wind murmuring through tree tops and the soft swoosh of waves washing against rock.

Dropping a load of sticks, Jess plopped down and curled up next to the fire. She couldn't remember ever being so hungry. That morning, when the boys had fried fish, the scent had made her mouth water. Her stomach had even growled. But except for some broth, she'd refused their offerings. She was determined to keep her pledge never to eat meat, regardless of its source. A promise she'd made because of her mother's unexpected sudden demise.

In celebration of Jessie's birthday, the family of three had gone out to eat. Jess chose a small neighborhood cafe specializing in offbeat cuisine. They'd had a fun time, laughing, teasing, and savoring the meal. Except that when they returned home, her mother became ill.

Just a touch of the flu, she'd said. Nothing a night's sleep wouldn't cure. But she'd been wrong. During the dark hours of early morning, her mother had become violently ill; too weak to even reach the bathroom before vomiting. Dad urged a visit to the ER. But her mother refused, saying it was foolish. She was sure that by daylight the symptoms would pass. That she'd soon be feeling better.

But that hadn't happened. By the time the sun lighted the horizon, her mother was so ill an ambulance had to be summoned. Arriving at the hospital, she sank into a coma; never to regain consciousness. Despite doctors' heroic efforts, she'd passed away the next day.

At the time the events had all seemed surreal. A bad dream—a nightmare Jess would awaken from. These things happen to others, not to your own family.

But it hadn't been a fantasy. According to the medical examiner, contaminated meat had been ruled the culprit; a rare and deadly form of the E-coli bacteria. And because the meat hadn't been thoroughly cooked, the deadly germs had multiplied in the meatloaf; transformed into a lethal toxin. Jess and her father hadn't suffered so much as a stomachache. She never told anyone, but she felt that she was a little bit to blame. After all, she'd chosen the restaurant.

As her mother's coffin was being lowered into the ground, Jessie made the silent pledge. To honor her mother's memory, she'd vowed never again to let meat touch her lips. She learned that she could live on cereals, bread, fruits and vegetables, and an occasional sweet treat or two.

Coughing came from the shelter, returning Jess to reality. Her uncle was awake. She scrambled to her feet and hustled to the tent. Bob was lying sideways on the sleeping bag, misty blue eyes opened wide.

"Hi, Uncle Bob. How're you feelin'? Would you like a drink or something to eat? We have plenty of cookies and those dried meaty strips you brought along."

The old man took a shallow breath, closed his lids as if he were in deep thought, and sighed.

When he spoke, it was barely above a slurred whisper. "Oh, Jazzi. You're too good to me. Yup, a cookie and sip of water might be just what the doctor ordered," he croaked, opening his eyes once more.

The wet-eyed stare made Jess uneasy. She'd had time to mull over the boys' warnings—that they were in the middle of nowhere—without any way of reaching help. Her uncle needed medical treatment: oxygen, prescriptions, IV tubes—a whole range of medical apparatus. How was that going to happen stuck out here in the wilds?

"Okay," she whispered, camouflaging her concern with a meek smile. "An order of cookies and water it is."

Jess hand-fed the man. Most of the cookies wound up as crumbs decorating the tent floor. But Bob was able to sip liquid, nearly a cup. When the skimpy meal was over, he mouthed a thank you and then patted her hand. He closed his eyes and in a few seconds was sleeping again.

For a time Jess sat still, watching the man snooze. Her

empty stomach gurgled as if competing with her uncle's soft snores. Never had she felt such hunger pangs. And the cookies looked so scrumptious, chocolate chip, a favorite. Stuffing a handful into a baggy pocket, she returned the package to the tent sack, and went outside.

After tossing a few sticks on the fire, she flopped down so she could savor every nibble. Finished, but still feeling famished, she reached into the big baggy pocket one more time. When her hand emerged, it was closed around a pack of cigarettes. Maybe a quick smoke would mask the signals coming from her empty middle.

She'd just finished the cigarette when the squeak of boat oars caught her ear. Turning toward the irritating squeal, she saw a little red-bottomed boat working its way along shore. For a moment or two her spirits soared. Help had arrived.

But then, as the vessel drew closer, she recognized the occupants. Her heart dropped like a stone in an empty well. It was only the scouts coming into camp. A second thought sparked. Where would they have acquired a boat? Answer—a fishing outpost! There had to be a camp close by, maybe even a resort. Jess jumped to her feet and started working her way along the shore.

When she came near enough that the boys would hear, she yelled at the top of her lungs. "You found help! When are we gonna get out of here?"

Seth stopped stroking long enough for Travis to yell out a reply.

"Sorry, Jess. This is all we found, an old boat. How 'bout you? Did ya see any pontoon planes?"

Another wave of despair washed over the young woman. "Nope, haven't seen a thing."

Without another word she spun on her heel, and with head down and shoulders slumped, started traipsing toward camp.

Three mushroom-shaped shelters squatted in evening shade. Nearby on the flat rock, the teens sat on their haunches, staring blankly toward the fire.

"It's almost seven-thirty. Fish should be biting pretty soon," Travis remarked after checking his watch. "We've got several hours of good light left."

Seth refocused his gaze, studying the dark wall lifting over the horizon. "Yeah, maybe so, but check that out," he muttered, motioning off in the distance. "It looks like we'll be gettin' rain before morning. Best we catch as many big ones as we can. Just might get weathered in for a few days."

He turned toward the girl. "Jessie, we picked a pan of raspberries. They're not really ripe, but they're safe to eat."

"Yeah, and we have some lily pad roots. I think what you do, is peel off the skin, cut 'em up, and boil 'em."

"So how do you know that? You ever eat one?"

"No, never have. But I've read up about edible plants," Travis said, meeting the girl's stare.

Seth took over. "You see, Trav and I have had some really bad luck on these camp outs. Do you remember that I mentioned we were trapped by that big wind storm? Well, all we had to eat were fish. Since then, Trav has made it his mission to read everything written about wilderness food. Oh, by the way, we didn't find any bird nests, so you don't have to worry about eating poached eggs."

For a time they were quiet. Travis broke the interlude. "Best we get to it. Seth and I are going out in the boat fishing for a while. We'll be back before dark."

He stood up, mulling over what he was about to offer. "While we're fishing, you can move your things into my tent. The 'Seth-man' and I'll double-up. If you want, you can use my mattress pad. Later, after supper, I'll toss some pine needles under our tent to cushion the ground. And besides, tonight I'll be in my own bag. Pooped as I am, I'll sleep like a log."

As was becoming the pattern, Seth tagged on a second set of instructions. "Make sure you keep the fire going. And be sure to check on your uncle every now and then."

He was about to leave when he added, "Hopefully, by tomorrow, Search and Rescue should be doing their thing. With luck, they'll find us in a day or two. And don't forget, if you hear an airplane; stoke the fire with some of those green boughs you managed to hack while we were exploring."

"What is it with you guys?" she snapped. "Cutting a few sticks isn't exactly rocket science. Just get out of here. Go catch your supper. I'll take care of myself."

* * *

Once the boat was out of earshot, Seth couldn't stop grinning. "Looks like I rub that girl the wrong way," he quipped.

"Yeah, so I've noticed," Travis said, readying his rod to make a cast.

Travis flipped his wrist, propelling the multi-hooked lure near shore. He waited for the bait to settle, and then started a slow retrieve, cranking the reel in short bursts, the lure imitating an injured minnow.

"Ya know what I think? I think she likes you. Yup. There's no doubt in my mind," Travis teased, preparing for a second cast.

"Hey, see if you can row a little closer to that big rock. There oughta be a keeper or two lurking on the bottom."

* * *

"Soup's ready," Seth shouted, lifting the lid off the steaming pot. "Jess, you better have a cup. You can't live on just cookies and candy."

Jessie pushed up, trudged to the cooking set, and then picked up a metal cup. She hated to admit it, but Seth was right. She was starving. She'd tried nibbling a few berries while the boys were fishing. Still weeks away from being ripe, they were hard and bitter.

Following Travis's advice, she'd tried preparing a few of the skinny roots. One bite was all she could manage. She had to spit out the dime-sized sample. The odor alone was enough to make her gag. Reluctantly, she'd raided the treat stash, pilfering a few more cookies and even one of the boys' Snickers. And then later, to trick her stomach, she had slowly savored a Tootsie Pop.

The fishermen had returned sooner than expected. They'd almost caught her puffing a cigarette. She'd wondered what they would have done if they had seen her. No doubt freaked out and given her a lecture on the evils of nicotine. Not that she needed to be reminded. Her stepmother had already covered that territory, more than once, thank you.

Cigarettes, and the crowd she'd chosen to hang with, were two of the reasons she was now stranded in the middle of this mosquito paradise. That Uncle Bob actually looked forward to taking these scouts on this outing was insane. Their elevators must have been stuck in the basement on that decision. No sound person would choose to purposely camp out in bug heaven—miles from warm showers and electric lights.

Tucking away her private thoughts, Jessie mumbled, holding her cup out, "Yeah, I suppose. Just make sure there aren't any fish chunks floating around."

The curtain of menacing clouds had bullied overhead. Daylight was fading fast. The tree-line on the far shore was already a shadowy barrier. Only the tallest of the conifers were outlined against a dull black background.

A pair of loons silhouetted against the cove's mirrored surface; pencil lines of wake recording their progress. Without wind, and the temperature holding mild, hoards of hungry guests had winged into camp—each in search of an evening snack.

"Cripes! How can you guys just sit there and pretend these freakin' bugs don't bother you?" Jessie exclaimed, pulling the hood of her sweatshirt tight around her head.

Seth set his cup on a rock, jumped to his feet, and dug into his pocket. "Jeez, Jess, I'm sorry! You need use some of this industrial strength stuff," he said, offering the small bottle in an outstretched hand.

"It stinks, but it works great for keeping bugs from carrying you away."

Jess glared before snatching the bottle from his hand. She removed the cap and held the container to her nose. After scrunching her face in disgust, she snapped, "This better not be another one of your sick jokes. I tried boiling a few of those roots, just like you guys said. They were disgusting...almost made me throw up."

"Yeah, about what I told you earlier," Travis said sheepishly. "I goofed. I was thinking about it while we were fishing. I should have been looking for cattails. I read somewhere that their roots are vegetable-like, sort of starchy like potatoes. I think it's only moose that like lily pad roots. Sorry 'bout that."

Jess shook her head. In slow motion she rubbed repellent on her cheeks. She smeared on enough goop to ward off a whole generation of blood sucking pests. Then she replaced the cap and tucked the bottle into a pocket.

"Thanks. Since your mistake could very well have poisoned me, I'll take a turn at keeping this safe," she said, stifling a smile.

Turning, she started toward her uncle's tent. Halfway to the shelter, and feeling a little guilty for the harsh tone, she stopped. "By the way, thanks for the chowder. It was better than I expected."

Reaching the shelter, she unzipped the door and peeked inside. To her astonishment, her uncle was awake. He lay twisted to one side, eyes open, and a crooked grin curling one side of his mouth.

"Jessie, what did I tell you? Don't be giving those fellows such a hard time. They're trying to do all the right things," the man snorted, his words easier to understand than earlier.

"What? Have you been just hanging out here, listening?" Jessie grinned, relieved to see improvement.

"What else I got to do? Tell you what, kiddo. I gotta go out to do some business. Why don't you be a good sport and ask the boys to give me a hand."

The boys were pleased, that with effort, and though he was stiff from lying so long, Bob could almost manage on his own. With the call completed, and after insisting he try a sip of chowder, they'd tucked him back into his bag.

A cool mist had begun to dribble down, bringing with it the cover of night. As the soft rain dropped, the temperature did the same; sending most biting bugs to bed.

The boys had donned rain suits and were sitting tight to the fire. Moments earlier, and with only a quick "good-night, see you in the morning", Jessie had disappeared into Travis's tent.

Seth stirred the coals with a stick, sending up a fiery shower of sparks. From far out on the water, the loons took turns wailing; their haunting cries echoing off the distant shore.

"So? What's our plan for tomorrow? Use the boat to tour the lake or stay close to camp?" Seth asked while pushing the stick around in red-hot ashes.

Travis waved a hand in the air, trying swat a pesky mosquito that hadn't been told meal time had passed.

"I guess it depends on the weather. At least we don't have to go fishing. We still have a couple smaller fillets from those cute ones I caught. Plus a big slab from that blind finny cripple you snagged."

"What d'ya mean snagged? It was skill and patience that put that old fish in the boat," Seth protested with a wide smile tinted orange by firelight.

In truth, luck had played a big role in bringing the largest of the three fish into camp. It happened as Seth was cranking in a small walleye. A much larger northern pike spotted the smaller fish struggling to break free. As the big pike slashed in for an easy meal, one of its eye openings snagged on the lure's second treble hook.

"Yeah, right," Travis retorted. "That fish was so feeble it had support braces on its fins. Good thing we used it for soup. A fish that old probably tastes worse than dead carp, not that I ever tried eating one."

Seth unexpectedly turned somber. "Not to change the subject, but Bob seems better. When we walked him to the woods, he pretty much did it his own. I didn't carry much of his weight. What about you?"

"No, I thought you had him. And did you notice? He's talking much better, too. Maybe by morning he'll be back to near normal," Travis said softly, doubting the words would ring true.

The two pals kept quiet for a time, vacantly watching the fire change over to coals. Rain was beginning to pelt down as droplets grew in size and volume.

"I've had it. I'm turning in," Travis sighed.

"I'm more than ready. I can't remember when I've been this tired. It's hard to believe we just left home yesterday. What with all we've been through, it seems a whole lot longer."

"Yeah, it seems that way to me, too. I'm so pooped I could sleep for a week," Travis yawned. Then, after unsteadily rising to a standing position, he plodded toward the tent.

Chapter Eight

CHAPTER EIGHT

Morning arrived with a snivel and a whimper. But that was fine with the boys. The pitter-patter of drizzle on tent fabric only encouraged the teens to stay tucked deep in their sleeping sacks.

"Trav, you awake? I think it's way past time to get up." Seth moaned in a throaty whisper long after first light.

"What? It can't be time already. It's still pretty dark out," Travis groaned, poking his nose out of the sleeping bag. "Oh, man! I feel like an old pack mule...used, abused, and put away wet. I'm so stiff I don't think I can move."

"Same here. But I suppose one of us should check on Bob. We need to make sure he gets plenty of water. Isn't that what they do a hospital? You know, hook up a tube and let liquid drip."

"I guess. I'll go check," Travis volunteered in a voice husky with sleep. "I gotta get up and go in the woods anyway. Just give me a minute or two. I forgot to put needles under the tent. It feels like I slept in a rock-spring bed."

Seth let out a long yawn and then cleared his throat. "Uh-huh. As if you didn't get fifty winks or more last night. Cripes, from the way you were snoring, you must have a big pile of kindling sawed, split, and ready to burn."

"Oh, is that so? And, what about the weird noises you make? I woke up to such snorting, I thought I was gonna have to go out and scare away a moose."

They kept mute for a time, listening to the tapping of rain drops falling on the tent fly. And trying to will stiff muscles to get on with the day.

Finally Seth sucked in a big breath, and then exhaled loudly. "Are you gonna get up or not? There's not enough room in here for both of us to get dressed at the same time."

"All right, already. Stop with the nagging. If you're in such a big rush to get going, do it. It isn't gonna hurt my feelings," Travis grunted.

"All right, I will," Seth snapped, working the bag's zipper.

He squatted on his sleeping sack, struggling into damp clothes. Pulling on his rain suit, all the while wearing a scowl, he stooped through the door opening. When he was outside, he stood tall, arms over his head, working kinks from complaining joints.

A cold drizzle slapped his face before he realized he hadn't pulled up the hood of the jacket. After snuggling it tight to his cheeks, he stood scanning the surroundings.

Looking like a scene from a scary movie, foggy vapor hung over the water, obscuring the opposite shoreline. Behind camp, needles and leaves drooped low, saturated from an all-night soaking. All in all, it was very depressing start to a brand new day.

Seth made one optimistic observation. The drops showering the tent cloth sounded larger than they actually were. The rain was more of a mist than a downpour. He sighed. It was probably best to get a blaze burning before checking on Bob. If they had to walk the man to the woods, the old timer would no doubt become wet. They'd need fire to warm him up and dry him off.

"A real butt ugly morning, huh?" Dressed in camouflage rain gear, Travis was bent low, fastening the tent flap.

"Sure is. I didn't hear you come out. Why don't you check on Bob while I work on the fire?" The request sounded more like a command than a question.

Travis stared at his friend for a moment. "Well, one good thing, we have plenty of fish. A guy could catch a cold out there today," he noted, nodding at the fog shrouded waterway. "You want me to help with the fire? With everything so soaked, it won't be all that easy to get going."

Seth glowered. "What's that supposed to mean? Don't ya think I know how? I've started lots of fires on wet mornings. Or did you forget that I helped guide canoe groups through the Boundary Waters last summer?"

Travis raised arms in surrender. "Man! Did one of us get up on the wrong side of the bed or what? I need to sneak back in the woods before anything else. If you wait a few minutes, I'll bring back some birch bark."

"Don't need any birch bark," Seth muttered. "I'll cut some shavings. Go ahead. Do your thing. I'll have the fire going before you're back."

Jess had been awake for hours, curled tight in her silky bag, full of worry and dread. She heard the boys talking. Even though the words weren't clear, the tone said something was amiss in Mosquito Bay.

Not able to sleep, she'd had lots of time to think about the mess they were in. But her uncle had been right. It wasn't their fault that they were struck by a storm, and they'd have to work together.

Still, she couldn't help feeling that she was a little bit to blame. Uncle Bob had changed his flight plans to ferry her to the resort where she was supposed to spend the rest of the summer. The new route had run them right into the storm.

So the least she could do was start pitching in more. But right now she had to sneak off. Listening to the rain dance on the tent top only increased the urgency. It wouldn't take a minute to get ready. Because her sleeping bag wasn't all that warm, she'd slept in her sweatshirt and jeans.

Decision made, Jess slipped into her uncle's rain jacket, tied the laces of her Nikes, and scrambled out of the tent. The first thing she saw, besides thick fog, was Seth. He had his back to her, clearly concentrating on something.

When she was still several feet distant, she stopped, cleared her throat, and then asked, "Is there something I can help with?"

"Damn! Don't be sneaking up on people! Look what you made me do!" Seth snarled, dropping the knife and clutching his thumb.

He unclenched his fingers to look at the wound. Bright red blood oozed from a cut just above the knuckle. "Yeah, you can help! Go get a bandage from the first aid kit before I bleed out."

"Gosh, I'm sorry! I didn't mean to startle you. That's why I coughed."

"Well, I didn't hear you. You obviously didn't cough loud enough," Seth spat, putting his thumb to his mouth.

For a moment they stood glaring at each other. "Oh, forget it; just stand there like some stupid statue. I'll go get one myself." Annoyed and angry, he grasped the thumb in his free hand. Mumbling a curse under his breath, he stalked toward his tent.

Travis returned moments later, surprised to see Jess stacking branches in the fire ring.

"Morning, Jessie. Where's Seth? I thought he was gonna be the fire-bug today."

Jess turned from her work. "Oh, hi," she said softly. "Your friend's in his tent. He sliced his thumb and thinks that it's my fault. Right now he's looking for a bandage."

Travis scrunched his brow, trying to sort out what might have taken place during the short time he'd been away. "How could it be your fault? You weren't holding the knife...were you?"

She didn't answer, reaching under her rain jacket instead. Her hand emerged clutching a pink lighter. "What do you think? Think I can get this pile going?" she posed, pointing to the misshapen stack of soggy twigs and sticks.

"Ah, I don't want to criticize, but no. It won't. You'll need some of this," Travis said, unzipping the front of his jacket. Tucked inside like balled-up newspaper were curls of white bark. "Unless the twigs are small and dry, you have to use birch bark. It has oily stuff that burns like gasoline. Here," he said, tearing several of the curls into smaller pieces. "Sneak these scraps under the pile."

Jess was impressed. The fire started with just one flick of the lighter. Even more surprising, Travis had helped without being mean-mouthed, not at all like his bossy sidekick. She felt a little braver and calmer.

* * *

Seth was able to staunch the bleeding and bandage the wound. On closer inspection, the cut wasn't all that serious. He had done worse to himself while filleting fish back home. But the upcoming injury to his ego would prove far more serious.

He'd poked his head out in time to see the girl starting the fire. Within seconds flames had flared; and the pile began burning in earnest. What Seth hadn't witnessed was Travis slipping off into the woods, searching for more kindling, which left Seth thinking that Jess had accomplished the feat by herself.

Travis slogged back several minutes later toting an armful of sticks and branches. Satisfied the fire would burn on its own, he said, "Jessie, what say we check on Bob? He probably needs to get up and out."

Jess returned a small smile in agreement, pleased that at least one of the scouts was acting civil.

"Uncle Bob? You awake?" Jess asked when they'd trudged to the tent flap.

The query was rewarded. Sounding stronger and a bit more like his old self, Bob slurred, "Is that you, Jazzi? Where are the boys? What are those two polliwogs up to this morning? I've been hoping they'd show up soon. I need to go out."

"I'm right here, Bob," Travis said, working the zipper open. "Are you staying dry in there? Any leaks?"

Bob hacked out a raspy cough before replying. "Yup. Dry as day-old popcorn. But I won't be for long if I don't get up soon."

Although no more than five feet high, Bob's tent was wide enough for several campers plus a bit of gear. There was enough room for both teens to enter. Inside, Bob lay on his back, one arm out, the other tucked under the cover of his sleeping sack.

The dismal light filtering through tent fabric made it difficult to get a good read on the man's coloring, but it seemed pretty normal. A moment of awkward silence ensued as Jess and Travis stared.

"Are you two tadpoles just gonna sit there gawking, or are you gonna help an old man get up and take care of business?"

"Wow, Uncle Bob! You're sure sounding terrific, so much better," Jessie beamed, stripping off the raincoat.

"Here, let's get you sitting up," she continued. "As you can tell from the tapping on the tent top, it's raining. Not real hard, but enough to get you soaked if you don't wear this."

"All right, let's do it! And then see if you can sweet talk one of the boys to start fryin' some fish. I'm ready for some real food."

* * *

Seth lay on his bedroll, seething. Seeing Jessie start the fire had only added fuel to his already foul mood. Who in the world did she think she was—ruler of the campsite?

Up to now she hadn't lifted a finger, wouldn't even listen to simple directions. And then, after she causes him to darn near cut off his thumb, she had the nerve to take over his job.

For that matter, he fumed; she was the cause their problems in the first place. If they hadn't had to sidetrack and deliver the skinny witch elsewhere, they'd have made it to the fish camp with time to spare. Besides, since the original destination was nowhere near here, they probably would have missed the squalls altogether.

He rolled onto his side, and checked the bandage for seepage. Nothing. The cut had been clean, and although it was deep, pressure had quickly stanched the flow. But Seth knew the downside of such a wound: water. For a while he'd have to keep the bandage from getting wet. And worse, to keep the thumb from becoming infected, make certain no fish slime entered the injury.

Flopping over on his back, Seth stared at the ceiling. Human chatter rose above the din of the rain. Voices, first Travis's, then Jessie's, even Bob's slurred gravelly baritone, followed by a burst of laughter. What could be so darn funny on such a miserable morning? More than curious, Seth stuck his head out the tent door.

Jess was kneeling under the rain fly of the larger shelter, a seldom seen smile lighting her face. Bob, with only a bit of support from Travis, was shuffling into the woods, mostly under his own steam. Some of Seth's earlier annoyance faded. The man's condition had drastically improved. Maybe their luck would do likewise.

* * *

Seth began preparing breakfast while the others were busy with Bob. Having a supply of fish fillets on hand, he chose to fry a few and use another for soup. By the time Travis rejoined him at the fire circle, he had both a pan and a pot steaming away.

"Good news, huh?" Travis said, pulling up his hood. "Bob's walkin' and talkin' so much better. He's even sitting up. Right now he's propped against his duffel waiting for you to bring him something to eat."

"Great. At least it looks like he's gonna survive this stroke thing. But I gotta tell ya, bud, we aren't about to get rescued today. Not with this cloud cover."

Travis slugged his friend lightly on the shoulder. "Is that why you're so glum? Hey, remember, it's June. We aren't gonna freeze. And with the boat, we can always catch plenty to eat. Lighten up. Like the song says, the sun will come out tomorrow. It always does."

"Oh, I suppose you're right," Seth reluctantly agreed.

"Say, why don't you stir the soup? I need to flip the fillets, make sure they don't burn."

After breakfast, and per Bob's request, everyone crowded into his tent. Although muscles and nerves on one side refused to fully cooperate, he was feeling better. Good enough, he thought, to hold a meeting.

"Jessie, go ahead and dig into the snack sack. Pull out a couple of those chocolate bars for desert. You've all done good. You deserve a treat," Bob said, a tinge of a smile curling one side of his mouth.

Jessie flushed. "Ah, maybe we should save them for an emergency," she muttered, examining the wrinkles in the fabric floor.

"Ah, Jazzi. Might someone have already sampled a few of the treats?" Bob asked in his halting speech. "It's all right. Just be honest."

Jessie nodded yes, eyes still fixed on the floor. "Sorry. I was so hungry I couldn't help myself. But except for one Snickers bar, I didn't touch any the boys' stuff."

"Well, after this, check with us first. We don't want to make plans for things we don't have. Well now, why don't you share a couple of those Tootsie Pops in trade? By the look on Seth's face, he could stand some sweetening up."

Bob kept mum until each had his or her mouth wrapped around a sucker. "I think it's time to make plans for the rest of the week. Lying around doing nothing, I've had time to consider our options. The way I see it, there are only two. We stay camped on this lake and hope we'll be located; or study the maps and see if there's a safe water route out of here."

He cleared his throat and then looked at Seth and Travis. "Boys, since all we've had to eat were fish, I'm assuming you weren't able to get the cooler. Is that correct?"

"We tried, but the water's so cold we couldn't do it. Seth got your flight bag, though. And we dried all the maps. We think that Jessie even located this lake," Travis reported, flashing a small smile in Jessie's direction.

Bob gave a slight tip of his head. "Good, that's a start. But there's something else I need to tell you. There might be a good reason we could end up needing those maps. Not all of these wilderness lakes are being used this year. This could very well be one of 'em."

"No, that's not right," Seth interrupted. "Trav and I went exploring up that creek we crossed the other day. We found an old Lund fishing boat at a little lake that feeds the stream. If somebody stashed a boat way back there, there's gotta be others hidden along the big water."

The man bobbed his head in partial agreement. "Maybe. I hope you're right. Problem is, outfitters might not be using 'em this year. It seems some lakes were getting too much fishing pressure...at least by wilderness standards. Most of the trophy-sized walleyes and pike have been pulled out."

"What's that got to do with us?" Travis asked.

"Well, from what I heard, fly-in operators came to an understanding. They'd let some lakes sit idle for a spell. Give fish a chance to make a comeback, let 'em grow up as it were."

"Yeah, but even if this lake's off limits to fishermen, won't planes still be passing over?" Travis queried.

"What about Search and Rescue?" Seth threw out. "They're bound to check every lake, right?"

Bob slowly shook his head. "Well...I'm not so sure. They could, but maybe not. There are thousands of lakes in this part of Ontario. And we're a long way from my original flight plan. Chances are that every aircraft within a hundred miles will be listening for our ELT signal. But since we didn't crash, and the airplane is bobbing around upside down, they won't hear a thing."

Jessie spoke, the quiver in her voice a giveaway to how she was absorbing this package of bad news. "What's an ELT? Sounds like a sandwich."

Seth gave Jessie a withering look. "Not a BLT, it's an ELT. An emergency radio or somethin' like that. Right, Bob?"

"Yup, you're pretty close," Bob slurred. "It's a special transmitter that sends out a signal when a plane comes down hard, like in a controlled crash."

The man took a couple of raspy breaths, cleared his throat, and continued in his slow drawl. "But our landing was smooth so it wouldn't have been activated. Besides, right now it's strapped down in the rear of the airplane. It wouldn't do much good even if it was working."

Seth popped the sucker from his mouth and asked, "Is it something I could get at? You know, once the weather warms."

Bob used his good hand to scratch his whiskery chin while he thought it over. "I don't think so, Seth. If you couldn't get at the cooler, I doubt you'd have any luck with the transmitter. You'd have to remove the back panel to get at it. It'd be tough dive. Let's hope we're home before the water warms enough to even consider going after it."

Speaking was still a burdensome task. The man paused, collecting his thoughts and catching wind. "Here's what I think. In a day or two I want to spend some time going over the maps. Hopefully, with each passing hour I'll get a little stronger. You boys do what we planned in the first place: some serious fishing. Catch enough to dry some fillets over the fire. You know, Seth, like Rollie does in the smoke house at the resort."

After another break, Bob had just enough energy to

make some final suggestions. "Jessie, maybe you should try to gather enough wood to keep the fire burning night and day. That, and look in on your old uncle from time to time. And keep your fingers crossed that the rain stops. You're bound to feel better in sunshine."

Seth was about to leave when Bob added one final comment. "And kids, try to get along. We're in this together. Let's work as a team."

* * *

Although the day remained wet and gloomy, murky light made for great angling. When the boys rowed in several hours later, a dozen fat walleyes trailed behind on a rope stringer.

Travis went to work weaving together a web of live branches. The idea was to support the mesh over the coals. That way the fillets could be dried, preserving them. After cooking up a pot of chowder, leftover fish slabs were placed on the matting. With forked limbs supporting the web, the idea was put to use.

While the scouts went fishing, Jess kept busy gathering wood. Each trip nibbled at her fear of becoming lost. And except for quick checks on her uncle, she'd worked non-stop. When the boys beached the boat, they were introduced to an impressive mound of fire sticks.

Travis was quick to give praise. Seth remained temperamental. Cranking in the biggest catch of the day had done little to improve his disposition. He was growing weary of eating only fish, and by his reasoning, Jess was the cause of one-course meals.

When a pot of chowder was cooked, Travis filled two cups; one for Jess, the other for Bob. The girl took a cup in each hand, gave Travis the slightest tilt of her head, then without a word, walked to her uncle's tent.

With lunch over, and fillets drying over smoldering

coals, the boys retreated to Seth's shelter. Their rain gear had done its job. Only leather shoes had become sponges, causing chilled feet. Inside, they cocooned themselves in sleeping bags, ready to nap.

Chapter Nine

C H A P T E R   N I N E

By early evening the drizzle had slowed to a sporadic face-wetting spit. Thick tangles of gray cotton continued to whirl over the lake, only occasionally letting slivers of sunlight sneak through.

Following a short nap, the boys pulled on rain gear before trudging out into the gloom. After breathing new life into the fire, each had kept busy by either rotating drying shoes or flipping fillets. From the lack of pleasant chit-chat, Travis sensed the short sleep session had done little to improve his pal's disposition.

Jess joined the duo, hoping to make small talk. But failing to engage Seth in any meaningful conversation, she returned to the shelter; preferring her uncle's company, ailing as he was, to Seth's.

It didn't take long for Travis to make the connection. He recognized the cause of Seth's unhappy attitude. His buddy was worried they wouldn't be found before the weekend. But being who Seth pretended to be, a teenage tight-lipped macho man, he'd never admit to it.

Hoping to shake his pal free of his doldrums, Travis chose to try a little humor. "Mr. Springwood, did you hear the one about the kid who came home from school and ate his homework?"

Seth turned his head and frowned. "No Trav, I didn't hear about the kid who ate his homework. Why, I suppose you want me to ask, did he do that?"

Travis beamed. "He thought he was following the teacher's directions. She'd told him the work was a piece of cake."

A low groan escaped Seth's lips. "Real funny. Come on, Trav. If you can't do better than that, don't even try."

"Okay, how about this one? Grandpa comes downstairs and finds his young granddaughter pecking away on the computer keys. 'What are you working on?' he asks. 'Oh hi, Grandpa.' she says. 'I'm writing my first novel.' The old man walks over and looks at the monitor. 'What's it about?' he asks. The girl looks up at him with a puzzled expression. 'How should I know?' she answers. 'Ya know I don't know how to read yet.'"

Seth shook his head. "Trav, will ya just let it go? A comedian you aren't. Don't give up your day job."

"Well, if you weren't such a grouch, you would've laughed. You could have at least chuckled." Travis mumbled, standing on tip-toes to avoid smoke curling toward his face.

For a time they stood without speaking, staring at a group of gulls gathering down the bay. The large white water birds were squabbling over the latest fish remains.

"Look, I'm worried about our predicament...'specially about Bob. But there's nothing we can do about it until help gets here. In the meantime, we're camping and fishing just like we planned to do in the first place. Hey, it's summer. We've got lots to eat—although I grant you it's mostly fish. Try to put a more positive spin on our situation. If not for us, at least do it for Bob's and Jessie's sakes. Acting like the resident grouch isn't gonna get us rescued."

"So you think I'm being a wimp?" Seth challenged, tossing a stick in the fire. "That I'm afraid we won't be rescued soon?"

Travis bit back a reply, wanting to say more but fretting that he may have already said too much. Without a response, Seth shuffled to the fish drying rack and began turning fillets. No words were spoken until every fillet had been flipped.

"Yeah, but Trav, you forgot something. My mom's getting married next Saturday. I'm supposed to be the one to give her away. And you...you're the best man. By now, she and my sister must be nervous wrecks. We gotta get out of here soon or she's gonna be a basket case." Without another syllable, Seth grabbed his shoes, slipped them on, and clumped off to his tent.

Travis was left standing by himself, pondering what else he could say or do to lighten Seth's load. He shivered, remembering Bob's words right after the first squall. "A rescue might take longer than you think," the old man had cautioned.

"It might take longer than you think."

* * *

Shortly before sunset the western horizon threw off its blanket. A slash of scarlet smeared the edge of the earth; staining lake ripples a rusty red. After tending to Bob, and gulping a meal of fish and chowder, the teens crouched near the fire, savoring the heat.

"You know what I think? I think we should move to another campsite," Travis blurted without waiting for a reply.

"Why? What's wrong with where we are?" Jess asked, fiddling with the zipper on her jacket.

"Yeah, I agree. What's wrong with staying put?" Seth grumbled. "The tents are pitched. This rock slab makes a terrific work and fire spot. And fishing's been good out in the bay. Why change now? One spot's the same as another."

Jessie zeroed on Seth. "Holy cow, you're actually considering something I said."

Seth looked down, scowling. "'Cause it's about the first thing you've said that does make sense," he snarled, feeding a stick to the fire.

Travis leapt into the fray, hoping to put a halt to heated words. "Would you two just chill out? There are a couple of reasons. First, when the weather warms, the bugs are gonna eat us alive back here. We're too sheltered to catch a night breeze."

Seth tossed a second stick on the fire, rocketing up a spiral of cherry sparks. "Okay, I'll give you that. So what's the second reason?" he asked, leaving off a little of the edge.

"That's obvious, if you think about it. If we hope to be spotted from the air, we need to be camped on the shore of the big lake. I hardly think any search flights would fly over these narrow bays. I'd bet they'll be checking bigger bodies of water first."

Seth furrowed his forehead before responding. "Yeah, you might be right. So where do you have in mind?"

Travis stood and ambled to the wood stack. He returned with a bundle of sticks and limbs.

After carefully placing most on the fire, he detailed the plan. "I was thinking about the end of this channel...over on the opposite shore. You know...where the bay opens up to the big lake."

Looking at the others for approval, he added, "There's a

stretch of sandy shoreline on the inside corner of the point. It'd be a good place to beach the boats. Probably a good place to swim or take a bath, not that any of us needs one," he grimaced, pinching his nose with thumb and forefinger.

The trio fell quiet, considering the proposal. From behind camp the hoot of an owl vied for the teenagers' interest; the call announcing the hunting hour had arrived. Almost as if an echo, a loon added its voice, a primal wail.

"Don't those howls ever spook you guys?" Jess shivered.

For the first time that evening, Seth looked directly at Jess. "There's nothing to be 'fraid of. They're only birds. Should a wolf pack start yappin', you'll have a new meaning for the word spooky."

"Uncle Bob said you guys were just kidding about wolves and bears. That none lived around here."

Travis couldn't help himself. He chuckled out loud. "Bob didn't say that they didn't live around here. He said they wouldn't bother us. And they shouldn't, 'specially with all the human stink we've left in the woods."

He paused and then stepped around the fire so Jessie could better see his face. "Remember, you asked me if I've ever read any fairy tales. Well, yeah, like lots. They're just make-believe stories to frighten little kids, especially tales about wolves. I know you won't believe this, but a wolf pup help save my life last winter. Didn't he, Seth?"

"Yup. I would never have found you if it hadn't been for your black, furry friend. Over time you'd just be name on a plaque, decorating the high school hall."

Jess sprang to her feet. "There, dang it! You're doing it again. Puttin' me on, trying to pull my leg. When you two can talk more like adults, clue me in. 'Cause, right now I'm going to bed."

After Jessie had disappeared into Travis's little green tent, both boys broke out in soft laughter.

"I tell you, Trav. That gal is sure somethin' else. She doesn't believe us when we're teasing; and she won't believe us when we're tellin' her the truth. Maybe tomorrow you'll have to put your little toe on display to prove your point. Or I should say where your little toe used to be before it got nipped by frostbite. Maybe she'll believe once she sees the proof."

Travis stretched, ready to trudge off to bed. "Oh, forget it. But she did accomplish one thing. Something I hadn't been able to do all day."

Seth also stretched, ready to follow. "What's that?' he asked, extending his arms and yawning at the same time.

"She got you to smile. I gave up on doin' that hours ago."

* * *

First light arrived bright and breezy. By the time morning chores were completed, the sun had climbed far above the tree-line. Over a breakfast of dried fish and liquid chowder, Travis ran his proposal by Bob.

"I think it's an excellent plan. The only hitch," he noted, "is how can I tag along if I can't walk or paddle?"

Travis had already considered the question. "That's a no-brainer. Remember, we have a boat. Seth and Jessie can take one of the duffels in the canoe. You and I will take the others in the Lund. It's a three-seater so weight won't be a problem."

Bob shot Travis a grin, but because of the stroke, it was little more than a lopsided gash across a whisker-filled face. "You've been doin' some good thinking," he slurred, spittle dripping from his lips. "Your pa would be proud."

At the mention of his father, Travis flashed on his family back home. They, just like Seth's mom, must be going wild with worry—three times in one year. Must be some kind of record, he thought, one he wasn't proud of.

Travis pushed the image aside and put a confident pitch in his reply. "I don't know 'bout that. It just seems Ma Nature keeps testing me. Like I told Seth yesterday, as long as you're holding your own, we haven't got a whole lot to worry about. The fishing's great, and unlike last fall and again this winter, the weather's warm. We're gonna be just fine."

Bob managed to hold a one-sided smile. "Son, I like your attitude. You're a chip off your old man's block, that's for sure. So let's do it. I gotta get up anyway. There's no sense wasting a trip."

* * *

Once tents were down and packed, all the camping gear was stowed in the boats. With help from Seth's broad back, Bob was placed in the rear of the Lund. Pulling hard on the oars, Travis soon had the little vessel pointed down the waterway. The two-boat flotilla was about to depart.

"Ever paddle a canoe before?" Seth asked while holding the slender craft bow first in the shallows.

"No, but how hard can it be? If you can do it, so can I," Jessie replied, tight-lipped.

Shoeless and dressed in a pair of cutoffs and the baggy sweatshirt, she waded out a few feet, ready to climb aboard.

"Whoa, wait a minute. You just don't jump in a canoe. It'll flip. What you wanna do is place your foot right smack dab in the middle. Then carefully bend over and grab both gunnels for support."

"Say what?" Jessie asked, stopping mid-step.

"That's right, I forgot. You're a rookie," Seth smirked. "I should have said grab the sides of the canoe. Next transfer all your weight to the bottom. Once you're in, sit down and stay low. And don't forget. Never. Ever. Stand. Up. Don't even think about it, okay?"

"Yeah, yeah, I got it," she mumbled, and then did as she'd been told.

Seth was impressed by Jessie's agility. She'd stepped in so gracefully that the Wenonah had barely wiggled. Even Travis, with years of experience, had never made it look easier. But Seth wasn't about to dish out any compliments, not this morning, anyway.

Once Jessie was settled, Seth found his voice and coughed up a second set of instructions.

"Okay, when you think you're ready, reach down and grab the paddle. Lay it crossways in front of you while I get in. When we start out, pull hard with your right hand. I'll let you know when it's time to switch."

"Aye, aye, Captain," Jessie answered with syrupy sarcasm.

Then, doing as she had been told, she held the paddle tight and sat still, fuming. Seth was such a jerk. She wished that Travis was sharing the canoe with her; at least he didn't hassle her about being new to the wilderness.

Once underway, Jess took to paddling like a young frog to a new pond. Within minutes the slender craft zipped by the slower rowboat. For the second time that morning, Seth was impressed, but like before, kept his mouth closed.

Travis was struggling to keep the Lund on a straight line. Battling a crosswind, the boat's path became a comical zigzag affair. If it hadn't been for Bob's gentle reminders, telling what oar needed stroking most, the teen could have easily rowed in a circle.

Travis had vast experience paddling canoes, but his rowing skills were rusty. Ever since he could take a boat out to go fishing on Poplar Lake, he'd had the use of an outboard engine. So it wasn't long before muscles and joints began putting up a fuss. Reluctantly, he prepared to accept that the Lund would be coming in a far distant second.

By the time the canoe reached the big lake, the rowboat was merely a gray-red smudge far behind. A sharp breeze gusted unchecked across open water, and choppy white-tipped waves crested and fell on its sky-reflecting surface. Seth had to stroke hard to keep from being blown toward shore.

It wasn't until they rounded the stubby peninsula that he could relax. "Right there," he said, and as if Jessie had eyes in the back of her head, pointed with the blade of his paddle. "We'll go straight in and let the canoe beach itself."

Still facing front, Jessie replied with what had become her standard reply. "Aye, aye, Captain."

The finger of land tempered much of the wind. Once the canoe was in calmer waters, Jess let Seth do the maneuvering. They were just about to bump the gentle slope of shoreline when Jessie spotted the cow moose disappearing into the woods with her calf.

"Oh!" she shouted, pointing. "Look at that!" And forgetting Seth's warning, stood right up. The canoe rolled, dumping them into the shallow water.

Spitting out a mouthful of lake water, Seth exploded with an open-mouthed bellow. "Hey! You did that on purpose! No one can be that stupid!"

"So what if I did?" Jessie retorted, sloshing ashore. "And I'm not stupid."

"Could've fooled me," Seth snarled as he pushed the canoe onto the sand. "I told you never to stand up in the canoe!"

"I've never been in a canoe before, so excuse me for making a mistake, Mr. Smarty Scout! Maybe your bath will wash away your rotten attitude."

Seth felt a flutter of regret, but was still far too angry to let it go entirely. "Fine," he growled, "I—"

"Just leave me alone," Jessie muttered, snatching her duffel bag and tromping toward the point. There she could get a good view of the boat and mark her uncle's progress.

* * *

Seth discovered they weren't the first to use the sandy beach. He explored the nearby woods while waiting for the boat to arrive. From what appeared to be years of use, campers had cleared and leveled several tenting sites. The openings were just inside the woods, perfect for catching both shade and a lake breeze.

The discouraging news was that most dead timber had been well picked over. They would have to wander farther into the forest for a fuel supply. And knowing how Jess feared getting lost, Travis or he would have to take on the role of fire-keepers.

But that was alright. Although he was still angry, he realized Jessie had pinpointed the problem. His attitude had needed a clean-up. And he had to admire Jessie's spunk. If she was telling the truth that today had been her first time in a canoe, she'd been amazingly good at it.

Seth realized he had to put aside the soaking. He wasn't made of sugar. A little water wouldn't make him melt. Acknowledging his mistakes never came easy. He'd work at building up enough nerve to say 'sorry', that he'd been acting like a jerk. But he could do all of that later. There were tents to pitch, wood to gather, and fish to catch. He could consider apologizing to Jess when the work was done; maybe after lunch, or possibly around the campfire.

Distant yelling caught Seth's ear. Looking up, he saw the Lund plowing around the point. From the way Travis was clumsily manning the oars, it was clear the boat's engine was beginning to misfire. Right now he had to trot to the beach. Bob would need his help getting out of the boat.

By the time Seth reached the beach, Jessie had waded into the water, ready to grab the boat before it banged against the beach. Travis was sitting backwards, pulling wearily on the oars, when suddenly the craft surged forward and stopped.

Startled, the oarsman twisted in his seat. He was surprised to see Jess bent over the bow, attempting to tug the Lund farther up on land.

As Seth drew near, Jessie coughed up the story of the mishap. "I jumped up and made the darn thing tip over." Referring to Seth with a tilt of her head, she added, "I would have helped your water-logged friend empty it, but I don't think I'm on his A-list right now."

Steadying himself with an oar, Travis rose up and turned to face front. Flanked behind Jess, hair plastered to his head and jeans dark with lake water, stood Seth; a hang-dog expression on his usual stoic mug. Only Seth's well worn Tee showed signs of drying—the faded navy-blue cloth tie-dyed with swirls of wetness.

A raspy chuckle came from the back of the boat. Up to this time Bob had taken it all in without comment. But he was obviously amused by what he had witnessed.

Directing his remark toward Seth, Bob drawled out a request. "Say...young...feller, how 'bout you slosh out here and give this old man a lift? And, from the looks of things, you might as well leave your shoes on. From where I'm sitting, it appears you've already had one swimming lesson today. What harm can a second session do?"

* * *

By the time the tents were set, and a meal of fish soup served, noon hour had come and gone. The campers quickly realized that this new site presented several perks. The tents were pitched on forest soil, not bedrock like the former location. Travis knew, come nightfall, he'd be the first to appreciate the difference.

While gathering firewood along a half-hidden path, Seth stumbled upon an unexpected bonus. One that Jessie and Bob would appreciate. He discovered an outdoor privy; complete with a weather-worn toilet seat and a tattered canvas privacy screen.

Travis had taken time to do a little exploring of his own. Fifty yards down shore he came upon a second camping site. Several possible tent openings were cleared just inside the brush-line.

He was delighted to find four fat log butts, cut from what had once been a very thick tree. The stump look-alikes were squatting in a semi-circle around a rock-lined fire pit.

Aha...a perfect job for Jess, Travis surmised. She could move them one at a time. She was certainly strong enough to roll the short logs along the beach front. Come dusk, everyone would have a stubby stool to sit upon; a place from which to enjoy the fire and appreciate the panoramic view of the lake.

Bob was exhausted and looked forward to an afternoon nap. Just the effort of being the passenger had worn the man out. And although he tried putting up a good front, it was apparent he faced an uphill battle. Minutes after of slurping a cup of chowder, he excused himself. Then with help from Jess, he was tucked into his bag, ready to catch some serious shut-eye.

Bob hadn't said anything, but he was disheartened by the lack of activity in and around the lake. That was peculiar. Late June was prime-time for fishing trips. Yet not a single boat and motor combo was pulled up on the beach, waiting for fly-in visitors to chase after big ones.

No doubt his earlier thought had been on target; that this lake had been declared 'off limits.' From what Jess had explained from viewing the air chart, this was the only large body of water in the area. All the other lakes were small or narrow. Fly-in trips were pricey. And because of the old maxim, 'bigger water—bigger fish,' anglers usually preferred being dropped off on larger waterways; much like this one.

What was this, the fourth day of their ordeal? Yet, to the best of his knowledge, not a single floatplane had passed overhead. But questions and possible answers could wait until evening. He'd be more alert after a snooze. They could discuss their situation later. Right now it was nap time. Even with Travis doing the work, the boat trip had emptied the man's limited reserves. His battery needed recharging.

Chapter Ten

Jess was the first to spot the overturned aircraft. Riding low in the water like a pair of giant silver-tinted alligators, the pontoons reflected enough light to attract attention. She'd been daydreaming at the time, resting on one of the four stumps she'd moved earlier that afternoon—as per Travis's subtle hint.

He hadn't bossed her into doing the job. As it happened, she volunteered. Travis had merely mentioned the find, and that the stubby logs would make good 'sit-upons,' whatever that meant. He even said that he'd do it himself, later, after gathering wood and hopefully catching a few fresh fish for supper. Unless she'd like to have a go at it herself.

After considering the comment, she decided that it was the least she could do. That job was by far much better than traipsing about in the forest, getting gobbled alive by bugs.

Jess wished the boys were here now, with the boat, able to assist her. The plane was as close to camp as it would probably ever get. They could use the boat to tug the pontoons closer to shore. Once there they could tie the airplane off, keep it from floating away. But the scouts weren't in camp, or even anywhere in sight. They'd left an hour earlier, heading back into the bay, hoping to have success with rods and reels.

If the plane was to be secured, she'd have to do it by herself, without delay. The wind was beginning to shift, fanning away from shore. Did she dare try doing it alone? In a tipsy canoe? And without a life jacket?

Why not? She knew how to handle herself in the water, probably as well, maybe even better, than the scouts themselves. Having spent countless hours playing at the pool, she was an expert swimmer.

Jess estimated the gap between the beach and the air-craft. No more than a couple hundred yards. Not all that far, less than eight laps in the pool. A distance she could easily manage should the canoe tip over.

The day had continued sunny and bright. Only an occasional cloud marred an otherwise uncluttered sap-phire lid. Despite cool air, solar rays covered the beach like a warm blanket. And because of the sunshine, Jess hadn't changed clothes. She was still clad in cutoffs and a sweatshirt. Besides, she flashed, there wasn't time to change into a swimsuit.

The spur-of-the-moment strategy was to paddle to the pontoons, tie up the canoe, locate the ropes, knot them together, and head back to the beach.

The combined cords probably weren't long enough reach shore. But they'd come close. Near enough, she hoped, that she could jump in and touch bottom. And if all went as planned, she could get the airplane secured near shore. Then they could rescue the cooler—and the delights it supposedly held.

It wasn't possible, Jess concluded moments later, to climb into a tipsy canoe without a partner holding one end steady. Attempting the balancing act had been an athletic dare.

Once the canoe was floating, she'd tried to get in. But the skinny craft nearly flipped. Only lightning reflexes saved her from duplicating the early morning stunt.

She stood barefoot on the beach, clutching a gunnel, frustrated. She recalled Seth's advice before they embarked on their short voyage. "Place your weight on the bottom...grab the sides...step in and stay low."

The canoe had a mind of its own. Like a pony that didn't want to be ridden, it twisted and wiggled at the slightest touch. In the meantime, the pontoons were getting a shove in the wrong direction.

She had to make a decision—immediately—before it was too late to even make an attempt. Choice made, Jess became a whirlwind. She tugged the canoe up on the sand, pulled the sweatshirt over her head, and ran into the water. When it was waist deep, she dove in and began stroking.

She hadn't gone far before realizing that the lake was a polar bear bath. Undaunted, she doubled her efforts, arms and legs propelling her across the surface at a record-setting pace.

Jess was more than halfway to the finish line when her limbs began complaining. It started with the toes on her right foot. The little digits curled inward like claws, the ache intense, as if they'd been jabbed by a dozen sharp sticks.

Next to protest the frigid undertaking was the lower muscle of her left leg. Its sinews and cords began constricting, the spasms deep and severe, and the limb becoming paralyzed with pain.

Pushing down a rising wave of panic, she stopped swimming altogether. How far had she come? Taking a glance behind, she judged that the pontoons were closer than the beach. Reaching them would be her only hope.

* * *

The boys were returning to camp, the fishing quest completed. Across the cove, the first dark shadows of evening were creeping from the forest, individual trees blurring into a mysterious looking barrier.

Hovering just above the tree-line, a plump golden balloon tinted the lake surface with a half-dozen shades of yellow. And with exception of a few mosquitoes, just awakening from daytime siestas, it was the perfect evening to be out on the water.

As had become the standard operating agenda, Seth was the engine providing the power. Travis was seated in the rear, clutching tight to rod and reel, trolling. He played out more line, hoping for one last strike before calling it quits.

"You know what, Trav? I'm getting fed up eatin' nothing but fish. Wouldn't it be great if we could get the cooler, add some freeze-dry to the menu?" Seth complained while tugging hard on the weather-checked wooden oars.

"I hear ya. Just be happy I caught a big laker. At least we'll have some variety tonight. But let's not use it for chowder. Trout tastes great baked over open coals. Just thinking about it makes my mouth water."

Seth swiveled his head to get his bearings, then resumed rowing, considering Travis's suggestion.

After a silence broken only by the grating of oar yokes, he shook his head and grinned. "I swear, Trav. You must have some bear blood runnin' through your veins. What with the way you like fish meat so much."

"Are you kidding? It's not that I like it. Well, I used to...before last fall anyway. Naw, I'm just thankful that we've got plenty to eat, even if it's a fishy deal."

They were approaching the finger of land separating the bay from their new camping accommodations. Travis raised the rod tip and began reeling. "So how many did we get altogether? Four or five?" he asked once the lure was secured to an eyelet on the rod.

"We caught five, kept four. Why bother cleaning a skinny jack when we had walleyes on the stringer? I never did care northern fillets in the first place. Too many bones. A guy could get one caught in his throat and choke."

"Yeah, but they're okay for soup or chowder," Travis considered. "Sure wish Jess would try a little fish meat. You know, having to cook special for her is becoming a real pain in the rear. There's no reason she can't start cooking for herself."

About to row around the point, Seth brought the boat closer to shore. "Speaking of which, I wonder if she kept the fire burning. We'll need to keep reminding her to keep an eye out for planes. If she even thinks she hears something, she should toss on some of those spruce boughs I hacked up. They'll make lots of smoke, don't you think?"

"Yeah, they will. I used some last winter...."

Suddenly Travis's eyes went wide as dinner plates. He sprang to his feet, causing the boat to wobble.

"Holy moly! Seth, look! Out there!" he shouted, aiming the rod tip past the bow. "Somebody's out on the lake, waving at us!"

Seth released the oars and spun in his seat to see what the fuss was about. Sure enough, far out on the open water, he spotted a single figure, arms flailing wildly in the air.

But at such a distance he couldn't make out any water-craft. It appeared that the person was standing on the rippled lake surface.

But Travis had the eyes of an eagle, better than twenty-twenty vision. "My God, Seth! It's Jessie! She's standing on one of the airplane floats, waving at us. And partner, from what I can see, she isn't wearing much in the way of clothes."

Seth didn't wait to be told. He grabbed up the oars and put everything he had into the first stroke. The boat surged forward, pitching Travis off his feet.

Plunked in his seat, Travis chuckled. "Hey, I didn't say she was naked. I only said she wasn't wearing much."

* * *

It was close, but by keeping her wits and not panicking, Jess reached the pontoons. The last part of the swim had been done on her back, stroking with hands and arms, legs dangling low and useless.

She had resolved that she wouldn't give up—she wouldn't die—not this way. After all, it was only water and she'd learned to swim as an infant. Swimming was second nature to her—something she never even thought about—an activity as familiar as walking or running.

Reaching the aircraft proved to be only the first stage of the quandary. Climbing onto the pontoon was the second. Once her head bumped metal, she frantically searched for a hand hold. With the exception of rivet bumps, the metal surface was smooth and slippery as a newborn's bare bottom.

Keeping one hand on the float for support, she splashed with her free hand to the pontoon's narrow, tapered end. And because the floats were low in the water, she was able wrap her arms around and rest for a moment, catching her breath. Then she called up the last of her reserves. Through determination and willpower, she wiggled and pulled herself aboard.

What a difference getting out of the water made. Jess flopped full length on the flat part of the float. Warming rays from the late afternoon sun felt scrumptious. Within minutes circulation began returning to normal. Thankfully the cramping subsided.

Feeling better, she sat up. Butterflies immediately fluttered in the pit of her stomach. While she'd been warming and catching her breath, the distance to shore had nearly doubled. Swimming back to the campsite wasn't an option. She had only one choice—sit tight—wait for the boys to make a rescue.

* * *

"Say, sailor! Need a lift?" Travis yelled as the boat drew near. "Looks like you've got a little problem."

Seth stopped rowing and then turned to face front. "What in the world were you thinking?" he croaked. "The ice just went out a few weeks ago. Water's still too cold for swimming. You could have drowned before we had a chance to save you."

"Well, a cheery hello to you, too," Jess said mockingly. "But I didn't drown, did I? And if you have to know, I was hoping to tie off Uncle Bob's airplane before it floated away. But as you can see, my plan didn't work. So cut the crap and take me to shore."

Seth was still nettled by her risky swim. "I don't know. What's it worth? Float trips on these wilderness lakes are pretty pricey. How did ya plan on paying for the ticket?"

Jessie clenched her teeth, trying hard to contain her temper. "You are one big-mouthed know-it-all, aren't you?"

Then she paused, biting back words she'd only regret if they flew out unfiltered. All of a sudden her mind went clear. There was a way to make payment for being rescued. As long as the boys were here with the boat, why not try for the cooler?

She'd recovered enough from the earlier swim to make the attempt. And if she was successful, she'd kill two birds with one stone—food and payback all in one sweet package. Jess rose to her feet, careful not to slip on the metal surface.

"Here's my offer," she said, looking for a suitable place to enter the water. "How about I pay with a package of veggies?"

Without waiting for a reply, she dove beneath the surface. Seth and Travis sat speechless, staring at the bubbles burbling up from the unforeseen plunge.

After a few seconds of stunned silence, Seth broke out in an ear-to-ear grin. "Like I told you the other day, buddy—that gal is sure somethin' else."

Travis didn't respond. He had become a beehive of activity, stripping off sweatshirt and tennis shoes. Next, he unbuckled his belt and began pulling off his jeans.

"What're you doin'?" Seth yelled, his grin replaced with a fly-catching gape. "Don't tell me you're going in after her. You don't like tight places. I better be the one."

Without waiting for an answer, Seth pulled his shirt over his head, kicked off his shoes, and before Travis had a chance to protest, jumped feet first from the boat.

Then, gulping in big breath of air, the youth dropped beneath the surface and disappeared.

* * *

As a youngster, Jess had spent many afternoons playing water games. One of her favorites was a contest diving for nickels and dimes. On hot summer days her mother—her real mom—would toss a handful of coins into the pool. Then it was a race to see who could gather the most money in the shortest time.

Jess was no dummy. She always searched for dimes first. One thin dime was worth two of the bigger nickels. She usually won the contest and was allowed to put the hard-earned cash into her little pink piggy bank.

So when out of the blue she had plunged off the pontoon, it wasn't something unfamiliar to her. Only the temperature was foreign. The pool had a heater.

Dropping below the surface here was like diving into a can of ice-cold Coke—dark and chilly. There would be only one chance to get it right. But Jess didn't like losing. She felt she had something to prove.

The task turned out to be quite simple for someone with her underwater expertise. Because of Seth's earlier effort, the cockpit door was wide open. That was one less thing to deal with.

Filled with Styrofoam insulation, the Coleman cooler had stayed put. It was tight against the floor. Only now, with the plane upside down, the bottom was no longer the floor—it was the roof.

Jess had considered that scenario earlier. She'd pictured the scene in her head after the boys returned empty-handed. Seth had explained how he had to rip the flight bag free from a seat lever. But unlike the cooler, the carryall was fabric and would have become water-logged. Tucked under the seat, it would have wanted to stay put. Not so with the food box. It would want to float to the surface.

So that's where Jessie looked—up. Sure enough, through murky light, and with blurry vision, she spotted its rectangular outline. Ignoring the ache already starting in her legs, she swam inside the cabin. Pulling herself under the upside-down seats, she grabbed onto the cooler's carry strap.

Then, with a firm push off the seat, she exited the aircraft, the strap clutched tightly in her hand. When she and the Coleman were clear of the door, she released her grip and let the container float free. With a flutter kick, she followed the treasure box to the surface.

A heartbeat later, Jessie popped up between the floats. The chunky green box was bobbing alongside, waiting to be hauled from the water.

Without another moment's delay, she clutched onto a crossing brace, and then pushed and pulled her way onto the pontoon.

Next, by lying flat, she reached down and snagged the strap. She pulled until she could grasp onto a side handle. Exerting a herculean effort, she heaved the cooler up on the float. She sighed and smiled simultaneously. She'd done it. The treasure chest was ready to be placed in the boat and rowed back to camp.

* * *

Seth had no way of knowing Jess was on her way up when he was on his way down. He'd begun the lung-testing workout from the far side of the Lund. That meant he had to swim under both the boat and the pontoon before reaching the cockpit. By the time he arrived, Jess was already out of the water—catching the last rays of the day.

With eyelids opened wide, Seth frog-kicked through the door opening, hoping to make a heroic rescue. But even in limited light, with the exception of an orange preserver pushing up against the floor, he could see that the cockpit was empty.

His pulse raced even faster. He was too late. She was already missing—no doubt sinking to the bottom of the lake.

An image of the dark-haired girl resting on the rocky lake bottom splashed across his brain. Despite the cold and gloom, bile rose in his throat, nearly forcing him to expel his breath.

His lungs felt ready to rupture. He had to get a grip, had to save himself. The frigid water was taking its toll. He needed to get topside—immediately—before the watery graveyard called the next number.

Grasping the life preserver, Seth pushed out of cabin. He tucked the flotation aid under his chest, thrust with his legs, and rocketed toward the surface.

Seconds later his head banged the bottom of the boat. For a terrifying instant he thought he was trapped. Releasing the preserver, he kicked and paddled sideways. Several lung-searing ticks passed before he broke into daylight, gasping like an old man who'd just finished a marathon.

Then he lunged for the boat, laboring to catch his breath. Gulping mouthfuls of air, he grabbed onto the gunnel. Travis quickly shifted to the opposite side, worried the small craft would take on water if they didn't keep the weight equalized.

When Seth's panting slowed, Travis bent forward so he could see his friend's face. "Toss the life vest in and work yourself 'round to the back. I'll pull you in," he directed, cautiously moving to the rear.

Seth's grip on the far side of the boat meant that the pontoons were out of his sight-line. He had no idea Jessie was sprawled flat, relishing the last heat of the day.

The youth's breathing eventually slowed enough for speech. "My God, Trav! She's gone! I couldn't find her!"

It suddenly dawned on Travis that his friend had no clue Jessie was safe. He leaned back so Seth couldn't see him wink at Jess. Maybe he could coerce a confession before the cat was out of the bag.

"What d'ya mean? You couldn't find her? How can that be? She was here a second ago." Travis said, leaning back to keep his smile secret. "And what do you care, anyway? From what I could tell, you weren't all that fond of her in the first place."

Seth let go with one hand and used it to hammer on the side of the boat. The thin aluminum hull became a bass drum, deep and tinny. "What the heck's matter with you? Don't you get it? I mean she's gone, Trav— like in forever! Drowned!"

Again Seth pounded with his fist, only this time the blows were much less severe. "I tried! I really tried, but I couldn't find her. The cockpit was empty!" Seth lamented, sounding close to tears.

Travis had heard enough. Anymore would be cruel and unusual punishment.

"Maybe you just didn't look in the right place. Come on; let's get you in the boat before you become a cold prune."

Seth pulled himself along the gunnel until he arrived at the stern. With both hands on the transom, he started to do a pull-up. Once his head cleared the curve of the motor mount, he got a clear view of the float—and the girl who lay face down on its shiny surface.

"You dirty rotten son-of-a-birch tree! Why didn't you tell me? You owe me, buster, big-time!" Seth bellowed, muscling all the way into the boat.

"Hey, go 'buster' yourself! I never said she wasn't here. I just said you probably hadn't looked in the right place. And I was telling the truth. You hadn't."

While the boys bantered, Jess sat up, ready to leave. Travis turned toward her with an ear-to-ear grin smeared across his face. He pointed at the cooler, and then said, "Say Seth, look at the pirate chest Jess brought up from down deep. Now that she knows you care so much, she'll probably share somethin' with you."

Travis turned to witness Seth's response. "So what d'ya think, Jess? Don't you think he might deserve a treat or two for making the effort? After all, it's not his fault you're a regular otter."

Jess stepped lightly onto boat's front seat, and then turned to grab the cooler off the float. After placing it on the boat's floor, she said, "Oh, I thought we decided on that before I went down-under. As I recall, I was supposed to pay for this rescue with a package of veggies."

Seth was pulling on his sweatshirt when he caught the remark about payment. He wasn't certain if he should pout or laugh. For the second time that day, the gutsy girl had bested him. She had a regular nine inning shutout going.

His comeback was feeble. "Aw, Jess, the veggies were for a ride to shore. But now, what with me jumping in after you, the ante went up. Like maybe one of those T-bones we got bundled up inside. That is, if they're still good after four days of swimming with the fishes."

Chapter Eleven

C H A P T E R   E L E V E N

Never had food warmed over an open fire tasted so lip-smacking delicious. Four filled-to-the-brim campers lounged in the smoky aftermath—stomachs stuffed. The teens' eyes were drooping from a day of fresh air and bright light. But the senior's lids were opened wide. He'd snoozed most of the afternoon. The gentleman had concerns he wanted to share.

The return voyage had proved uneventful. Within minutes of Jessie boarding the boat, Travis had rowed to shore, Jess in front, Seth in the rear. Soon as the boat was beached, Jess leapt out, pulled on her sweatshirt, and had run straight to her uncle's shelter.

The man had been awake for a while, curious as to why camp was so quiet. Bob was pleased to see his niece and learn of her success. More importantly, the long nap had worked short-term wonders. He shared that he was feeling better and was up to eating a real meal.

The seal on the Coleman's cover had done its job. No more than a few dribbles of moisture had leaked inside. And because of the coolness of lake water, the ice chunk had yet to melt. Nothing had spoiled.

After four days of mostly fish, the meal was more of a

banquet than a simple supper. Jess was true to her word. She rewarded her rescuers by sharing peas, potatoes, and a vanilla pudding treat for desert.

Seth quickly staked claim to two of the T-bones. They returned the remaining steak to the Coleman to be savored another day.

After cleaning fish, Travis instructed Jess how to prepare powdered rations, an easy undertaking: pour the powder into a pot, add water, stir and heat; wait for the contents to cool. Jessie laughed at the simplicity. She found it hard to believe that the dull, sand-like concentrate could change into real food, but magically it did.

Seth took charge of the beef slabs. He first sliced several strips from each to be shared with Bob. Next, he placed the pieces on the wire bread-toasting grill.

Then he propped the lightweight grid on flat stones set adjacent to the fire ring. With the aid of a forked stick, he'd pushed and prodded until a half dozen red hot coals smoldered beneath the meat.

While Seth worked with the T-bones, Travis prepared the trout fillets. He'd salvaged a piece of foil from the cooler. Wrapped tight in aluminum sheeting, the fish-filled package was placed on a large rock at the fire's edge. Soon the succulent scent of sizzling beef mingled with the aroma of baking trout, causing three sets of lips to water in mouth-tingling anticipation.

Although the steaks smelled tempting, Jess kept her pledge. She dined totally on the reborn vegetable treats, savoring every spoonful, filling her belly until she thought it would burst.

Sometime during the late supper hour the sun had retired. In the lingering twilight, hordes of mosquitoes hovered over the dinner party, each with hopes of feasting on a first class banquet of its own. The invasion had sent Seth and Travis scurrying for rain gear.

After drawing up the top of her sweatshirt, Jess made a beeline to the tent. Moments later she returned with Bob's rain jacket slung over her arm. She helped her uncle into it, and then pulled up its hood to cover the man's head.

"Hey Jess! Where did you put the bug goop?" Travis bawled from inside Seth's shelter. "I can't find it."

Jess felt heat crawl up her cheeks. She'd forgotten all about the little bottle. The bugs hadn't been so vicious in sunshine. A blast or two from the aerosol can had been enough to keep them away. Not tonight. They'd need the industrial strength ointment or risk being carried away. Her embarrassment being, she couldn't remember where she'd put it.

"Aw, hold your horses. I'll get it in a minute," Jess stammered, stalling. When had she used it last? "The lotion's probably in the tent. I'll go look."

After a fruitless search of her bag, Jessie's anxiety started to rise. The evening had been so pleasant. She knew she'd get a hard time if she'd lost the bottle. Finally, Jess found it hiding in the pocket of her old jeans. Right where she had tucked it the day the boys had returned with the boat. A sly grin played across her face. Sorry guys, my rules. First come—first served.

After smearing lotion on every smidgen of exposed skin, she returned to do the same for her uncle. Meanwhile, in a futile attempt to keep biting bugs at bay, Seth and Travis had inched closer to the fire. They stood; bent at the waist, faces toward the flames, letting swirls of smoke curl around their heads.

"Come on, Jess. Hurry up!" Seth pleaded, waving a hand furiously in front of his forehead.

Jess closed the container and then threw it underhanded

to Travis. "Here, you take it. Your friend underestimates the power of the word please."

Snatching the bottle out of the air, Travis smiled triumphantly at the lucky catch. But apparently a truce had yet to be called. He was hoping that since Jess had gained big time points with the cooler, the tension line had been cut. Obviously it hadn't.

Once everyone was insect-proofed, and they were all seated, Bob began. "First off...you did good, Jess. The boys and I want to thank you for supper. Seth, Travis...the surf and turf was also delicious. Well done."

He stopped, drew in a ragged breath and then coughed. "Okay. Let's get to it. Let's chat about this campsite. Boys, did you notice that it hasn't been used yet this year? Not even any boats tied up on the beach. What d'ya think that means?"

Seth was quick to respond. "This place was probably getting tramped down. Maybe the guides moved everything to a new site, someplace with a fresh wood supply."

"Possibly. That might be the answer. But think about this. It's been four full days and we haven't seen or heard any air traffic. I wonder if maybe my notion the other day doesn't ring true. That this is one of the lakes set aside for trophy fishing and is off limits for a few years."

Bob made a feeble swat with his good hand, attempting to brush a mosquito from his cheek. "There's something else bothering me. Something I haven't mentioned."

Seth and Travis glanced at each other with raised eyebrows. Then they leaned forward, wanting to hear every word.

"It's about that flight plan I filed with air control. It had us zigzagging on radio beacon routes. The problem is, once we gassed up, I chose to use the GPS and fly a direct approach to the resort."

When Bob took breather, Seth jumped in. "Why's that a problem? We couldn't have gone that far off your plan. After the lightning strike, we only flew another fifteen minutes or so before landing."

The old man scratched his cheek and nodded. "Yup, that's about right. But that detoured us another twenty-five or thirty miles. What you don't know is that I'd begun sidetracking long before the storm hit. Soon as I saw the dark clouds, I started changing the heading. I thought we could fly around that squall-line."

This time it was Travis who interrupted. "So what are you saying? That we're nowhere near where we should be?"

Bob turned to lock his rheumy eyes on the teen. "Exactly—now you're startin' to catch my drift. But I'm not certain just how far off-track we went. Maybe tomorrow I'll feel well enough to plot it all out on the charts."

He paused, cleared his throat, and then continued, "My best guess right now would be sixty to seventy miles off the original route. But it could be more. That'd be far enough to put us out of the loop for search flights."

Jessie pushed off the stump and then knelt in front of her uncle. "So what are you saying? Are you telling us not to expect help? That we're stuck out here forever?"

Bob stretched out his good arm and stroked the girl's closely cropped locks. He curved his lips in a lop-sided smile and dropped his hand to her shoulder.

"No, Jazzi. We're not going to be here forever. One way or another, we'll figure a way out. And thanks to you, for a few days we'll have more than just fish on the menu."

Bob gestured at Seth with his good arm, indicating he wanted help getting up.

"It's been a long day for all of us. The good news is my belly's plumb full, but my head's growing weary. Kids, let's leave the dishes 'til tomorrow. We all need a good night's rest. We'll get a fresh start in the morning."

* * *

Jess awoke with a start. She lifted her head, straining with both ears in an attempt to hear what had interrupted her sleep. The only sound was that coming from her uncle's tent pitched on the other side of the evergreens. There was a ragged, nasal honk every time the man sucked in air.

Outside, looking like a setting for a stage play, a pale crescent moon hung low over the lake. With its rays shimmering off the water, it was just bright enough to push a candle of light through the thin-skinned shelter. Jessie appreciated the light—it rubbed the edge off the otherwise cave-like interior.

For a time she held her breath and stayed perfectly still, listening for any clue to what had awakened her. But with the exception of her uncle's raspy breathing—there was no sound whatsoever—not so much as a bird chirp.

The longer she lay wondering, the more she realized she needed to go out. Maybe that was the reason for waking up. If she wanted to fall back to sleep there was no postponing the event. Waiting for first light would entail a risk of a flood, not to mention the discomfort.

The thought of the boys mocking her fear of the dark was all the motivation she needed. Working out of the bag, she reflected that she'd gone all day without a cigarette. With everyone sound asleep, this would be a good time for a smoke. And if there was enough moonlight, she could even wander the beach without worry of getting lost.

Slipping outside, she didn't bother to zip up the door flap. This was that deep time of night when biting bugs seek a place to hide and reload. So why bother?

Besides, she'd only be away for a few minutes.

Jess trod quietly to the water-line, turned, and then trudged toward the point. The slice of pale moonlight supplied more than enough illumination. And although the world lacked color, she had no difficulty finding her way along the beach.

When she reached the narrow spit of land, Jessie took care of her need, and then found a place to relax. Sitting on a windfall, she was amazed at how much she could observe—all the way across the lake in two directions.

The distant shoreline was a ragged dark streak. The uneven tree-line silhouetted itself against a charcoal curtain spattered with pin-pricks of white light. Hundreds of stars, thousands of stars, dotted the sky—more stars than she could have ever imagined.

She lit a cigarette, inhaled, and suddenly started coughing. She stared at the cigarette, and realized with a small shock that she didn't even want it. Without a second thought, Jess flicked the cigarette toward the lake; a miniature red missile followed by a short hiss as it hit the target.

Then she lay back and gazed up. The heaven directly above was alive with sparkles—dappled against an ocean of black velvet—tiny white dots clustered so thick they'd be impossible to count in a hundred years of trying.

How was this possible? This couldn't be the same sky as the one overhead where she lived. There, near the edge of the city, constellations were occasionally visible, especially on nights without smog. But never like this. This was a two-page photo from a coffee table book—a scene from a movie—a lightshow without the fireworks.

The pre-dawn air was cool, and after a few minutes Jess became chilled. She wasn't dressed warm enough to stay out for long. So despite the appeal of the peaceful night, her sleeping bag was calling. She pushed up, took one last look at the heavenly light show, and then in a brisk walk, headed for camp.

* * *

The hungry forager had crept close hours earlier. With a nose many times more sensitive than any human, he'd scented the aroma of fried meat and baked trout from miles away. But he knew enough to be cautious. Because mingled with the tantalizing scents was the repulsive reek of man. And although the would-be thief was young, he was crafty enough to stay out of sight.

The shaggy bandit waited until the camp grew quiet. Then on soft paws, he padded silently to the fire site. Many mouth drooling fragrances still hung about in the air, but except for a few empty pots and pans, not a scrap of real food remained.

His sensitive snout directed him next to a fragile structure filled with a host of sweet smelling treats. Red meat, bacon, eggs, cookies and bread—even the luscious scent of chocolate—wafted through the damp night air. He could enjoy a buffet if only the human stink would go away.

One stealthy step at a time, the midnight raider approached. So many wonderful odors wafted from within that he couldn't help but push his muzzle tight to the fabric. He made a second attempt, harder than the first. But this time the taut material popped back with a muffled snapping noise, startling him.

From inside came the sound of movement. The human was stirring. Silently as he'd padded in, the black-furred bandit made his retreat. He had no need to go far—only a few yards into the dark, shadow-filled forest. There he could lie and wait without worry of being seen.

Moments later the young bear couldn't believe his good fortune. No sooner had he settled onto the forest floor, when the human walked away. He watched with night seeing eyes—mouth slavering—as the form trekked to the water's edge, turned, and then disappeared.

He could feast until he was full.

* * *

Jessie tramped toward the tent, feeling good about the day's events. Not only had she proved her worth by recovering the cooler, she'd handled the dark without being handcuffed by fear.

Added to the plus column was pitching the cigarette. The tobacco stick had tasted foreign, awful. Besides, without friends taking part in the ritual, smoking had lost its appeal. It was something she could learn to live without.

As she approached the campsite, Jess paused to take one last look at the lake. The panorama was so breathtaking it gave her goosebumps. It was as though she was standing in the middle of a three-dimensional work of art.

The sliver of moon had become pumpkin-colored as it settled near the edge of the earth. Tipped on its side, it had dipped low enough that it appeared to be resting on the tree tops of the distant shore.

Yellowish rivers of light shimmered on smooth water, broken here and there by ripple rings created by surface-feeding fish. A few hundred yards out a pair of loons glided ghostlike across the level surface—their watery trail a brush stroke on silvery paper.

For the first time, Jessie began to appreciate why Bob and the boys enjoyed camping out. This simple moonlight stroll was more convincing than words would ever be.

Unexpectedly, a big yawn rose in her throat and bubbled out her mouth. Rather reluctantly she turned and started padding quietly toward her tent. She was exhausted and needed more sleep.

Tomorrow would come soon enough.

* * *

Seth and Travis were jolted to life by a piercing screech. Both had been deep in slumber and it took a moment for them to gather their wits. Meanwhile, the screaming continued, soon followed by the sound of approaching footsteps.

"Wake up! Wake up!" Jessie hollered hysterically, grabbing at the tent fly and shaking it hard.

"What? What's the problem?" Seth mumbled with a dry mouth, his tongue thick as a piece of ham.

"Get up! Get up! There's a bear in my tent. A really big one!" Jessie bawled, sounding hysterical.

"A bear in your tent? Not possible! Not while you're in it!" Travis snorted, coming wide awake.

The boys had put themselves into their bags wearing T-shirts and shorts. Each was frantically feeling in the dark for jeans. Regardless of the hysterics taking place by the tent door, they weren't about to pop out nearly naked.

Seth was the first to pull on his pants. He found the flashlight tucked under the mattress pad, flipped the switch, and crawled on all fours through the opening.

Travis had located his Levis and was in a wrestling match to get his feet pushed into the legs.

Jess was too frightened to hang around for help. In the short minute it had taken the boys to dress, she'd dashed to the beach, shoved the boat out into the water, and had climbed aboard. When Seth came out with the light, she was gone.

"What d'ya think, Trav?" Seth asked, slashing the flashlight beam in a full circle "Is this one of Jessie's jokes? Is she trying to get even with me for giving her a hard time?"

"I wouldn't think so. Let's take a look in her tent."

Out of respect for her privacy, Jessie's shelter had been pitched behind a small copse of evergreens. The boys slowed to a snail's pace as they neared the needled boughs.

Travis had reclaimed his flashlight from the pocket of the duffel. The youths tiptoed toward the tent, playing the narrow beams front and back, nervous about what they might stumble upon.

Seth was the first to see it—the open Coleman—lying alongside the shelter. Behind the cooler a trail of eggshells, plastic packaging, and paper wrappings littered the forest floor.

"Damn! Jess was right. Looks like a bear did raid her tent," Travis grumbled, peeking around Seth's broad shoulder for a better view.

"Never heard of a black bear being that bold," Seth muttered. "I can't believe it clawed its way in with a person inside. Come on; let's see if we can salvage something."

Seth edged closer, all the while stabbing the light beam helter-skelter into the woods. When he reached the Coleman, he stopped, knelt, and examined it. Not a thing remained inside. He set it down, and then ambled slowly around the tent, searching for the entry rip. Uneasy, Travis stayed put, shining his light on the door opening, trying to put two and two together.

"You know what?" Seth asked, and then before Travis could respond, went on. "There aren't any holes or tears in the nylon that I can see. That food-stealing ball-of-fur must have used the door. Either that or the cooler was left out for the night."

Travis lifted the entrance flap and played his light inside.

"You're right. I think it did use the door. My guess is that for some reason Jess went out and didn't zip the door shut behind her. But that really wouldn't matter to a bear, would it? Sealed or not, one swipe and it'd make its own opening. At least this way I still have a tent to use when we get home."

Before Seth could respond, a frantic yell shattered the night air. Jessie was calling for help. In unison, the youths spun and sprinted toward the beach.

Jessie had a problem. The boat was drifting away from shore. Having never gripped a pair of oars, she wasn't certain how it was done. The fact that she was panicked didn't help matters.

Even in the murky lake-side lighting, the Lund was easy to see. The boys came to an abrupt stop at the water's edge, looked at each other, and chortled. Jess was hunched over in the middle seat, facing front. She was making a brave attempt to bring the little craft to the beach; problem being, she was rowing in a circle.

"Were you planning on taking a trip without us? Or would you rather come in?" Seth hollered, failing to conceal his amusement.

Jessie released the oars and shouted back an angry reply. "What's it to you, hotshot? It's obvious that you think this is pretty funny." She sat straight and picked up the handles. "Travis, help me out here. How do you make these things work?"

Travis reached out and clutched Seth's upper arm. He squeezed lightly, bent close, and whispered. "Come on, cut her some slack. I can understand how she's feeling. Remember that old bruin that swiped our food last fall? I never told you, but I was so scared I almost lost my lunch and more. If that big thing had come in the tent with me, I probably would have wet my pants."

He released his grip and waited until Seth gave a nod of agreement. Then Travis cupped his hands to direct his voice. "Tell ya what, Jess. Just stay put. We'll come out in the canoe and get you."

Bob had slept through the first of the noise. It wasn't until she yelled from the lake that he awoke. Then he stayed statue-still, laboring to hear the conversation drifting from the beach.

Though his niece's frantic call had first caused grave concern, Seth's question about taking a trip eased the man's worry. Whatever it was, it sounded like the situation was under control. Besides, in his current condition there was little he could do but wait it out. He'd hear about it in the morning.

The rescue was simple. The boys paddled out in the Wenonah. Then holding tight to the side of the Lund, Travis climbed into the boat's stern. Meanwhile, to balance the load, Seth simply shifted to a kneeling position in the middle of the canoe.

The transfer of weight hadn't gone unnoticed. Jessie now knew how one person could paddle solo in a featherweight watercraft. The technique appeared so simple and was definitely something she could learn to do on her own.

She stayed mum on the short row in. Travis could feel her fear. He'd been there himself several times during the past year. So he only said two things. The first was to watch how he held the oars and how they broke the surface to stroke deep in the water.

The second comment was about the bear. "Don't beat yourself up, Jess. It's not your fault. If anyone's to blame, it's me and Seth. We were too lazy to take a rope and pull the cooler high in a tree."

He paused, recalling just how terrified he'd been that dark and fright-filled night the past autumn.

"We learned that lesson the hard way on the portage trip. A really big bear stole most of the freeze-dry packets our first night out. We lived on fish for nearly a week."

As soon as the boat bumped land, Jess hopped out, gave the bow a quick tug, and started toward her uncle's shelter. But after a half-dozen steps she stopped, did a one-eighty, and reversed course.

Travis had his back to her, pulling the Lund farther up on the beach. Jess came up behind, and then lightly touched his shoulder. In a voice so soft he could hardly hear, she said, "Thanks. Uncle Bob was half-right about the two of you. You're an okay guy."

Chapter Twelve

C H A P T E R   T W E L V E

Nothing fishy would be on the menu the next morning. Breakfast would consist of a cup of juice, two strips of bacon for the meat eaters, oatmeal, and one poached egg apiece.

The reason being, before turning in for the second time, the boys had scoured the path behind Jessie's tent. Her shrieks had apparently startled the marauder far back into the forest. Except for a few tracks, small and hardly intimidating, no sign of a bear was heard or seen.

They discovered that not everything edible had been trashed. In addition to a half-dozen powered food packets, the scavenger hunt turned up four unbroken eggs, a sealed parcel of bacon—it did have teeth marks—a tube of juice concentrate, and a small box of oatmeal mix. The boys were pleased. It was more than either had anticipated.

Items ruined or missing included the T-bone, the fresh fish fillets—no problem, they could be replaced—the loaf of wheat bread, a good number of the freeze-dried veggie packs, a carton of instant cocoa, and most of the eggs.

While the boys rummaged about in the woods, Jess had briefed Bob about the burglar. When she finished her spiel, her uncle sympathized, and then told her to go get her sleeping bag. He said that with Seth and Travis traipsing about, leaving lots of scent, no bear would come close. Regardless, she could spend the remainder of the night in his tent.

Bob had dropped off in minutes, his snores alone loud enough to keep any wild creature from creeping close. The problem for Jess was she couldn't fall asleep with a nose trumpet continually tooting a one-note tune in such close quarters. Only when first light arrived was she able to nod off, soon to be awakened with the call to "come and get it."

It looked to be another pleasant day. A peek through the forest crown revealed a high blue ceiling. Rising above the distant shore, a warm yellow globe beamed a big smile, its breath wrinkling the lake surface.

Four campers hunched on stumps, chomping down breakfast. Seth finished munching a piece of bacon, gulped, and turned toward Jess. "So tell me again, Jessie. Just how big was this bear that raided our food supply?"

Jess fixed her eyes on the fire, certain that if she looked up she'd snarl something she'd later regret. "You weren't there. At the time the thing seemed enormous," she mumbled. Then in a bigger voice, "Besides, you could have said something about hanging the cooler in a tree."

Bob smiled his unbalanced grin and agreed. "You're right, Jazzi. But it's as much my fault as the boys'. I should have paid more attention. Out here the rule is you never leave food where critters can get at it. I should have made sure the fellows strung the cooler far out of reach."

He waited until Jess gave a nod of acknowledgment and then went on, "Now then...what's on the agenda? You guys planning on fishing first or working on the wood supply?"

Travis turned to view the lake. Though early, without a cloud in sight, sunlight was already intense. It was bright enough to have already pushed larger fish into deeper water.

He stood and scratched his head. "Seth and I can gather wood. Jess can do the dishes. Afterwards I think we should take another look at the maps, make certain we haven't missed something. What d'ya think, Seth? You wanna gather firewood first?"

Seth got to his feet, stretched tall, and stared up at the tree tops. "Jeez, I don't know, Trav. D'ya think it's safe? We don't have any bear repellent. Wandering about in the woods could be risky. From studying those tracks, I'd say that bruin has to go at least a hundred pounds, maybe even a little more."

Jess wasn't certain if she should be upset or laugh. In the bright light of this gorgeous new day, the bear incident seemed more like a nightmare than reality. So she did neither.

Instead, she pushed up, smirked, and declared in a clean clear voice, "Tell you what. I'll help this polite gentleman collect firewood. Meantime Mr. Macho-man, you can do the dishes."

* * *

A short while later Travis and Jess trudged the narrow trail, soon vanishing behind boughs and brush. Before starting on the dishes, Seth had stomped to Bob's tent with the flight bag. The man didn't want to wait. He wanted to study the charts while he had the energy.

* * *

Jess, edgy about leaving camp, never ventured more than a few yards from her workmate. But that was okay with Travis. He was enjoying her company. She'd opened up enough that they'd actually had a few laughs—several at

Seth's expense—especially when they'd carried in the first load. And after that, to Travis's astonishment, she'd shared a multitude of personal tidbits.

The first chuckle had occurred while Seth was working at the lake's edge, washing the metal cookware, unaware of Jess and Travis's return. As the wood-gatherers were about leave for a second load, Jessie had hollered in a voice that would have made a cheerleader proud.

"Hey you there, down by the water! Be careful you don't get a case of dishpan hands. They'll feel all scratchy next time you're stroking your over-inflated ego."

In the short time it took Seth to turn from his work, the twosome had vanished from view. They jogged for a half minute before Travis made an abrupt stop and began laughing. Jessie pulled up alongside, tipped her head, and asked, "What's so darn funny?"

Then she couldn't help herself. It started as a small snicker, worked its way up to a giggle, and before she could contain it, the laugh became a side-splitting gut-buster.

"I'm sorry...I think," Jessie chortled, wiping at tear-filled eyes. "It's just that your buddy rubs me the wrong way."

Travis bit his lip and then burst out in a second round of belly laughs. Soon, he too, was swiping at his eyes.

"What? What did I say that was so darn funny?"

Travis bowed at the waist and sucked in mouthfuls of air. When he could talk, he stood straight, looked at Jess, and started chuckling again.

"Hey! Are you gonna let me in on your secret or not?" She demanded between bouts of giggles.

"Yeah, I am. It's what you just said...'rubs you the wrong way.' When we were fishing the other night, Seth used exactly the same words talking about you."

He took a few more big gulps and then continued. "But you know what I think? I think you two have a lot more in common than you realize. Problem is, neither of you has taken the time to look in a mirror."

Jessie had fallen silent then, mulling over what Travis had just said. But the exchange had thawed the ice. Before long they were talking about a variety of things.

For Travis, the information gleaned that morning was an eye opener. He now had a handle on why Jess appeared to be, as Seth had so crudely stated days prior, an 'oxymoron.' Travis listened without comment as Jess told about her mother's untimely death. And he'd paid close attention to the explanation why Jess didn't eat meat. A reason he could only respect her for holding tight to.

And Jessie couldn't believe how easy it was to talk to this straight-arrow kid from Who-ville. But he seemed trustworthy, honest and, more importantly, caring.

That hadn't been her experience with kids she'd run up against at her new school. So many had been judgmental, pigeon-holing her before they even knew who she was or what she was about.

It felt good just to say out loud all the angry, frustrated things she'd been bottling up.

The past six months had been terrible, the second worse time in her life. Her father remarried and the family moved to a new residence, requiring her to transfer schools. The worst was the year her mother died.

The two were plodding toward camp with the third load when Travis posed a question. "So let me get this straight. Your dad remarried last December and then you changed schools after the holidays? So just how far did you move?"

Jessie came to a standstill and let the armful of sticks

and broken branches drop. Tired and straining with his own load, Travis did likewise.

Jess turned so she could face him. She scrunched up her mouth and considered the answer. For a few seconds there was near silence, only bird chirps in the background.

"We just moved from South Minneapolis to the suburbs. But as it turned out, it might as well have been to a foreign country."

"Why's that? What made the new school so different?"

Jess selected an aspen tree to lean against, brushed a mosquito from her forehead, and then studied Travis through narrowed eyes. "Listen, I've been running off at the mouth all morning. Are you sure you want to hear this? It really doesn't concern you."

Travis picked up a short stick and then used it to draw small circles in the leaf littered earth. "Hey, I'm all ears. Go ahead. Lay it on me."

He sensed Jess was reluctant to share, so he added, "Really, I'm not going anywhere. I've got all the time in the world and I'm pretty good at keeping secrets. Who knows, maybe there's something I can help you with. Stranger things have happened."

After giving a small waggle of concurrence, Jessie lowered herself against the tree until she was sitting. Then she looked up to study a patch of blue peeking through a small opening in the leafy canopy.

Keeping her gaze skyward, she began. "The thing is, kids at my new school travel in cliques. You know...groups of girls who think they're better than everyone else. That their pee is perfume—and heaven help them—if their nose should run, it'd only drip Perrier, not snot like us common folks."

Travis shook his head. "No, I don't know. I don't even know what Perrier is. There might be some of that at our school—cliques, I mean—but I'm not aware of it. But you've gotta consider, most of the kids in my grade have been together since kindergarten. I don't know if that's a good thing or not, but we don't have many secrets."

"Yeah, that sounds a little like my old school. It wasn't all that large. Only a couple of grade schools fed into it, so I knew most of the kids. But the big difference was that at the old school there were students of all colors—white, black and every shade in-between."

Travis stopped doodling in the dirt and stared at Jessie. "What's color got to do with anything? I mean at your new building?"

Jessie dropped her gaze and clutched up a stick of her own. After a short lull, she looked at Travis. "Well, duh. As if you haven't already figured it out. It's pretty obvious I'm not a lily-white Norwegian like you. I'm only half white. I don't fit in anywhere."

It was his turn to stay quiet. This news came as a bit of a shock. He hadn't given her heritage a second thought. If anything, she was fairer skinned than Seth—who had bragging rights to Ojibwe blood coursing through his veins.

After an awkward moment, he managed a comeback. "Really, I never paid any attention to what your background might be. It doesn't matter to me. But just for the record, what continent are we talking about?"

Jessie stuck the stick in the ground, stood, and brushed her backside free of debris. "Southeast Asia. Vietnam," she said softly. "My mother came to the states a few years after the war. She was five."

Travis digested this latest of information. "So getting back to what you were saying before...that you don't fit in at your new school because of your skin color? Is that what you're telling me? 'Cause I find that hard to believe.

"You know, don't you, that Seth's not one-hundred-per-cent white either. But he's never had a problem with it. Jess, I don't want to seem 'butt-insky' here, but if you gave your classmates the same welcome you gave Seth and me, I can understand why there might be a problem. And I don't think it's because you're not lily-white."

Jess bent and began gathering her wood supply. She didn't speak until they were loaded and ready to head out. "It's pretty easy for you to give an opinion when you don't know the whole story. I haven't even mentioned my new step-mom. What a pain in the rear end she is—always bossing me around—'don't do this, don't do that.'"

"Is that why you took up smoking? Are you trying to get back at her?" Travis asked over his shoulder.

"What! You know about my smoking! Have you guys been spying on me?" Jessie screeched, racing up behind.

"Relax. No, we haven't been spying on you," Travis protested. "It's just that first morning I got up early and went outside. I saw you sitting by the lake, puffing on a cigarette. I didn't want you to think I was spying, so I went back in the tent. Okay?"

"Are you serious? You saw me and never said anything about it? I wouldn't have expected that."

She cut her sentence short and then answered the original question. "And no, I didn't take up smoking to irritate my step-mom. It just happened. I fell in with a crowd of kids who smoked."

Travis ground to a halt and spun around. Jessie was trailing so close that she bumped into him, losing most of her load.

"Jeez! Next time use your stop lights. One of us could get hurt!"

"Sorry," Travis apologized. "But there's something else you should know. A couple years ago Seth's dad was killed in a car accident. It was a rotten time for him. He knows what it's like to lose a parent."

For a couple seconds Travis remained mute, studying Jessie's face. The expression she was wearing was one of concern, one of real interest.

He decided to prattle on. "Now, you didn't hear this from me, but one of the burrs under his saddle all week is directly related to his mom. She has wedding plans for this weekend."

"Believe it or not, Seth's been looking forward to the wedding. He's supposed to be the one to give her away. Right now he's worried we won't get out of here in the next day or two. Here's another thing: Seth knows his new step-dad can't take the place of his real father."

Travis paused to observe a whiskey jack—the far north version of a blue jay—perch on a branch over Jessie's head. The plump gray bird sat tight, clutching the limb, studying the young people below. Curious to why Travis was staring up, Jessie tipped her head skyward. The movement startled the jack, and with a sudden rush of wings, the bird rocketed away.

Travis returned his gaze to the girl. "Everyone's different, Jess. Seth doesn't want this new guy, Doug, pretending to be his real dad. The main thing though, is that Seth has gotten to like him and his mom seems happy. You might find things that you like about your step-mom. And maybe cut your dad some slack, 'cause I'll bet he misses your mom too."

Using the toe of her tennis shoe, Jess began pushing sticks and branch parts into a pile. When she had them in a jumbled stack, she looked up. "You're certainly full of advice today. It better be free. I hate to think about paying the bill."

Travis grinned. "Hey, even if she's a total pain in the rear, there's only a few years until college."

Jessie sighed, then smiled. "I suppose. Come on, I'll race you to the woodpile."

* * *

They dashed back to a quiet campsite. Travis finished first; though he suspected Jess purposely slowed so he would win. Then, after dumping their loads onto the ever growing wood stack, they trudged to the water.

Travis was the one to notice that the boat was gone. He scanned the lake in all directions and came up empty. The little red and gray Lund was nowhere in sight.

"So what's your take, Jess? Did Seth take Bob back in the bay to do some fishing? Or is he so teed off at us he wanted to get away by himself?"

Jessie splashed a handful of water on her face and then stepped back. "I don't know, but we can find out easy enough. Let's check my uncle's tent."

They found Bob wide awake, poring over an air chart. The man had been so engrossed he hadn't heard the teenagers approach.

"Oh! Jazzi, it's you. You startled me," Bob exclaimed, peering over a pair of old-fashioned bifocals.

"Yup. It's just me and Trav. What did you think? That you had drop-in guests for lunch?" Jess teased, unzipping the screen door.

"So where's my other half?" Travis asked, once sprawled on the fabric floor. "Did he go fishing by himself or is he just upset at Jessie's joke?"

Bob formed a crooked grin and answered in what was now a familiar drawl. "I can picture a little of both. But he was nice enough to ask if I wanted to go along. Told him I don't think I'm quite ready. But I am feeling better. It must be your cooking, Trav. You did a great job with breakfast."

"So where'd he go, Uncle Bob? We didn't see him on the lake."

"Well, Jazzi, I'm not certain. My guess is he rowed back in the cove. He's probably fishing the shady side. Gotta tell you though, he didn't seem very chipper. What did you two rascals go and do?"

Travis chose to slant the reply. "Aw, it's nothing he won't get over. Truth is, he's worried we won't be out of here before the weekend. Remember, his mom's gettin' married on Saturday. Seth's shook up because he thinks he'll mess up all the plans."

Bob let that go without comment and then pointed to the map. "Well, kids, after going over these charts, he might be right. Jess, that lake you located the other day, I don't think it's the right one. I know it looks like it, but I've found another that matches up even better. It's got the right number of arms and a couple islands."

"Really?" Travis said, moving on all fours to get a better look. "Is that good or bad? Say, hold on! You said Seth might be right. What d'ya mean?"

Bob cleared his throat—a loud raspy 'herrump'—and began to explain.

"First off, these charts are meant for airborne travel. They don't have the same type of info you might find on an atlas or road map. That being the case, I've narrowed things down."

Travis interrupted a second time. "Wait a minute. Is this even the same chart we were looking at the other day? I don't see the red flight path."

"Good eyes. You're right. It isn't. This map uses a different scale. It shows a larger picture."

Bob extended his good hand and then placed a finger on a tiny blue spot. "This here," he said tapping the map. "This is where Jess thought we might be. But I don't think so. We had quite a tail wind. Our ground speed had to be higher than I first figured."

He trailed his finger farther up the colorful sheet until it pointed to another splotch of blue.

"Here's where I think we are. Just off the edge of that map you were scouring the other day. Have a look at this lake. Don't you think it resembles the one out front?"

Jess had edged up next to Travis. Because both were on hands and knees, their heads nearly bumped. They were so close Travis could almost taste the Juicy Fruit gum tucked away in the girl's mouth.

"It sure does. Don't ya agree, Jess?" Travis asked, opening the space between their foreheads.

Jessie scrunched up her nose. "Yeah. Jeez, I'm sorry, Uncle Bob. This lake matches up perfectly."

Bob curled in his arm and then let it rest on his chest. "There's nothing to be sorry about. I'm the one who got all mixed up. Once we started detouring, I figured I could use the GPS to get us back on the correct course. I'm the one who should be apologizing. And I am."

Travis thumped the map with his forefinger. "So now we know where we are. What's next?"

"We're farther north than we originally thought," Bob said. "But this lake has an outlet. Once it gets past all these smaller lakes, the stream passes under a seasonal north-south highway."

"Tell you what," Bob sighed. "It's time I go out. Trav, how about helping me hike to the privy? Once you've filled Seth in on the details, we can talk about this some more."

* * *

While Travis was learning more about Bob's map find, Seth was hard at work treasure hunting. The youth wasn't sure what he was looking for. But he was convinced that it must be something special. Why else would Jess have splashed around in ice cold water before anyone else was even awake that first morning?

For the second time in a couple of days, the young man was soul seeking. He was stressing out about his mom's wedding, and that stress was turning him into a sourpuss. It just wasn't like him. He was performing out of character, and that bothered him—much more than he'd ever admit.

Sure, he loved to tease and pull tricks, but always in a friendly manner. But mean was what he'd been all week, taking his frustrations out on Bob's niece. Why— why—why? He mulled over and over while pulling hard on the oars.

There had to be some way to say 'sorry, this isn't the way I really am.' If he could locate whatever Jess had been trying to find; then maybe, just maybe, it would give him a way to apologize.

So while Travis was tending to Bob, Seth was wading about in shallow water, straining to see anything unusual or manmade lying on the lake bottom.

He had told Bob that he was going fishing. He just didn't say what he was going fishing for. He'd even asked the ailing gentleman to come along, knowing full well what the answer would be. And so what if he came back with an empty stringer? That was to be expected on such a bright sunshiny day. He'd give it his best shot.

Chapter Thirteen

C H A P T E R   T H I R T E E N

It was a rare diamond of a day. Not too warm, not too cool, with just enough breeze to keep bugs off the beach. Three stranded campers basked under a lazy sun, savoring a small meal and tossing around friendly chit-chat.

Travis had put together the midday snack. He recalled that not all the smoked fish packets had been put in the cooler. Several wraps had been squirreled in with the cookies and Tootsie Pops.

Naturally, not everyone relished fish for lunch. Jess opted for a cup of reconstituted peas and a partial bag of dried peaches.

Yet to return, Seth missed out completely.

Completing the skimpy meal, Travis rubbed his belly, pretending to be stuffed. "Jess, I'm gonna trek 'round the point, look for the boat. Want to go?"

Jess was busy licking the last smidgen of pea paste from a metal plate. Stopping long enough to answer, she said, "Thanks, but I'm gonna pass. I'll stay here and keep my uncle company."

Bob twisted about so he would face the teens. "Don't

you be worrying 'bout me. I'll be fine. It's such a nice day I'm gonna take my nap right here in the sun."

The shriek of rusted oarlocks stopped all conversation. The Lund had rounded the point and was bearing down on the beach. As if competing for a first place prize, Seth was bowed at his work, stroking fast and furious.

"I guess we can forget about the walk. Let's wait and see what he's been up to," Travis suggested, rising off the stump.

Jessie also stood. "You don't need me for that. It might be best if I clear out for a while. Your buddy's probably still steamed. I'm gonna stroll the beach...way down there," she said, pointing toward a segment of shoreline yet to be explored.

She walked a few yards, and then stopped. "Ah Travis...let me know when it's safe to return. Okay?"

Travis threw a quick glance at the water. The Lund would be kissing shore in mere moments. With a half-dozen quick giant steps, he halved the distance to Jess.

"And just how am I supposed to do that? What d'ya want me to do? Chat you up on your cell phone?"

Jess could see that the boat would soon be bumping land. "Be creative," she quipped, flashing Travis a wily grin. "Maybe paddle down and pick me up with the canoe. I'm not going all that far. Besides, the workout will do you good."

And with that she was gone, striding away with long, graceful strides and her head high.

"Weren't biting, huh?" Travis said a moment later, taking note of the empty stringer coiled on the bottom of the boat. "I didn't think they would be. It's still too bright. We'll have to wait 'til just before sunset."

Travis may have received a more pleasant reply speaking

to a shrub. At least tree boughs sometimes whisper. Seth's short comeback was only a snorting, "Uh-uh."

Travis's trouble-shooting radar went on alert. Apparently Seth was still steamed.

"Hey. I've got some news; some good and some not so good. What d'ya wanna hear first?" Travis asked, tugging on the boat's bow.

Seth jumped out, and then stood with hands on hips, rotating his torso, working out the rowing kinks.

"Where's she going in such a big rush? Thought she told us she was scared to be alone?" Seth wondered out loud, nodding in the direction of Jessie's shrinking silhouette. "What's she up to?"

"How should I know? Maybe it's nothing at all. Maybe she's just playing around."

The boys looked on for a moment, and then went about their business. They trudged to the tree-line where Bob was stretched out under the midday sun. With eyes shut and a frail smile wrinkling whiskered cheeks, the man was laying face up, drinking in warm rays.

The duo checked Bob's breathing and determined he was just fine. Then, without a word, they moseyed to the stools and parked. For a time there was a fat wedge of prickly silence. Finally Travis took a chance. With whispered words so as to not disturb the sleeping senior, he said, "You missed out on lunch. You must be starving."

"That doesn't begin to describe the hole in my middle. So what did I miss? Was there anything but seafood on the menu?" Seth demanded, staring over the lake.

"No, you're right 'bout that. Jess did fix some freeze-dry. Bob and I had a couple of the smoked fillets. If your gut's really empty, raid the tent sack. There are a few bars and beef sticks left. You need something in your belly."

The breeze suddenly freshened, and where they sat in shade, the air cooled. Travis focused his gaze far into the distance. Like a herd of wooly buffalo heading over a high hill, plump shaggy clouds were gathering, preparing to forage a new range.

"I think another system is comin' in," Travis observed. "Fishing should be good later on. For that matter, if it clouds over early enough, we should think about going out well before dark. Agreed?"

"Yeah, I think we should. But I thought you had something you wanted to tell me. You said something about 'good news, and not so good news', remember?"

Travis tugged at his ear while continuing to gaze over the water. Before moving on, he wanted to say sorry. "Look, 'bout this morning. Jess was just teasing, you know."

Looking Travis straight on, Seth's face broke out in a broad smile. "I know. Just like I've been doing to you right now."

And then Seth laughed. As if he'd shrugged off a back-pack, Travis felt a weight lift from his shoulders. He had no need to continue with a head game of Scrabble, searching for acceptable words. His bud was back.

Seth leaned forward, and then like an actor flaunting an exaggerated grin, asked, "But do I sense you got to know her pretty good today? You got something going on you're keeping locked up under that Twins cap?"

Travis was caught completely off guard. "What! Me?" He managed to sputter. "Open your eyes you hairy-headed tree dweller! It's not me she's interested in. But yeah, I got to know her better, but like a friend, that's all. Period!"

Seth suddenly shot to his feet and dashed to the water's edge. He braked to a halt and then peered toward the double island end of the lake.

"Trav, I hear a plane. Off that way!" he bawled loud enough that even Bob sat up to look.

"Stir the coals and get the fire going! We need to make smoke before it disappears."

Unfortunately, no seaplane would be landing on their lake anytime soon. The fire was too puny, the aircraft too distant. All the boys could do was flap their arms and jump up and down in hopes of being noticed.

Without so much as a wing wiggle, the blunt-nosed flying machine droned on, and then like a honeybee in a large garden, buzzed out of range.

"Gall-dang it! It's Jessie's job to keep the fire going!" Seth groused as they plodded back to the stools.

"Hold it right there. Jess had nothing to do with this. I've been in camp for a couple hours. If it's anyone's fault, it's mine. But you know what? It just isn't worth it to keep a hot fire roaring all the time. It uses way too much wood. All we'd be doing would be cuttin' and haulin'."

Seth's comeback contained a surprise package.

"You're right. It isn't her fault. I was sitting here right beside you. I could have tossed wood on the coals."

The senior had been taking it all in. A spark of an idea flared. There was a way to make smoke without continually lugging in fresh wood.

"Fellows, come here a minute, would you?"

"Cripes, Bob. We didn't mean to wake you. How are you doin' anyways?" Travis asked, plopping alongside his elderly friend.

"Not bad. I feel stronger after every nap. But first off, don't be fretting over that seaplane. There was nothing you could do. That old bird was a long way off, probably farther away than you think. Now then, let's talk about the fire. Why don't you fellows float the boat along shore and scour up some driftwood? Gather up a few old logs, the wetter, the better."

"Ahh, I see where you're heading," Seth said, bobbing his head. "If we were to stack 'em over the fire, Lincoln-log style, they might take to smoking like big cigars. They may even smolder for a day or two before we'd have to start over."

There was a brief interlude as each pictured how it would work. Bob broke the silence by asking, "Trav, did you tell your bud about this lake?"

"Not yet. I was just 'bout to when we heard that plane. I'll explain when we're out in the boat."

* * *

Jess stopped where the wide, sandy shore tapered and transformed to a narrow strip of bleached rocks and small boulders. Seeing so many light colored stones brought about a sudden inspiration. Maybe she could use of the stones to spell out an SOS. Step one would be to scratch the letters in the sand. Picking up a stick, she put her plan in motion.

The simple three-letter project was more demanding than she could have imagined. Dozens of rocks and undersized boulders had to be pushed, pried, and bullied from long established burrows. Once free, they then had to be lugged or rolled to the sandy section of beach. It was rough work, especially on her hands. A fingernail splintered, deep enough that it not only pained, it bled.

She knew the only way the plan could work was if each letter was huge. Anything small would be a waste of time. Things on the ground looked minuscule when viewed from an aircraft. In order for the SOS to be giant-sized, hundreds of rocks had to be moved to a new home.

After nearly an hour of back-breaking labor, and not quite finished with the first S, Jess threw in the towel. Maybe in the morning she could get the boys to help. From what Travis had mentioned earlier, Seth should be more than eager to lend a hand. He wanted a speedy rescue as much or more than she did herself.

Plodding toward camp, Jess was surprised to see the boat heading her direction. Travis sat in back; Seth was working the oars. As the distance closed, she was undecided if she should shout a hello or continue on without comment.

Travis made the decision for her. He chirped out a friendly greeting. "Hi there, fellow woodchuck. What have you been doing?"

Seth stopped stroking just long enough to turn and give Jessie the slightest nod of his raven haired head. Jess was mildly shocked by the act of civility.

"Ah, I was working on a poster. I think I'll call it 'Writing with Rocks—Composition One-O-One.'"

Travis wasn't at all certain what that meant, so he faked it. "So, did you get it done? Did you want us to give it a grade?"

Jessie plowed a groove in the sand with the heel of her shoe. "It's not ready to be graded. I've only finished one letter...a big S...you know...like in SOS."

The boat, just yards from shore, had turned perpendicular to land. Seth was now facing Jess. He gave a tip of his head and lit a small smile.

"Good thinking. It sounds like a great idea. If we have time after scrounging up driftwood, we'll let you borrow our backs."

Jessie studied the ditch she'd etched in the beach. Water was seeping into the trough, eroding its sides. Using the ball of her foot, she filled in the furrow.

"Thanks. But let's finish tomorrow. Right now I need to go get a bandage."

* * *

When the boys returned, five small soggy logs weighed down the boat's rear. There'd been plenty to discuss while searching for wet wood. Travis had clarified Bob's map finding facts. The not-so-good news; this wasn't the lake they'd picked that first day of checking the charts. And also, that they were farther north than they'd originally thought. But the lake had an outlet. The tributary emptying from the lake flowed through several smaller lakes before joining a larger stream.

"After about twenty or thirty miles, the stream goes under a seasonal road. It looks like an old railroad grade that dead-ends at a fishing camp farther north. So we have to decide: do we stay put—or do we paddle and row for the road?"

Seth threw back an instant retort. "You said about twenty miles by air. How many miles would it be using the creek? If they're lots of twist and turns, a float trip could be twice that far."

"It's hard to tell. When we get back to camp you can look for yourself. For sure it'd be more than twenty miles. But the main stream looks to be pretty straight-forward. If it's not plugged with windfalls or beaver dams, we could probably travel that far in a day. No more than two or three at the most. And once we reach the road, it might be only a matter of hours before a car or truck comes along."

Seth had gone silent, digesting this new data. If it wasn't for his mother's special day, he knew what the answer would be. He'd opt for waiting right where they were, let help find them.

His mentor and resort supervisor, Rollie Kane, had instilled that rule before Seth had gone on his first canoe trip. The old man had repeated over and over— that if you wanted to be located, make sure you stayed put. Don't be wandering about the countryside.

"What's today? Is it Monday or Tuesday?" Seth asked after a lull.

Travis had to think about it. "Well, we left on a Thursday. And what is this, the fifth day out? I think it's Monday."

Seth had gone quiet again, letting the oars rest. "Tell me Trav, if we were to pack up and leave at first light, do you really think we could make the road before sunset?"

Now it was Travis's turn to chew on the possibilities. After another pause he expressed his opinion. "We could, but...and it's a King Kong of a 'but'...only if everything goes right." He paused again, picturing all that a float trip would entail.

"Now, if it was just you, me, and a bit of gear in the canoe, it'd be no problem," Travis started. "But I don't think we should split up, 'specially with Bob out of commission. And even though we'll be heading down-stream, it's gonna be slow going using the boat."

After another pause, he went on. "Plus, there might be times when we have to portage. It'll take the two of us to carry the Lund. That means we'd have to make return trips for the other gear, including the canoe. And don't forget, there won't be any packed trails like in the Boundary Waters."

Despite the probability of obstacles, Seth was warming to the thought. If it went well, they'd be out in a couple days, tops. He'd be home in time for the wedding. And even if the journey didn't go as fast as they hoped, they'd still reach the road before the weekend.

"Yeah, but you and I could take turns rowing. Jess can

stay with the canoe the whole time. It isn't that heavy. She's strong enough to carry it by herself. And we don't have to bring all the gear. We can leave at least two of the duffels at the campsite. Don't you think once we contact Search and Rescue that they'll fly a big 'copter in to pull the Cessna from the lake? At the very least there'll be planes coming and going once they know what happened to us."

"Sounds like you've already made up your mind," Travis said, not convinced that taking off was the thing to do without days of planning. But for the time being he'd keep that opinion sealed tight. He wanted to hear Bob's take before committing one way or the other.

* * *

The old outdoorsman was snoozing in his tent. He missed seeing his idea put into practice. Once the boys had a hot blaze roaring, they stacked driftwood on the fire. Imitating a turn-of-the-century locomotive, wet wood was soon spiraling up a plume of white steam.

While Travis and Seth worked on the fire, Jessie retreated to her tent to bandage her finger. When she emerged, her expression was bright and full of life, more like it had been when they were joking around and getting firewood.

Without a word, Jessie walked softly to the blaze. Seth was balanced on a stool, watching white vapor spiraling skyward.

"Seth," Jessie asked, using his name for the first time, "were you the one who found my bracelet?"

Glancing at her briefly, Seth mumbled an answer. "Um, yeah. We saw you sloshing around down there really early that first morning. I figured you must've lost something pretty important." He poked at the fire with a stick.

"Thanks," she said, turning the bracelet over in her fingers. "My—my mom gave it to me before she died, so...thanks." Jessie gave him a quick smile.

Seth looked her in the eye, more than just a little surprised. "You're welcome," he replied with a smile of his own.

"Well, I'm going to go check on Uncle Bob." Jessie spun on her heel and headed for her uncle's shelter.

Seth remained perched on the stump; looking pleased with shades of embarrassment tinting his face.

Travis grinned at Seth across the fire, glad that those two had done some fence mending. There was already enough worry in their brain streams without personal problems muddying up the waters even more.

* * *

"I think you're the cat that swallowed the canary. Are those yellow feathers fluttering about your lips?" Travis taunted once the boat was some distance from shore.

Unfortunately his earlier forecast had been accurate. Dim, grumpy clouds drooped over the lake, threatening to dribble on anyone foolish enough to look up. Without the sun's heat, the temperature had plunged. Cool enough that the boys donned rain suits before rowing away with rods and reels.

Instead of answering, Seth fumbled with the hood of his jacket. Once his head was covered, he went back to propelling the boat.

"Feathers, huh?" Seth grunted, pulling hard on the oars. "D'ya know what I think? I think you're the one full of feathers—bull feathers from the colonel's chicken ranch. Probably because you're jealous that I'm number one on Jessie's list. 'Specially the way the two of you were carrying on this morning."

And then Seth could no longer control the muscles of his mouth. He broke out in his give-away grin, unable to continue the pretense.

"Really Trav, all I did was a little wading where we hunkered down during the storm."

Travis gestured a double thumbs up, pursed his lips in approval as he waggled his head up and down. "You did good, partner. I think you made a friend for life. Who knows, maybe a very special friend, if you get my drift."

"Yeah, I'm sure," Seth mumbled. Then after training his eyes on the sky, he added, "Why don't you drop the subject and start fishing before we get soaked? I'm running on empty."

The fish seemed as famished as the castaways. Within minutes three plump walleyes were trailing behind the boat. After racing back to camp, the boys quickly cleaned the catch and had five fillets frying in the one heavier pan they'd brought for that particular purpose.

In the event Jess wanted to make chowder, Travis held one piece in reserve. He'd guessed correctly, and for the first time the young woman handled the water boiling and pot stirring on her own.

Distant thunder rumbled as the foursome gulped down supper. When plates were empty, the discussion turned to the upcoming day.

"Have you decided, Bob? Are you feeling strong enough to take a boat ride in the morning?" Seth asked politely.

Bob pondered his reply. After a spell he said, "Well, Seth. I've been asking myself the same thing all afternoon."

A series of thunder claps of echoed over the lake, putting a stop to all words. As if expecting to see a band led by an oversized bass drum, everyone turned toward the water.

A misty haze distorted the shape of the far shore. Four pairs of eyes measured the rain's movement as it marched up the lake.

With no further sound effects forthcoming, the senior continued, "I don't know, Seth. Maybe it'd be wise to wait another day or two. Let the nasty weather pass over."

His gaze fixed on Seth. "I know you're hopin' to get home in time to hear your mom's vows. We can't blame you for that. But it'd be this fellow's opinion we should wait at least one more day, let the weather warm up. It wouldn't be much fun totin' and paddlin' in an all-day soaker."

He paused to catch his breath. "It could prove to be risky. No matter how we dress, we'd be bound to get drenched. And remember, Jess didn't bring any rain clothes along. In no time at all she'll be chilled to the bone."

Travis nodded. "Yeah. Let's use tomorrow to get ready. You know...finish the SOS project...maybe smoke some fillets to eat along the way. We'll need a bunch if we don't complete the trip in one day. That, and figure out just what we need to pack along. Maybe even leave a written message for Search and Rescue."

Bob's head bounced up and down. "Atta-boy, Trav. Good thinking. Better to plan ahead than rush off half-cocked. Who knows, maybe we'll get lucky and be located before then. Right now I'd say we better batten everything down. The rain is right on our doorstep."

Chapter Fourteen

C H A P T E R   F O U R T E E N

It proved to be a dreary night. A chilly breeze teamed with a steady downpour, keeping four bodies tucked deep inside bags. Only through the miracle of modern technology were the campers able to stay close to comfortable. The waterproof double-layered roof of each shelter did what it was designed to do: keep moisture out and the occupants inside dry.

Seth and Travis were both awake when the murky light became strong enough to punch through fabric. Having been holed up for nine hours each needed out. The steady patter of rain on the tent top, accompanied by water dropping from tree limbs, increased the urgency.

Seth was the first to pull on rain gear and make a dash behind the nearest tree. He returned moments later, more than eager to crawl back into bed.

His report wasn't promising. "It's a monsoon out there. Make sure you pull up your hood or you'll get drenched."

Travis did as suggested and then rushed out to take his turn. As soon as he'd gone, Seth shed his outer layer and slithered into his bag. He lay awake, waiting for his partner to return. They had plans to make and things to talk over.

He scrolled down a mental to-do list in preparation for breaking camp. They had fish to catch and fillets to smoke, gear to sort and a bag to pack, a map to study and route to memorize.

The SOS needed completing and a message had to be written on paper, and then posted in plastic in plain sight. They also had to pack up the leftover items into the remaining duffels, and probably a half-dozen other tasks he couldn't bring to the forefront at the moment.

The youth reviewed the list several times. What was he forgetting? And where was Travis? He should have finished his business and been back long before now. Seth was about to get up and go check when his partner popped through the door.

"Where ya been? I thought I was gonna have to round up a search party and go out looking for you."

Travis knelt at the foot of his sleeping bag and sloughed off the wet jacket. Then he plopped on his rear and started removing soaked shoes and rain pants.

"I went to see if Bob needed help. He did. That took some time. But Seth, he's not doing well. He's come down with a cough, probably from lying around so much."

"How bad?"

Travis brushed the question aside long enough to slide into his bag. "Don't know. But he doesn't sound good. He was coughing up lots of junk, just like you did last fall."

Seth thought about that, recalling how his own lungs had become filled with fluid after an injured ankle kept him from moving about in wet weather.

"Yeah, but we've had nice days. Yesterday he was even able to snooze in the sun."

Travis rolled over to face his friend. "True, but remember, he's not exactly a spring chicken. Maybe the stroke lowered his resistance. Whatever, if he gets any worse, we'll have to come up with a different plan."

"Yeah, but let's cross that bridge when we get to it. While you were out, I went over all the things we gotta get done today."

Travis listened closely as Seth ran down the list. When completed, both lay quiet. Rain continued to pelt the tent, hammering the taut nylon in sporadic bursts. Occasional gusts shook the shelter, rattling the fabric fly over the entry door. Doing anything outdoors was not going to be fun.

There was an interlude before Travis spoke. "Okay, I'll be honest. Before hearing Bob's cough, I was gonna cast my vote for staying put. But now I'm not so sure. He needs to get to a hospital, or at least see a doc. I think you and I better get up and at 'em. If the weather's even halfway decent come tomorrow's sunrise, we need to be ready to boogie."

* * *

Preparing breakfast was a soggy undertaking. Saturated by the all-night drizzle, the fire had gone stone-cold. It took more than an hour to rekindle the blaze, boil some water, and stir up a pot of several freeze-dried vegetable packs.

The campers crowded into the big tent to partake of the odd cuisine, a green pudding-like mish-mash of undetermined heritage. But no one criticized. The gluey offering was warm and slid into empty stomachs without complaint. The downside was that the pot was bare before tummies were full.

With breakfast over, Seth took it upon himself to lay out the day.

"Jess, I was thinking about your SOS project. It's gonna take a lot of time to complete. We'd be out in the rain for hours gettin' it done. But I think I have a way to accomplish the same thing without so much work."

Jessie hadn't slept well. She'd spent the night in her uncle's tent, curled inside her satiny bag, clad in two sweatshirts and a windbreaker. It seemed that just as she'd drift off, Bob would hack out a cough, startling her wide awake.

With her lack of sleep and half-empty middle, she was glad to hear that she might not have to shove boulders around in the rain.

"Great," she smiled. "Let's hear it."

"Well, I'm just borrowing your design. I thought while me and Trav are fishin', you could keep busy with the prunin' saw. 'Cause instead of using rocks; we could weave spruce and cedar boughs into giant letters. Sound like a plan?"

Jessie rolled her eyes. "Well yeah, it makes perfect sense. Why didn't I think of that before I broke my back lugging all those boulders?"

Bob coughed, a chain of chest-wrenching whoops that made the teens wince. When the hacking subsided, he added his two cents. "It's a great idea. Maybe also make an arrow pointing to the campsite. Even if you kids tote me off in the morning, we can leave a message saying where we're headed."

The old man hacked again before completing the thought. "Jazzi, just make sure you bundle up in my rain suit. You don't need to be catching a cold. That's my area of expertise."

The day remained wet and windy, with only one check mark in the plus column. Fishing was fabulous. The boys only had to circle the point and wet their lures. Walleyes seemed to relish the gloomy weather. Fish bit on nearly every cast. Within an hour a dozen keepers were skewered on the stringer, ready for a date with the fillet knife.

Back at camp Travis went right to work with the blade. Seth trotted down the beach to where Jess was slashing away with the saw. During the short time the boys had been on the lake, she'd cut an impressive mound of needled boughs.

Seeing Seth approach, Jess threw a branch on the pile and then stood still, waiting for a comment to be tossed in her direction. She wasn't disappointed.

"Wow! Good work. Looks like you've got enough stacked to start forming letters."

"Thanks. I discovered that I can stay warm as long as I keep cutting. But my arm's tired. Why don't you take a turn while I start weaving the first letter?"

"Sounds good," Seth said, reaching for the saw. "How big d'ya figure they should be?"

Jess drew a line in the sand with the toe of her shoe. She took four long strides toward the water, stopped and made a second scratch. "What do you think? Big enough?"

"Perfect. Let's get to it."

* * *

Later, with the SOS complete and the fillets drying over the fire, the teens regrouped. They stood close to the smoky heat, warming cold hands.

The shower had slowed to an on-again, off-again spitting contest; with just enough moisture to make rain togs mandatory. At least there had been a shift in the wind. It was now blowing parallel to the shoreline, no longer huffing into camp.

Seth made the observation. Without looking at anyone

in particular, he remarked, "What d'ya wanna bet that we're on the rear end of a low pressure cell?"

Jess looked up, lips twisted in a puzzled smile. "Say what? The rear end of a who? What the heck are you talking about?"

The sing-song way she'd said it caused the boys to chuckle. Travis beamed a grin her way and then said, "Low pressure cell. Low pressure usually brings rain or snow, depending on the time of year. With the wind shifting 'round, it means the center of the system has probably passed. Hopefully a high pressure's pushing in behind. If it is, we might see the sun before the day is over."

Still wearing a look of confusion, Jessie asked, "How d'you guys know so much about that stuff? Are you two planning on being TV weathermen or something?"

"Not hardly," Seth said, stepping back as a chunk of wood settled onto the coals, rocketing out a shower of sparks. "When you live as far up the road as Trav and me, you take a special interest in the forecast. Not that they always come true."

He gave out a laughing grunt and then moved closer to the heat. "The plane ride out here is a good example. They said 'blue skies for the rest of the week.' Yeah...sure, you betcha."

Travis grinned in agreement. "Right, sometimes it seems a coin flip would be just as accurate. But I gotta admit, more times than not, they're right. I don't know about Seth, but in the winter I always check the news before going to bed. Never know when we'll get a snow day. We have a twenty-five mile bus trip down the Gunflint Trail to Grand Marais. And we only live halfway to the end. Some kids ride nearly fifty miles one way. So if it sounds like a blizzard or snowstorm's heading over the Boundary Waters, we stay home."

Jessie thought that over. "Don't you go stir crazy having to hang around inside all day, doin' nothing?"

"Who said we stay inside doin' nothin'? Heck, snow days are a blast. Trav and I are usually the first ones to ride the snowmobile trails. That or fishing out on the ice."

"Don't you get cold standing knee-deep in a snow drift?"

Seth formed a smile and said, "Not as cold as hanging out here in the rain. You gotta remember, in the winter we're dressed for the weather; snowmobile suits, boots, mitts, facemasks...."

Travis completed the thought. "That and a portable fish house with a heater, hand warmers, thermal underwear...."

Jessie shut her eyes and shook her head, "Spare me the details. I can't imagine going out in weather like that on purpose. I'm freezing right now. But as long as you brought up gear, do you guys think we should start packing? From what you just said, the sun will probably be out in the morning. We'll be good to go, right?"

Travis dug into the cook set and came up with a pancake turner and a large spoon. Handing the spoon to Jess, he said, "Help me flip the fillets. There's no sense letting 'em burn. Then we can start getting things together."

* * *

After a lot of discussion—and a few minor differences— the teens determined not much could be put into duffels until it was time to leave. The essential items would be in use until they broke camp. Pots and plates, tents and sleeping bags, mattress pads and rain gear had to stay in place until sunrise. Then, if it looked like the weather was willing to cooperate, they'd pack up and eat on the run.

By late afternoon, and although the sky was still wall-to-wall gray shag, the drizzle ceased. But without sunshine, the temperature remained unseasonably cool. A sharp breeze swept the length of the lake.

Away from the shelter of the stubby peninsula, frothy white-crowned waves chased each other, running a marathon toward a distant finish line. The boys were content to stay in camp, glad they'd fished earlier.

* * *

"So, are we gonna take off in the morning or not?" Seth asked, his stare fixed halfway between his wet feet and the red coals nestled at the bottom of the fire circle.

Huddled forward on the stumps, the four campers were sitting upwind of the blaze, relishing its radiant warmth. Earlier Jess had helped Bob hobble out of the tent. The constant coughing was taking a toll. The ailing man's already meager energy seemed to be fading.

Seth and Travis wanted to get several things done before dark. Besides nibbling an early fish supper, the boys sought a decision on the upcoming day.

Seth had his mind made up—if dawn broke clear and calm—he'd cast a vote for heading out. Travis was uncertain, torn between leaving or staying put.

The image of the autumn ordeal floated to the front of his brain. Had he not wandered off, he would have been rescued the very next day. But by heading into roadless area on his own, he'd nearly become a column on the obituary page.

Bob whooped up some mucus, turned his head, and spat. He was ready to speak. "Ordinarily, I'd say our chances of being discovered would be best if we stay here. But since the boats have been pulled from this campsite, I gotta believe the lake's temporarily off-limits."

He began to cough again, a series of wrenching gasps,

followed by another discharge of phlegm. The teens kept silent, and embarrassed to stare, fixed their eyes elsewhere. Jess was worried the coughing episode would cause her uncle to experience a second life-threatening stroke.

The young people waited quietly for the spell to run its course. When the coughing eased, Bob gulped in several breaths and continued in his slurred intonation. "The bottom line is that I'm in no shape to be of any help. I'm going to be excess baggage. But if the three of you want to strike off to that road, I'll go along with your decision. Let's hope I read the map accurately, and if I did, that the road's being used."

"Trav, what's your opinion? Go or stay?" Seth asked once he realized Bob had said all he was going to on the subject.

Travis looked first at Seth, then at his old friend. "I guess what Bob just said stands to reason. We've been here almost a week and not a single plane has come close. Search flights must be looking elsewhere. And the part about the boats being pulled makes it even less likely we'll be getting visitors anytime soon."

Up to this point Jess had remained silent. She was taking it in, processing all.

With a lull in the conversation, Jess decided it must be her turn to talk. "I don't know much about rowing and paddling, and nothing at all about portaging. But if we only have to travel—what, twenty-five or thirty miles—it wouldn't have to be done all at once. What's the big deal if it takes a few days? Once we reach that road, sooner or later someone is sure to come along. Wouldn't you think?"

"Yeah, seems reasonable," Travis agreed. "I was leaning toward staying here. But if tomorrow comes at us bright and sunny, let's go for it."

Chapter Fifteen

C H A P T E R   F I F T E E N

The boys' forecasting was on the mark. The day opened clear as glass, but cold, close to ice-making. Arctic high pressure had pushed away the soggy cloud cover, bringing crisp clean skies.

"Holy moly! It's colder than a plumber's butt on a winter day!" Seth whined, stepping out of the tent.

Pulling on his all-weather jacket as he went through the door, Travis trailed close behind. He scrunched his face. "It is freezing out here. At least it shouldn't stay cold for long," he said through chattering teeth, gesturing with a fist to the yellowish glow lighting the lake.

It was only half past four, but the big star would soon be waking up. Already enough sunlight spilled skyward to touch wisps of high clouds, tinting a few lingering vapors in pastel pinks and violets, and dozens of shades in-between.

Adding to the scene, a thin blanket of bluish-gray fog shrouded the lake; a hazy watercolor painting.

"Whoever decided sunsets are supposed to be on postcards never got up early. Man, that's about as pretty as she gets," Seth said, captivated by Mother Nature's artwork.

"Agreed," a voice chimed. "You know, I'm starting to get a feel for why you guys like camping so much. I've never seen anything quite like that before," Jess declared, sauntering around the evergreen thicket.

At first startled, Travis regained his composure. "Good morning. You're up early."

"Yeah, morning," Seth smiled. He strolled to the beach and scanned the horizon. Satisfied with what he saw, he turned toward the others.

"Hey, it looks like we're gonna have lots of blue today. Let's pack up and get the boats in the water."

* * *

The teens became a cyclone of activity. The first chore was to temporarily move Bob into Seth's shelter. Bright blue and pitched where it would be more visible from the air and water, the tent was left standing. They'd use it as a warehouse for items they couldn't take along.

Because the boys wanted to tote only one carryall, extra clothing, most of the cookware, the mattress pads, all but one fishing rig, the Coleman cooler, Bob's flight bag, and any other personal items had to be left behind.

Like the stripes on a zebra, it became plain to see that once the tents were folded their plan wouldn't work. No way would four sleeping bags, two shelters, a tackle box, a cooking pot, packages of smoked fish, and the few remaining foodstuffs cram into a single bag. Even if it did all fit, the bag would be too heavy to lug.

The fix was to divide the gear into two loads. Jess could manage one, and Travis and Seth could take turns toting the other if portaging became a necessity.

Full daylight didn't wait for tasks to be finished. A ripe peach had elevated over the edge of the planet; giving cheery approval to the upcoming expedition. From all indications it was to be a glorious morning. Even the lake fog had taken note of the rising sun and had silently evaporated.

After buckling Bob into the one and only life vest, Seth helped get him in the rear of the boat. Setting the heavier duffel in the front, the brawny teen heaved on the bow, gave a hearty push, and jumped in.

Travis and Jess were busy readying the canoe. Both looked on as the Lund and its crew bobbed on the water. Then, with Seth yanking hard on the oars, the tiny vessel began its voyage to a distant arm of the lake.

"You about ready?" Travis asked, arranging the half-filled bag on canoe floor. "If not, there's no big rush. We'll catch up in no time."

"Yeah, I'm set. Let's go. I don't want Seth to get too far ahead. I'd like to check on how my uncle's getting along. I'm worried. All that coughing is starting to scare me."

Now that Jess had a bit of paddling history, it was only a matter of minutes before the canoe drew alongside the more cumbersome rowboat.

"How you two doin'?" Travis shouted. "Or should I ask...do you know where you're going?"

Seth stopped mid-stroke. He gave Travis an overly dramatic scowl. "Hey man, you studied the map as much as I did. If we read it right, we need to head to the far end of the lake and then paddle down a crooked bay," he said, tilting his head in the direction of travel.

Jess rested her paddle across the gunnels. "How are you feeling, Uncle Bob?"

Always the gentleman, Bob twisted about to face his niece. He rumbled a low chuckle, and then drawled, "Doin' fine, sweetie. I'm doin' just fine."

Then he turned toward the front and nodded at Seth.

"But I do feel sorry for young Mr. Springwood here. The lad's got his work cut out...what with having to haul this sorry bag of bones everywhere he goes."

"Tell ya what," Travis said, "since you two are doin' fine without us, Jess and I'll go on ahead. Maybe we can locate the stream and scope it out before you guys get there."

Hearing no disagreement, Travis and Jess dipped paddles and started pulling. As if it had a hidden engine, the canoe surged forward, leaving the Lund wiggling in its flat wake.

A half hour of steady stroking brought the voyagers to the channel opening. Their one brief pause took place when Jess spotted the overturned pontoons. She'd stopped churning water, fixing her eyes on the far shore. Curious as to what she was staring at, Travis did the same.

Hunkered low, barely above the surface, the stepped-bottom floats were difficult to see. Neither knew what to say, so they sat quiet—resting—taking one last look at their overturned air taxi.

At last Jess swiveled her head, making eye contact, but keeping mum. Travis responded with a slight shrug of his shoulders. What could be said? The aircraft was a goner. It wasn't the first to be abandoned in the wilds, and no doubt wouldn't be the last.

* * *

A short while later the canoeists were thrilled at their find. The outlet appeared to be where the map indicated, directly at the end of a spidery arm. But after paddling up close, their joy was to be short-lived.

Mother Nature did her best to hold the lake in check. Huge slabs of glacier-tipped granite teamed with round-shouldered boulders in an attempt to block the exit.

Not to be denied an escape route, torrents of water thundered through gaps and openings. The frothy liquid gathered speed as it raced downhill in a series of white-water chutes. Then, before it even had chance to catch its breath, the little river boiled around a sharp bend.

A lump formed in Travis's throat. Unless the stream slowed after making the turn, a float trip would be fool-hardy and dangerous at best. He'd had a close call with drowning during the autumn fiasco. He wanted no part of this whitewater. One brush with a watery grave would last him a lifetime.

He gawked for several seconds and then went to work. Digging deep with the paddle, he pointed the canoe's bow toward a gravely section of beach well away from the rapids.

Jess caught on quick. She immediately added her arms to the effort. Moments later they had the canoe resting safely on shore. With Travis leading the way, the pair scampered along the lakefront.

Nearing the river's stony lip, they made a startling dis-covery: a narrow walking path paralleled the streambed, and from its appearance, the trail had been worn down by years of foot traffic.

Jess had to holler to be heard over the babble of cascad-ing water. "Looks like we're not the first ones here," she said, pointing at the trail. "Where do you think it goes?"

Travis considered the question. "I think it's good news," he yelled. "The river must pool up around the bend. Fishermen would be told that it'd be a terrific place to wet a line. Lunkers would gather there, looking for an easy meal."

Jess thought for a second and then sent Travis a warm beam. "So what are we waiting for? Let's go see."

* * *

The teens had just started hiking the trail when the ambush came without warning. Rocketing in from the rear, a pair of wide-bodied birds swooped in on the intruders. The first attacker zoomed past, nearly knocking the cap off Travis's head. Not to be outdone, the second assailant zeroed in on the hood of Jessie's sweatshirt, brushing the fabric as it zipped within millimeters of her skull.

Stunned by the unexpected attack, the teens dropped to the earth like they'd been hit by a club. Then after flinging up hands to protect face and eyes, they scrunched against the ground, nervously awaiting a second assault.

Having lost the element of surprise, the birds chose instead to hover over the trespassers, squawking harsh and raucous peals of disapproval.

Travis chanced an upward glance. The young outdoorsman recognized the birds for what they were—ospreys—eagle-like fish eaters of northern lake regions. He'd had similar run-ins with the fish-divers near his home on Poplar Lake.

Each time he had been just as startled. Yet, as with most of his outdoor experiences, he'd garnered a nugget of knowledge. There was nothing to fear. The birds were simply making a statement. 'Go away—our nest is near.'

Feeling confident the ospreys wouldn't make actual contact; Travis stood and started flailing his arms. "Shoo! Scat! Get outta here you crazy birds! Come on, Jess, make some noise! Show 'em who's the boss!"

Grudgingly, Jessie poked her nose out from under the brim of the hood. Then she rose to one knee and observed as Travis continued to beat the air and holler. His efforts were having an effect. Though still screeching, the winged assailants had flapped to a higher altitude.

"Come on! Let's make a run for it. They won't hurt us. They just want us to leave," Travis yelled, starting down the path.

"How can you be so sure?" Jessie shouted, hands and arms wrapped around her head as she trailed a step behind.

Travis suddenly jerked to a stop, bent, and broke a dead branch from the bottom of a spruce. He started whirling the limb over his head while nodding toward a huge evergreen.

"Up there," he said, jabbing the stick toward a tall tree. "See that big bundle of twigs and branches near the top? That's their nest. Probably have some young ones in it. They aren't gonna hurt us. They're just trying to scare us off."

Although she had nagging doubts, Jess saw no choice but to follow. But it appeared Travis had nailed the answer. Soon as they'd trotted a few yards down slope, the aerial attack was over. The birds circled one more time and then winged a retreat.

Jessie stopped mid-step to watch—intrigued—as the eagle wannabes flapped to the tree top, and with precise timing, dipped lightly onto the nest.

"How'd you know they'd do that?" Jess asked.

Travis rotated so he could look at her straight on. He was happy to have guessed right and his lips involuntarily formed a smile. After pretending to scratch monkey-like under an armpit, in his deepest voice, he boomed, "Tarzan knows all about crazy critters."

It was said in such a funny way that Jessie had to laugh. Still giggling, she took several small steps forward. Then, without a clue it was coming, she slugged Travis on the shoulder.

Before Travis could respond, Jess dashed ahead, and without looking back, bounded down the narrow path. Travis was left standing alone, shaking his cap side to side.

* * *

Although it was not yet seven o'clock, Travis thought he was having a pretty good day. He was two for two. First the answer about the birds and now his educated guess regarding the stream. As he had suspected, as the rapids turned the corner, they made an abrupt alteration. Having completed the fall, the river leveled, and the torrent slacked.

Thousands of years in the making, a pool had been carved after the river's last hurdle. A fisherman's paradise, Travis reflected. Too bad his rod was in the boat. A keeper probably would be caught on every cast.

Jess lured the young angler from his thoughts. "Don't you think we better get back to the canoe? Seth's gotta be wondering what we're up to. We told him we'd let him know if this was the right place."

"Huh? Oh...yeah, you're right," Travis mumbled. Then in a louder tenor, "We better go see if they've reached the bay."

Breaking into a mischievous smirk, he punched Jessie on her arm, spun, and yelled over his shoulder. "Come on, slowpoke. Last one to the canoe has to carry it."

Unlike the day of wood gathering, Jess gave it her all. And as Travis had suspected, she must have let him win that race. The long-limbed youth had just crested the slope when something thumped his shoulder. The roar coming from the rapids had camouflaged Jessie's footsteps. She was right behind and ready to pass. With a burst of speed, Jess sprinted by as if wearing jet-propelled Nikes.

Recognizing that the contest was lost, Travis slowed and

then stopped. Seth had hit the mark that first day—this girl was full of surprises.

"So who's the slowpoke now?" Jess chided moments later. "Looks like you'll be the one doing the lugging. That is if we're really gonna do it. What do you think? Are we?"

"You know, don't you, that I had to let you win. I gotta save my strength. Figure I'd be the one doin' the carrying regardless of who won," Travis bluffed, tipping the bill of his cap toward the canoe.

He expected a flippant reply, but Jess didn't say anything. However, the glint in her eyes told Travis she wasn't buying tickets to this act.

"Yeah, we'll probably go for it. I don't see why not. Once the river drops over the rocks, it seems harmless enough. There's plenty of water. That'll make for a quick trip, what with the current and all."

Jess was no longer listening. Her attention was focused elsewhere. "There they are!" she yelled.

That they were so close, so soon, was surprising to Travis. He hadn't expected the boat to arrive at least for another ten or fifteen minutes. But sure enough, Jess was right. The Lund was rounding the last crook in the channel. From the machine-like way the oars dipped in and out of the water; Seth was clearly anxious to leave this lake.

With a quick heave, Travis plucked the duffel from the canoe. "Let's open the pack and dig out something for breakfast. I don't know about you, but I'm starving."

Jess stared at Travis. "Well, yeah! Of course I'm hungry. I've been famished since the first day. Trouble is, except for your smoked fish, I don't think there's much in there for me to munch."

Travis hoisted the bag unto his shoulder. "Not to worry! We'll come up with something. Come on. Let's move away from this racket. Over there," he said, looking toward a large flat block of split rock farther downshore.

Using his teeth, he pulled up a sleeve and checked his watch. "It's only quarter to seven. We never eat this early, anyway. If you round up some twigs and sticks, I'll get a fire started. We'll eat something warm before we tackle the portage."

* * *

Seth was pooped. Despite the cool temperature, and having shed his jacket early on, he was wringing wet. Rowing was hard, sweaty labor. So after helping Bob climb out of the boat, and too tired go exploring, he plodded to the flat rock and flopped down.

After catching his wind, he wheezed, "Bad news, huh? From what I can see from here, it looks like the river idea was a waste of time."

Just then Jess trudged up, arms spilling over with limbs and sticks. "Wow! I bet you're tired," she said to the human form sprawled flat on the ground.

Seeing only a weary waggle of Seth's head as an answer, she turned her sights on Bob. Still buckled in the orange flotation vest, the grizzled man was parked on boat's bow. Jess let the stick collection fall. Then, spinning on her heel, she trotted to the boat. Once there, she gave the man a one-armed hug and started unbuckling the vest.

Travis quickly constructed a small tepee of dry twigs, sticks, and bark. With a flick of his lighter he set flame to the fire nest. A thin wisp of gray curled into the air, followed by a flare of yellow and red.

As fire began nibbling fuel, Travis gave Seth an update. "Actually, you're wrong. I don't think the trip was a waste of time at all. We had time to take a hike. There's a path worn alongside the stream. It snakes down to a fishy looking pool just past the end of the rapids."

Travis interrupted himself to throw a few broken branches on top the fire. Satisfied the flames could feed themselves, he continued with the report. "Anyway, once it drops over the slope, the river really mellows. Do we chance that this is all the major whitewater? Remember, once we decide to portage downstream, it'll be darn near impossible to turn around."

Seth sat up, eager to take a look for himself. "Are you puttin' me on? There's a trail around the rapids? Cool. Hey, maybe this is a canoe route. And maybe if there's more whitewater ahead there'll be trails there, too."

"Wouldn't count on it," Travis contradicted. "I think the path was made over the years by fly-in campers. The pool looks real fishy."

Rising to his feet, Seth started fluttering his arms, loosening cricks and knots from arms and shoulders. "What's with the fire? Are ya cold?"

Still dressed in his rain suit, Travis shook his head. "Naw. Just wanted something warm for breakfast. While I'm getting to it, why don't you take a hike? You can go see for yourself. I should have something ready to eat by the time you get back."

"Yeah, think I will. Anything else I should know about?"

Recalling the air strike, Travis chuckled. "Funny you should ask. Make sure to cover your head. There's a pair of dive-bombing lovebirds nesting over there in that tall tree. A couple of ospreys that won't want see your mug, homely as it is. Just make sure you go full throttle over the top and you'll be fine."

After filling the pot with water, Travis dropped in several smoked fillets. He picked with a fork until the meat was mashed. Once the water began boiling, he dumped in the remains of a freeze dry pack. Then he stirred and stirred until every lump dissolved. He let the contents boil, steaming off liquid. Finally satisfied the concoction was as done as it would get, he slopped the goopy brew into four cups.

Bizarre as it was, no one found fault. Everyone was operating near the empty mark. When hunger pains were corralled, it was time for a decision: remain at the lake or go for the road.

Restless to be underway, Seth steered the discussion. "I think once we portage the rapids, we should have an easy time of it. Wouldn't you agree, Bob?"

Bob scratched the week-old whisker patch on his chin. If it wasn't for the stroke and chest congestion, he'd exclaim in a heartbeat—'go for it!' Twenty-five miles of paddling downstream should be sweet. In his younger years, some days he'd gone that far and more before stopping for lunch.

That wouldn't be the case now. He was feeling so frail—so exhausted—too tired to be anything but a weary passenger. Yet, it wouldn't be fair to the teens to nix the plan.

Although they'd been missing a few meals, the kids were able-bodied. At their age, rapids or no rapids, beaver dams or log jams—they'd be able to portage their way down the river and reach that gravel road. For their sake, he saw no other choice but to give the go-ahead.

"Well, what do we have to lose but time? That stout SOS you made along the beach should be easy to spot from the air. And don't forget, we left a message in plain sight at the campground. So I don't see why not. Now then, if you all don't mind totin' this codger along for the ride, let's do it."

Chapter Sixteen

C H A P T E R   S I X T E E N

Getting gear around the rapids proved to be an easy endeavor. Jess helped her uncle hobble along the path. While she was busy with Bob, the boys carried and slid the boat to the pool.

Travis and Seth readied the watercraft, and then went back for the Wenonah and heavy duffel. While the boys took a break, Jess returned for the smaller bag. In minutes she came bouncing down the hill with the sack slung over her shoulder.

After getting Bob settled in the rear, Seth hunkered between the oars, waiting for Travis to shove the boat from shore. With the current providing a push, the rowboat took off like a rabbit. Travis and Jess slipped into the canoe and followed.

All were in high spirits. They were ahead of schedule. They'd cleared the first hurdle and it wasn't yet eight o'clock.

Unlike battling wind and waves out on the open lake, Seth found rowing with the current pleasurable. Muscles and tendons took a vacation as the oars were used mostly for steering.

Likewise for Travis, easy, relaxed strokes were enough to keep the canoe on course. And the river itself cooperated. The channel was wide and free flowing. Even the depth was perfect—deep enough not to scrape bottom—shallow enough to wade should the need arise.

Jess sat with her paddle resting sideways across the gunnels. That had been Travis's suggestion. The canoe sliced the surface with such little effort that if they were to both to pull, they'd zip past the Lund.

They didn't want that to happen. The plan was to stick together. Whatever surprises waited downstream—good or bad—they'd discover as a team.

In the meantime Jess was intrigued with staring into the water. Even with a tannic hue, the depth was such that she could easily see bottom. She yipped "Oh look!" the first time she spotted a fish.

The boys laughed. After that she stayed tight-lipped, but kept count of how many fish she saw. By the time the flotilla arrived at the first narrow lake they'd be crossing, she was up to fifteen.

"That went well," Seth said, standing alongside the boat's bow. "Only one set of rapids, if you could even call them that. Let's hope the rest of the way should be so slick. Heck, at this rate, we might make the road by mid-afternoon."

They'd pulled in to take a bathroom and map-reading break. Travis didn't want to head out on a strange lake without checking the chart. He'd experienced the feeling of being confused during the autumn storm. That had been a liver and chopped onion event, definitely something he didn't want to taste twice.

Travis arched his back and shook his hands, flexing fingers and wrists. "Yeah...time will tell. But let's not count chickens before we know what's in the egg. The next river could be a logjam. That's what happened last fall when I tried to paddle out for help. The first two channels were clear as window glass. The third stream was a nightmare; trees were tossed every which way."

Finishing a few knee bends, he said, "Dig out the map, would ya? I'd like to see how far we've come compared to how far we've got to go."

Jess had traipsed down the rocky shoreline where she'd disappeared behind a cedar clump. Bob kept to his perch in the back of the boat. He hacked out a couple of harrumphs before mumbling that he could wait. That he had no need to get out.

"Here," Seth said, digging in a pocket of his rain jacket, and then holding the chart in front of his friend. "We shouldn't have any trouble finding the outlet. It's straight down the other end of this lake."

Travis studied the chart. He slid a finger from where they had been to where they were now. It wasn't hard to see that they had many miles yet to go. He'd used Bob's red pen to mark the route. Now, looking at the complex collection of lines and numbers speckling the map, he was glad he had done so. It'd be more than easy to get mixed up. There was as much blue ink as green printed on the paper; rivers and lakes by the hundreds.

While preparing for this fishing trip he'd come across the estimated number of lakes and ponds dotting the Ontario landscape: approximately four-hundred-thousand.

So maybe it wasn't unusual they had yet to see an airplane. There were just too many spots of blue. The odds of company dropping out of the sky anytime soon were lousy.

Travis finished tracing the line and then handed the map to Seth. After a mental calculation, he said, "Yeah, I think you're right. It looks like this lake is just a wide spot in the stream. I come up with three to four miles in length. What d'ya figure?"

"Somethin' like that, I guess. You can wait for Jess. We're gonna get going. Bob and I need a head start. I'm sure you guys will catch up."

It didn't take but a few pulls for Seth to be reminded. Unlike the river tour, lake rowing was wearisome labor. Within minutes he began perspiring. Once again the jacket came off. And he was correct about the canoe crew. He'd only propelled the boat a couple hundred yards when Jess and Travis streaked alongside.

"Hey there! Do you need a push?" Jessie chided as the canoe slipped by several feet away.

Seth let oars drag as he wrenched his brain for a come-back. He failed to come up with a snappy retort, so he simply said, "No, but a tow would be okay. Really, you two go on ahead. We'll get to the other end sooner or later. Right, Bob?"

The senior tipped his head in accord. Then dredging up his biggest voice, he bellowed, "Yup, like good wine and ripe tomatoes, some things just can't be rushed."

Pushing back a cough, he added, "Jazzi, maybe after the next stop you'd like to take a turn driving this tug. It'll give you a chance to show the boys what you're made of...certainly more than sugar and spice."

Seth snickered. In words too soft to carry, he bent forward and whispered, "Oh, we figured that out right after the storm. Trav and me aren't surprised by anything she does. She's definitely something else."

Bob let out a guffaw that trickled off to a chuckle. "That she is, my boy. That she is. Yep. That gal has a mind of her own. And you know what, my young friend? That's a good thing. Anything else would be boring."

By the time the boat navigated the length of the lake, Travis and Jess had vanished from view. Seth brought the Lund into shore and beached it alongside the empty canoe. He hollered and then stood still, listening for a return yell.

Nothing—mostly silence—only the sound of waves lapping softly against the rocky shore.

No, that wasn't quite true.

There was a steady thrumming in the background. Just enough of a noise to cause panic bees to begin buzzing in the pit of Seth's near-empty middle.

Barely audible, like the din of distant traffic, a steady thrumming rumbled in the background. Seth was familiar with the hum, and had heard it before: the continual clamor water makes as it cascades over a cliff, tumbling and splashing on rocks and boulders far below.

Bob was also aware of the unique noise. Instead of his slanted grin, the man sported a warped frown. Even the furrows on his forehead seemed to have deepened, from small valleys into deep canyons. He understood his mistake too late, that his expression telegraphed his worry.

The last thing the teens needed was a fidgety old fellow looking at the glass half-empty. Attempting to put on a poker face, Bob muttered a cover-up. "It sounds like we might have a little problem ahead. But I'm sure it's nothing you and the others can't conquer."

He coughed and then swiped a hand across his lips, wiping away spittle. Before Seth could respond, the senior added, "If you help me out of this little ferry, you could go find your friends."

* * *

Arriving well ahead of the boat, Travis and Jess had

been greeted by the same distant din. Travis recognized the sound.

"Listen. Hear that?" Travis asked, tilting his cap toward the noise.

"Yeah, I do. What is it? Sounds sort of like a freeway, but that can't be."

Travis shook his head. "It's a waterfall, and from the sound of it, a big one."

He listened a little longer, pondering their next move. They may as well go check it out, he determined. Unless they wanted to return to camp, they'd have to find a way around.

"Come on," he said, "There's no sense wasting time. It'll be at least another fifteen minutes or more before the boat arrives."

Walking alongside the stream wasn't as difficult as Travis first thought. So much of the ground was exposed rock that the only growth it supported was spindly aspens and skinny spruce. For several hundred yards the river remained flat and calm. And despite a current, its surface appeared peaceful and non-threatening, certainly placid enough to float a boat.

But then without notice, as if seeking an easier route to the sea, the river abruptly changed course. And as it did, the teenagers had to holler to be heard over the thunder of tumbling water.

Moments later Travis and Jess were perched near the edge of a rock-faced precipice. Below them, littered with foam, lay a pool filled with frothy liquid. Looking like steam above a giant stone kettle, the air over the pond held a hazy silver mist; painting a shiny wet look to everything brushed.

"Wow! That sure beats that tiny falls we have in

Minneapolis," Jessie gushed, mesmerized by the sight.

"What? Oh, you must mean Minnehaha Falls. Yeah, I've seen it in pictures. This fall's gotta be almost as high but a whole lot wider."

Jess edged forward so she was standing slightly above and alongside Travis. "Oh, for sure. I've been to Minnehaha Falls. Believe me, it's a toy compared to this one."

Jess was standing so close Travis could feel each word on his neck. He wanted to turn and give a reply, but was afraid that if he did, their noses might touch. Falls or no falls, he wasn't prepared for that kind of close encounter. So instead of talking, he gulped and then wiggled his head up and down.

"Well partner, what's your professional opinion? Are we gonna be able to portage around it?"

Travis wasn't certain. The rock face was steep and treacherous looking. They'd have to talk it over, make a group decision. Without daring to swivel his head he yelled, "Not sure. Let's get back to the canoe. The boat should be arriving any minute."

Seth had just finished securing the Lund when Travis and Jess hiked into view. Anxious to hear about the waterfall, he jogged to meet them halfway. Closing the gap, he boomed, "So how big is it? Can we get around?"

"I think so. But let's talk it over with Bob. See if he's up to the hike," Travis answered, buying time to consider all angles.

Travis had little doubt that they could lower everything past the falls. Portaging downhill wasn't the problem. He was troubled that this was truly the point of no return. Making a one-eighty and having to carry everything up the cliff-like slope would be next to impossible. So before pressing on, he wanted to be certain everyone knew the risk.

Once Travis had summed up what lay around the bend, Jess put in her two cents. "I'm for taking a chance. It's barely nine o'clock and we've already come this far. Anyway, from this spot it'd probably take most of the day to get back to the big lake, what with going against the current and all."

She strode over to where her uncle was parked on a rocky wedge, resting. Sitting next to him, she asked, "What do want to do, Uncle Bob? Go back or chance going around the falls?"

The elder couldn't help but feel pride for the way his niece was handling the dilemma. She was more like the girl he'd known in the past, before her mother died.

Clutching the girl's wrist with his good hand, he stared her straight on and said, "Let's do it. Think of life as a trip, my dear. Not a destination."

Looking up to make certain the boys were listening, he added, "Go for it. Even a turtle wouldn't get anyplace if he didn't stick his neck out once in a while. And what's the rush? From here it's all downstream. We're bound to run into that road sooner or later."

* * *

As the teens began tackling the cliff face, two float-planes landed near their vacated campsite. But because of the thundering waterfall, they had no clue help was so near.

Bob had been almost correct about new fishing regulations. But fishing hadn't been banned altogether, as he'd speculated. Rather, the lake had been classified as 'Catch and Release.' Anglers could land 'lunkers' to their hearts' content, but all large fish had to be put back in the water. Fishermen were allowed to keep only a few small 'eaters' to be consumed around a campfire.

Seth's theory of an abandoned campsite was on target.

Due to overuse and lack of firewood, outfitters were establishing tent-pads elsewhere.

And Bob had also been accurate about boats being carted off. But not for the reason he thought. Old boats were being upgraded for new models, deep-hulled vessels equipped with modern non-polluting outboards.

This was delivery day. Two boats were strapped tight to the struts of a renovated Otter seaplane. A third was tied tight to the rigging of an equally ancient but refurbished Beaver.

Unfortunately for the stranded quartet, the pilots were much too busy managing their heavily laden seaplanes to notice the SOS and little blue tent. Only after a day of clearing brush, toting fire-ring rocks, and rigging boats would the pilots get a second chance to spot a three-letter call for help.

But by that time the castaways would be in the midst of a new and perilous predicament.

Chapter Seventeen

CHAPTER SEVENTEEN

"What's the skinny? Lug the Lund all the way around, or take a chance and float it close to the falls?" Seth grumbled, wanting to get underway.

Travis stared at the stream opening. "Well...it'd be real chancy to row close to the falls. The river's not wide, but the current's strong. What if you can't bring the boat to shore in time?"

Seth shot Travis a hard stare. "Do I have the word 'stupid' written across my forehead?" he scowled. "I didn't mean I'd be in the boat. We'll stay on the bank with a rope and walk it downstream."

"Jeez...cool your jets. No need to get testy," Travis mumbled.

Then in a louder voice, he added, "Sure, why not? It sounds like a good idea. It'll save time, not to mention my back. But don't ya think, to be safe, you better take the gear out first."

Jess had been chatting with Bob. Thinking the boys were about to make a decision, she walked over and said, "We're burning daylight. So, what's the deal? Are we gonna do it or not? 'Cause if we're heading downstream, it'll take a while to get my uncle down that steep slope."

Travis peered over Jessie's shoulder to study the man. The fellow seemed to be aging by the hour. Bent over in the midst of a coughing spasm, Bob appeared to be more an applicant for a hospital bed than the robust aviator he'd been days earlier.

"How's he really doing?" Travis asked in a soft voice. "Do you think he's strong enough to keep going?"

Jess stuck out her lower lip while staring up at the sky. "Doesn't make much difference," she muttered. "He can't stay here. He needs a doctor...the sooner, the better."

Seth had busied himself undoing the canoe's tie-off cord. Once free, he tied the rope to the Lund's bow line. Then, holding the lengthened cord in both hands, he shuffled backwards; jerking the line, testing the connection.

Satisfied, he hustled back to the boat, hoisted out the packsack and then spat out a set of orders. "Let's go. I'm gonna start walkin' the boat along shore. Trav, grab this duffel and follow me. I might need a hand. Jess, you start hiking with Bob. It's time to move."

Seth hadn't stayed put to hear objections. He pushed the boat into open water. Then, like a big kid pulling an oversized inflatable, he began towing the Lund toward the outlet. Once the boat hit the current, the roles would reverse; it would start tugging at him.

Sure enough, the boat swung with the current and the rope pulled taut. Careful not to stumble, Seth eased along the bank, leaning against the tug of the current.

Close to the waterfall, where the stream banks tapered and the current boiled and frothed, the knot let loose. All Seth could do was stand and gawk while the dinghy pitched and danced. One second the Lund was bobbing up and down like a cork, then poof, it went missing in action. Seth felt suddenly ill, as if he'd just finished a marathon and had been immediately punched in the stomach.

The boat was certain to be trashed, smashed to smithereens. It was built to take years of abuse from wind, waves, and the occasional rock strike. But no way could it survive a fall of twenty feet, especially with tons of water pounding on its thin-skinned shell.

As per his orders, Travis had been trailing. When the boat broke free, he dropped the duffel and dashed to Seth's side. For a long moment he was too bewildered to find his tongue.

After a time, he leaned in and bellowed over the roaring water, "What the heck! If ya couldn't hold on to it, you shoulda hollered for help!"

The words had just flown from his mouth when Travis noticed the cord clutched in his buddy's fist. "Cripes! The rope broke, huh?"

Seth turned and slowly shook his head. "Nope. The rope didn't break. The knot came loose. I was wrong. The word stupid must be written all over my face."

Travis felt sure that the Lund had to be a goner. After a pause he hollered, "Well...there's nothing wrong with our feet. We better check out the damage before it gets too far downstream."

The teens scampered down the steep slope. Just beyond the whitewater they spotted their transportation. Miraculously, the Lund had somehow survived. Dented and bruised, and with only an air chamber keeping it afloat, the boat was bottom-side up, snagged on the bony remains of a waterlogged windfall.

Unfortunately it was hung up on the opposite bank. Reaching the battered craft would require a trek down-river and then circling back. There'd be a delay getting to it. They'd have to find a safe place to cross over. The river here was narrow, but the current far too swift to swim.

* * *

Unaware of the boys' dilemma, Jess had her own difficulties. Bob had started the hike with a false sense of vigor. He appeared so energetic that Jess thought in addition to helping him, she could lug along the lighter of the carryalls.

They hadn't gone far when that arrangement fell on its face. Actually it was Bob who almost tumbled. For the better part of a week he'd spent most of his waking hours lying flat on the ground. No more than a hundred steps into the walk, he started fading fast, legs wobbling; unable to hike over uneven ground.

Jess saw no choice but to halt and drop the duffel. She draped her uncle's arm around her neck, and then half-carrying the man, they two-stepped forward. After a few minutes of awkward hobbling, Bob needed a timeout.

"Need to rest, Jazzi. Need to rest," the tired trekker wheezed.

Supporting most of his weight, she helped him totter to the trunk of a fallen tree. When he was seated, sucking air, Jess went back for the bag.

She returned to find Bob in the midst of a coughing fit. From the sound and duration of chest-wrenching wheezes, Jess thought he'd never catch his breath. She stayed hidden behind a sprawling cedar, waiting for the coughing to cease. After a time the man finally began breathe easier. Only then did she approach.

"You ready to make another go of it? If not, you can stay here. I'll run ahead with the bag, see how the boys are doing."

With a continuous background murmur, the man hadn't heard the approaching footsteps. He flinched at the first word, but then realizing who it was, let down his guard. He waited until she was close before exclaiming, "Jazzi, you startled me. I didn't expect you back so soon. Sure didn't take you long. What did you do, run both ways?"

Jess lowered the bag, came close so she didn't have to shout, and in a kind voice, said, "If you want to rest a while longer, I'll trot ahead. By now the boys should have the boat ready."

"Tell you what, kiddo. First find me a walking stick, one strong enough to lean on. Then you can go see what those scalawags are up to. I'll scuffle ahead at my own pace. I'm sure I won't get far but it'll beat sitting here doing nothing at all."

* * *

Travis and Seth were growing discouraged. They were tramping along the river's rocky lip, searching for a place to ford. They had yet to see a safe spot, one where the water didn't appear more than waist deep. At least the ground near the waterfall was mostly rock; only a smattering of vegetation took root. Because of the lack of thick forest growth, foot travel was trouble-free.

But as they progressed downstream the terrain changed. The farther they hiked, the closer the trees were spaced, until finally the bank became a dense mix of evergreens and aspen.

Coming upon a tangle of tipped trees, Travis tapped Seth's shoulder. "I just had a thought. It's so darn simple I don't why you didn't think of it from the get-go."

Seth brushed a fat deer fly from his cheek, squinted at his friend, and grumbled, "That's 'cause I'm operating in dumb mode today. If brains were gas, I wouldn't have enough to start a model airplane. Okay, what's your bright idea?"

"The canoe. We might as well turn around and get it,

the duffel too while we're at it. We can use the Wenonah to cross over."

Seth waved his hands in the air, attempting to scare away a cloud of gnats hovering over his head. "Who's got the bug goop? You or Jess?"

In the woods, away from the lake breeze, and with the temperature rising under a mid-morning sun, insects were buzzing; gnats, deer flies, mosquitoes—each seeking a snack.

"Jess, I think. I haven't used any today. Up to now bugs haven't bothered me. But you didn't answer the question. Should we go get the canoe?"

Continuing to flail his arms, Seth said, "Well yeah. If I didn't have that big 'S' on my face, we woulda done it that way in the first place."

* * *

Jessie's insides seemed to somersault. Unlike the day the storm trashed the airplane, she instantly grasped the impact of the scene. The boat—scarred, dented, and bobbing wrong-side up—was wedged over the skeletal remains of a dead tree.

But the boys were missing. An image flashed—a dreadful snapshot—a picture that made her legs weak and her heart pound. She brought her hands to her mouth. "My God! What were they thinking?"

A moment earlier she'd stumbled over the large duffel. At the time Jess thought it peculiar that the bag was casually plopped near the river's edge. She thought the boys would have put it in the boat. Certainly they'd have wanted to slide everything down in one trip.

But obviously they hadn't. The daredevils must have tried to shortcut the carry by riding the boat directly over the falls.

Seth was the first to see her, up high near the top, kneeling with fists to her face. He stopped short and waited for Travis to catch up.

"What? What d'ya see?" Travis panted.

Seth pointed to the top of the cliff. "Up there! It's Jess. It looks like she's crying."

Following Seth's finger, Travis saw his friend was right. Although the hood of her sweatshirt hid her features, it looked as if Jess was sobbing. She was on her knees, hands pressed tight to her cheeks. The waterfall noise made it impossible to hear, but from the way her torso wobbled back and forth, crying was the only explanation.

"Yo! Down here!" Seth bellowed. He may as well have whispered. The yell was swallowed by the din of the falls.

"Try again, on three. I'll holler at the same time," Travis said. "Ready...one, two, three—Yo! Jess! Down here!"

For a second time words were wasted. Jess didn't even flinch. Then, while the boys looked on in uncertainty, she rose to her feet. Stooped under the hood of the sweatshirt, she slowly trudged away.

Travis leaned in close. With his mouth only inches from Seth's ear, he said, "I wonder what's bugging her. She's seems really upset."

Seth turned so Travis could see his words. "Something must have happened to Bob. They both should have been up there by now."

Every nerve in Travis's tall frame tingled as if touched by a live wire. Of course! That had to be it. Bob must have suffered another stroke.

Grabbing his buddy's arm, Travis shouted, "Jeez, I hope not! We need to find out."

Jessie didn't know what to tell her uncle. The man would feel responsible—that all the horrendous happenings had been his doing. Being already stressed near the limit; this latest tragedy could put him over the edge. She shuddered. The mental picture was too chilling. There'd be only one person remaining, someone ill-equipped to deal with the wild surroundings—herself.

So Jess was in no rush to be the bearer of bad news. Her typical fast-clipped stride slowed to a shuffle. She didn't want to bump into Bob until she had a grip on her feelings, least not until the tears slowed and her eyes stopped burning. Hopefully her uncle was still resting on the tree trunk. At least he'd be sitting down when she gave her account.

Jess was dodging around a clump of evergreens when a flash of color caught her eye. Through an opening she caught a glimpse of the orange preserver, and then an instant later, Bob's mane of silvery hair.

She twisted sideways for a better view. With the aid of a walking stick, the gritty old-timer was hobbling her way, one small step at a time.

Tears or no tears, he had to be told. Jess swiped the sweatshirt sleeve across her nose, and then jangled her hands at her side, trying to regain a sense of composure. Taking one last deep breath, she bolted toward the bent figure, deciding it was best to get it over with before she broke down again.

Bob was leaning on the makeshift cane when his niece burst onto the scene. He waited until the girl halted a few feet in front before he spoke. "I swear Jazzi, the way you flit around; I think you've got wings instead of—"

Then he saw the remnants of tears and broke off the sentence. "What is it, Jess? What's the matter?"

Jess sucked in a big breath, then a second. "The boys—Seth and Travis...they're gone!" Then her shoulders shuddered as she tried to stifle a sob.

Bob took a shuffle step forward. He stretched out his strong arm and pulled the weeping girl tight.

"Calm down, Jazzi. Calm down. I'm sure they're just doing a bit of scouting. They'll be back soon."

Fighting off a tremor, Jess gulped in another mouthful of air. She held her breath for a few seconds before exhaling loudly. Then, pushing away, she gasped, "No. You don't get it. They're really gone, over the falls, drowned."

Bob reached out and grasped one of Jessie's wrists. "Slow down, slow down. Now tell me how you know all this."

After a break, and in the most gentle of voices, he continued the questioning. "Did you see them? Their bodies in the water I mean? I can't believe they'd risk taking the boat over a waterfall. It's not like either one to do something so foolhardy."

"Oh gosh...no! Not their bodies! They were probably washed down the river. But I saw the boat. It's caught on a dead tree, up-side down."

Bob began to breathe a little easier. There could be many reasons for the boat to be turned over. "Tell me, Jess, where's the boat, on this shore or the other side of the river?"

"The other side, I think," she stuttered, picturing the sight. "Yeah, I'm positive. There's kind of a pond just beyond the waterfall. You know, like the one we walked around earlier. 'Cept this one is all whirlpool-like. It'd be crazy to try swimming in it."

Looking over the top of Jessie's head, Bob caught movement in the trees some distance away. A soft smile curled his lips.

"You know, Jazzi, I believe you may have jumped to a hasty conclusion. 'Cause if you'd turn around and stand tall, I think you're gonna get a pleasant surprise."

Chapter Eighteen

C H A P T E R   E I G H T E E N

After explanations and apologies, the topic turned to salvaging the boat. Step one was to lower the canoe over the slope. Seth's unknotted section of rope proved a life-saver. They reattached it, and with three teens clutching tight as they let out line, the Wenonah slid downhill like a toboggan.

They lowered Bob the same way. Travis wrapped the rope around the preserver. Then, with Jess assisting on the slope-face, the boys played out the cord. He arrived at the lower level with nary a bump or bruise from the experience.

It was now time for the real test—a boat rescue. After discussing the risk involved, they decided that Seth, buckled tight in the life vest, would be the one to cross over. Once on the other side; he would attempt snag the bow rope. Then, tying the second section to the first cord, there should be enough line to stretch the width of the pool.

After securing the cords, Seth was to attach a stick to the rope. Using his best pitching form, he'd make an effort to hurl the limb across the opening. Jess and Travis would play outfield. Their job would be to catch the stick before it splashed into the pool.

Seth didn't dare paddle straight across the current. That would have been a blueprint for instant calamity. Turned sideways in churning water, the canoe would roll over like a dog doing tricks. Instead, he hunkered in the center of the canoe, and then paddling with gusto, angled the craft downstream. Despite a heroic effort, the canoe chased around the bend before reaching the opposite shore.

His next challenge was finding a safe place to run aground. It took another fifty yards before the river slowed enough that he dared jump overboard. By the time he beached the canoe, onlookers were out of sight.

Travis tried keeping pace by trotting along the river bank. He came to an abrupt halt where the windfalls formed a tangled barrier. All he could do was look on in nervous concern as Seth and the Wenonah darted out of sight behind the thick foliage.

Seth backtracked as quickly as the forested streambank allowed. A short time later he was waving across the river. Upon spotting his buddy, Travis cupped his hands and yelled, "You okay?"

"Yeah, it was a hassle but I made it. See ya at the falls." Eager to get on with the task, Seth slipped into the brush, and like an apparition, vanished.

* * *

Attaching the rope proved to be a perilous undertaking. Seth was grateful to be wearing a preserver. He discovered that the bow line had snarled around a branch. To free it, he'd have to get into the water. Once wet, he had to work his way along the tree trunk, grab the line, and pull himself, and the rope, to land.

Things were going okay until he was working his way back to shore. The limb he was clutching suddenly snapped, jetting him into the flow. Only the line, double-wrapped around his hand, kept him tethered to the boat.

Seth struggled frantically to save himself. Thankfully the preserver kept him from going under. Finally reaching land, and needing to recoup, he flopped flat, sucking wind. The unexpected swim had proved to be a bone chilling challenge.

All the others could do was to watch and wait while the water-logged teen caught his breath. Finally to the onlookers' relief, Seth got up and went back to work. After combining the cords, and as per the plan, he attached a thick chunk of wood.

Then, like a rain-soaked quarterback hoping to connect a touchdown pass, Seth cocked his arm and looked toward the end zone. Taking several stutter-steps, he hurled the chunk with everything he had.

Jess and Travis prepared for the catch. Their heads craned skyward as the stubby limb climbed, and then with the line trailing behind like a kite's tail, began losing altitude.

An eye blink later the line snapped taut. In the next instant the stick stopped playing ball and instead became a boomerang. Four sets of eyes followed the flight path as the limb wobbled over the water, then splashed down in the center of the pool.

Seth had no choice but to take another polar bear bath. When he lobbed the stick a second time, he did so like an old-timer pitching a softball—underhanded.

* * *

"It's almost free. Pull harder! Pull harder!" Seth encouraged.

Although Jess and Travis were tugging with every ounce strength they could muster, the snag refused to release the catch of the day.

"Hold up. I want a minute to think about this," Jess shouted to her coworker.

She stood tall, one hand holding the line, the other working a bug bite. After a moment of serious reasoning, she yelled, "I think we're pulling in the wrong direction. We need to move closer to the falls, get a better angle."

Travis concurred. He could see that they were fighting limbs by pulling sideways. And though the branches were dead, they didn't want to fracture. By tugging more upstream, there'd be a better chance the boat could slip free.

"You're right!" He yelled. "Over there. Out on that ledge. If the rope reaches, I think we can do it."

The line was just long enough. And true to Jessie's reckoning, with a couple well-timed tugs, the Lund was liberated. Immediately there was a new dilemma. Once released, and wanting to go with the flow, the upside-down watercraft became a battered and bruised red whale trying desperately to escape downstream.

"What now?" Jess shrieked frantically, clutching the line while struggling to stay on her feet.

Travis had already started scampering to keep pace. "We've gotta walk it along the bank," he yelled. "Find a tree...tie it off."

* * *

The Lund continued to act as if it an appointment elsewhere. The contest continued almost to barricade of tipped trees. Fortunately there the land leveled, the flow slowed, enough so that Travis was able to wrap the cord around a tree.

"Whew, that was work!" he wheezed.

"Tell me 'bout it," Jess panted, dropping fanny-first on damp needles. "What next? Wait for your pal or try to right the boat by ourselves?"

Travis plopped down alongside. "We'll wait. The boat's not going anywhere, at least not until it's flipped over. Why don't you go back and get Bob? We'll be taking off from here. There's no way we can paddle upstream to get him."

Jess sprang to her feet as if she were spring loaded. Standing over Travis, she asked, "What about the bags? Do you want me to bring 'em with?"

Travis cranked his neck to look up. "What...d'ya think you're Wonder Woman? Bring your uncle...oh yeah, and the cooking pot. We'll need it to bail."

* * *

Seth hadn't stayed to watch the whale taming. He'd trotted off as soon as the boat was released. Being on the wrong side of the river, the Wenonah had to be brought to the opposite shore.

Arriving at the canoe, he made a risky decision. Instead of paddling, he walked the canoe across. Luckily the water never became more than thigh high. If it had been deeper, he'd have been forced to let the canoe roam free.

Within minutes of Jessie's departure, Seth rejoined his pal. After fording the stream, he'd pulled the canoe up on the bank. Fast as the terrain allowed, he hoofed upstream.

The thorny part of the trek was getting through the tangle of tipped trees. It took a few tries before finding an opening. Even then he had to get down on hands and knees and crawl through.

Travis was surprised at his pal's quick crossover. After taking in the sopped and still dripping jeans, he asked, "What did you do? Swim over?"

"Yeah, sort of. I walked the Wenonah across. If I hadn't,

by the time I'd got to this side, I'd probably been halfway to the next lake."

Then he turned to study the boat. Struggling in the current like a big fat fish on a rope stringer, the Lund was twisting and bucking, trying to break free.

It suddenly dawned on Seth someone was missing. "Where's your girlfriend? I thought she was giving you a hand. I thought that the two of you would have the boat flipped and ready for bailing."

Travis took several steps forward and punched Seth's preserver. "Knock it off. How many times I gotta tell ya? She isn't my girlfriend. If anything, she's got eyes for you."

Seth flashed a responsive smile. "So where'd she go?"

"She went for Bob. And the cooking pot so we can empty the boat. Speaking of which, let's turn it over."

Standing knee deep along the stream bank each youth grabbed a gunnel, and with a big grunt, heaved. With a heroic effort, they managed to lift the edge of the Lund chest high, hoping to roll it over.

But without someone on the far side to grab and pull, the boat wallowed on edge. Then, caught by the current, the lower gunnel kicked into deeper water. They had no choice but to let go.

"Damn!" Seth cursed. "The two of us aren't gonna get it done. We need another body."

"Will she do?" Travis asked, nodding to the human mule lumbering along the river bank.

Turning, Seth was amazed to see Jess plodding through the brush. "Jeez! I don't believe it! What did she have for breakfast? Vitamin pills?"

Jess was plodding over the uneven ground, weighed down with both bags. The big one angled across her back, the carry strap curled around her shoulder like a rifle sling. The smaller duffel she clutched tight to her chest in a two-armed bear hug. Looking like a shepherd following a flock of one, Bob brought up the rear.

"I'll tell ya, Trav. If you told me that first day she would more than pull her own weight, I'd said you were crazy. Those bags must weigh darn near as much she does."

It was Travis's turn to display a wry grin. "Speaking of that first day, didn't I tell you not to be so quick to judge? Bob said she was an okay gal, and you know what? She is."

* * *

Jess and Travis did the lifting. Seth sloshed to the far side to catch and pull. The boat was turned over on the first attempt. Then the teenagers took turns bailing. The water was painfully cold, and much too numbing to endure more than a few minutes without relief.

Slowly, inch by inch, the sides began to rise as water was thrown overboard. When the boat was about half-empty, Jess asked, "Hey guys. What happened to the oars? Are they still above the falls? If they are, I can run up and get 'em."

Seth abruptly stopped bailing. He slapped his free hand to side of his head, "Double-dang! I forgot all about 'em...the fishing rig, too."

Travis grimaced but bit his tongue. He'd told his bud to take everything out just in case. Now it was too late. The fishing pole was taking a swim far under the falls.

Then he had a second thought. Oars don't sink. They're made of wood. "You know what? The rod's gone. Let's hope we won't need it. But the oars have to be some-where between here and the next lake. We'll find 'em."

Jess volunteered. "You want me to look for 'em? Maybe

they got caught up on a tipped-over tree or something along the bank."

Having returned to his bailing post, and hard at work sloshing water back in the stream, Seth grunted, "Naw, no sense in that. Trav's right. They gotta be floating someplace downriver. Once we get underway, we'll just have to keep a sharp eye out for 'em."

Chapter Nineteen

C H A P T E R   N I N E T E E N

Most of morning was gone before the flotilla was ready to depart. Bailing had only been step one in preparations to get underway. The boat was nearly empty when Travis noticed water gushing in between the seats.

One of the many new dents spanned a seam. Several rivets had jarred loose. Performing like a leaky faucet, a steady stream spurted through the broken joint.

To make repairs the Lund had to be pulled from the water. Then the teens tipped it sideways and propped it against a tree. Once it was secure, Seth banged away with a wedged-shaped rock on bent aluminum until the seam was flattened.

Next, with Travis holding a larger rock against the rivet heads, Seth hammered from the inside, forcing the fasteners together. Tight enough, they hoped that the leak would be slowed to a trickle; a flow they could bail as they traveled.

While the boys hammered on the boat, Jess tended to Bob. He was exhausted. Besides being pooped, coughing spasms returned; long bouts of lung-testing wheezes.

But other than bringing him water, there was nothing

Jess could do. Words of reassurance didn't slow the gurgling sounds burbling from his chest.

After an hour delay, and with the Lund once again straining at the leash, they were ready to leave. Jess was untying the line when Travis yelled, "Whoa! Hold on a sec. Seth, how d'ya figure you're gonna steer? You haven't got any oars."

Straddling the middle seat, Seth slapped his hand on his forehead. "Cripes! I thought with all the water work that 'S' woulda got scrubbed clean."

He turned to face his passenger. "Another delay, Bob. At least until Trav finds us a push pole."

The senior nodded. "There's no emergency. We'll get there when we get there."

Bob looked down at the dent repair. Water was seeping through the seam. He returned his gaze to Seth. "Now then, young captain, please pass me that pan. I might as well be ready when the tide comes in. You fellows have managed to keep my feet dry this far into the trip. No sense changing that routine."

The canoe crew had wandered off in search of a suitable steering stick. Jess sauntered along the stream's wooded bank. Travis disappeared into the forest. They returned within minutes. Travis came back first, a stout multi-limbed branch dragging behind like a giant broom.

Jess marched in moments later; a long bare branch propped smartly on her shoulder.

"Will this do?" she asked, suspending the sturdy limb out at arm's length.

Seth studied both offerings. "Sorry Trav, but Jess's find looks perfect. We're ready. Let's do it."

Undoing the ropes where they were hitched together, Travis flipped the shortened line into the boat. "See ya," he said, and then watched as the Lund, caught by the current, hurried downstream.

"Come on, Jess. Let's get this other line tied to the canoe and catch up."

* * *

After a few bends and twists, the land flattened and the stream slowed. No longer were banks made only of rock. Without so much exposed granite, thick foliage hugged the stream's edge, rising to form a canopy that curtained off the sky.

Travis noticed that the tree tops were becoming restless, swaying in a breeze that had yet to poke its way through the green roof. Without wind reaching water, he worked at ignoring deer flies dive-bombing exposed skin and the sweat dripping from his nose. Instead of complaining, he took frustrations out on the paddle.

Jess did likewise, pulling with the clout of one twice her size. Working in tandem, the Wenonah skimmed the surface like a water beetle. Several minutes of hard labor brought its reward. The boat was in sight.

"Check it out. Seth found one of the oars," Jess chirped.

Travis stopped stroking long enough to look. Sure enough, Seth was no longer steering with a stick. Instead, he sat facing the front, wielding an oar like an oversized paddle; stroking on one side, then the other. But because of flatter land and a tame flow, the boat had slowed considerably.

Jess peered over her shoulder. "How far to the next lake?"

"Not sure...couple miles, maybe. Why?"

Jess tilted her head toward the Lund. "'Cause they aren't going very fast. Besides, Seth can't keep that pace up all day. He's liable to have a heart attack."

"Yeah, for sure. Let's slow down. It's probably best that we stay behind anyway, at least until we find the other oar. And if we don't, we'll probably need to make a switch. Seth can take a turn in the canoe. I'll do the boat."

Travis slowed to an occasional pull with the paddle. He bounced his eyes from bank to bank, hoping to spot the second oar. How far could it have gone in a current that had slowed to a crawl?

One delight of river travel was that the teens never knew what new sight awaited them around the next turn. Shortly after making a lazy curve, the channel opened. Within a short space, the forest stream transformed into a wide, weed-choked marsh.

The Lund had rounded that bend moments earlier. As the canoe drew near, it appeared that the boat had run out of gas. Seth had reversed himself. He was facing the rear, bent at the waist, furiously bailing; the pot a blur as it dipped, rose, and emptied, dipped, rose, and emptied.

The canoe was nearly alongside when Jess yipped, "Over there! I see it! The oar! It's caught up in that swamp grass!"

Travis didn't wait to be told twice. Plunging hard, he spun the canoe to where Jess pointed. Seconds later the prize was snatched from its weedy rest stop. Jess placed the oar across the gunnels and then sat tight as Travis back-stroked.

"Thank you! Thank you very much! I appreciate the effort." Seth exclaimed in a poor Elvis imitation after taking the oar from Jess.

"One oar works okay when there's a current. But I'm gonna need both of 'em to get through this mess," he panted, indicating the clogged channel stretching into the distance.

Travis was clutching the side of the boat, inspecting the

dent repair. "What d'ya think? Is it leaking worse than when we started?"

Bob coughed up an answer. "Not so bad that we'll sink. I wanted to bail but your buddy insists on doin' everything himself. Says my job is to sit still and relax. Supposed to save my energy in case we have to portage again."

Jess pursed lips in agreement. "He's right, Uncle Bob. Listen to him. We don't want you having another coughing jag. Do we guys?"

"No way!" Travis concurred. "You just sit back and enjoy the scenery. We'll do the work."

He directed his gaze at Seth. "Speaking of which, do you want me to take a turn pulling on those over-sized paddles?"

Seth surveyed both sides of the swamp, looking for a place to pull in. The marsh lacked an edge-line. The shore was wall-to-wall reeds, rushes, and tamarack; a very uninviting place to beach a boat.

"Tell you what. I'll take it through this shallow water. If there's a good spot to switch at the other end, we'll do it. If not, we'll keep going 'til we reach the next lake."

They let the boat go ahead. Bob became a back seat tour director, instructing Seth which oar to pull to keep from rowing into weeds. Now out in the open, the breeze was a blessing. It kept most bugs at bay and brought a bit of cooling relief. Along with the wind, bits of cloud had formed, dotting the sky with shards of eggshells; white splotches of paint on a blue drop cloth.

Despite heavy vegetation, the canoe continued to skim the surface. Travis barely had to paddle to keep pace.

With little to do, his mind began to wander. The first thoughts were about family. His parents must be going crazy with worry. And by now, his little sister, Beth, must be having nightmares. How many times could her big brother disappear and return unscathed?

An unfed animal growled from his middle, reminding Travis of how little he'd had to eat. Other than the cup of chowder gulped for breakfast, and a couple of jerky sticks, he'd had only occasional sips of water. But best to keep mum about hunger pangs. No one else was whining.

Jess let out a shrill shriek, bolting Travis from his daydream. She was staring across the marsh.

"Look! Over there!"

The other three chuckled. Almost hidden behind swamp grass and willow shoots, a moose was standing knee deep in an opening, munching a water root. Spinach-like plants protruded from both sides of its long snout, giving the young bull a comical look. A set of hand-sized antlers, soft and furry, extended just beyond the animal's ears.

"I thought moose had big antlers," Jessie said.

Bob chipped in. "You're right, Jess. Big ones do. But that's a young bull, barely a year old. Probably out on his own for the first season. Give him few years and he'll have a head-dress that won't fit through a barroom door."

Jess considered that, and then asked, "What's with the fuzzy stuff?"

The canoe and boat were side-by-side, close enough to touch.

"That's velvet," Bob explained. "Deer and moose—the males anyway—grow a new set of antlers every spring. Come fall that furry coating will be long gone. They'll rub it right off."

The young bull had heard enough. Upset at having lunch interrupted, he spun and started wallowing through shallow water. The boaters looked on as the animal lurched to higher ground, and then with a couple of ungainly strides, blended into the background.

"Are they dangerous?" Jess asked once the huge mammal was out of sight.

The last years of Bob's extended wildlife career had been spent working with Travis's father. They'd spent countless hours in the floatplane, tracking radio-collared wolves and moose, searching for their secrets.

"Not usually, Jazzi," Bob said. "Like most wild critters, they just want to be left alone."

"Yeah, but a person doesn't want to cross a big bull during the rut," Seth interjected, throwing the comment in Jessie's direction.

Travis was glad his face was already red from paddling. Why did his pal have to mention the rut, a time when antlered animals became lovesick bullies? But before he had a chance to reroute the subject, Jess jumped in with both feet.

"What's the rut?"

Bob came to the boys' rescue. "It's that time of year when the mature males get the urge to start a family. They go around banging their antlers on trees, brush, and even each other. All trying to prove that they're the biggest and nastiest living thing in the woods. Then, if they impress the right female, the two will get together. Come spring there'll be another calf or two on God's green earth."

It was Jessie's turn to giggle. "Oh, you mean they act a lot like junior high boys, punching or shoving each other in the halls at school. I've always wondered who they really were trying to impress, their cronies or the girls in the corridor."

Seth had heard enough. This girl was good, flipping the answer over in the blink of an eye. With a thrust of his arm, he pushed the Wenonah away.

"We gotta get goin'," he mumbled. "We can discuss a moose's love life some other time."

* * *

If downstream river rowing could be compared to a gourmet meal, stroking the Lund the length of the marsh was a plate full of leftovers. Besides combating a weed-choked channel, Seth had to battle an ever-increasing headwind.

Travis tried talking his friend into trading places. Seth declined the invitation. He'd muttered that until they were beached, it might be too risky. Travis suspected a different reason—a Jessie reason—but he didn't go there.

He held his words and shrugged his shoulders. Sooner or later they'd have to swap. Seth couldn't keep working like a bionic robot forever.

After more than a mile of swamp grass, lily pads, and acres of reeds and rushes, the marsh narrowed and the current increased. The swampy shoreline became more defined as tamarack and alders gave way again to spruce and cedar.

The float trip had been an easy sail for the canoe crew. Little effort was needed to keep pace.

The opposite was true for Seth. He was dog-tired. Only visions of his mother's weekend wedding plans kept him going—stroke after pain-filled stroke.

Between bouts of coughing, Bob had cautioned the youth to slow down, to take a break. But the words fell on deaf ears. The only respite was when Seth traded oar handles for the bailing pot. Even then he went up and down, up and down, as if competing in a contest;

dumping gallons overboard non-stop.

He was busy throwing water when Travis guided the Wenonah alongside. "Hey, don't you think it's time you let someone else have a turn? It looks like there's a good place to pull in just beyond that windfall," Travis advised, tipping the bill of his cap downriver.

"Besides, Jess says she wants to try rowing, now that there's a current runnin' again."

Hunched up in the rear, feet to one side to avoid being tagged by the bailing pot, the gentleman dipped his silver head up and down. With an air of weariness, he looked at Travis. "I've been telling your friend to take a break but he won't listen."

The elder turned his eyes on Seth. "Please, would you stop? We aren't going to sink just 'cause there's a little H2O sloshing around."

With a straight, tight-lipped expression, Seth set the pot down, and folded his arms across is chest. "There, satisfied? I'm just trying to get us to that road before dark."

Bob bent forward to pat the youth's knee. "I know, I know. And you've been doing a fine job. But you can't continue working so hard. You need to rest once in a while. From the way you've been pulling on those oars, it wouldn't surprise me if you've raised a few blisters."

The man leaned forward and grasped one of Seth's wrists. With a gentle tug he extended the arm. "Let's have a look. You gotta realize, young fellow, that if you start growing bubbles, you aren't gonna be much use to yourself—or anyone else for that matter."

Reluctantly, Seth opened his fist, palm-side down. Once again Bob clasped the boy's wrist, slowly turning it over. He wheezed out a whistling sigh. He'd intervened too late. Like gopher mounds on open prairie, gray fluid-filled blisters bulged from the surface. The cut on his thumb also looked raw. Although partially healed and not bleeding, the injury was red and swollen.

"My God! I wish you woulda taken my advice an hour ago. There's no way we're going to let you keep rowing. Let Travis or Jess take a turn."

Self-conscious, Seth pulled in his hand, tucking it under an armpit. "It's no big deal," he said, staring off in the distance. "They don't hurt."

Bob grimaced, looked up at the cottony clouds, and then down at the water, slowly shaking his head. "Not right now. But later, when they break, and skin starts sloughing off, you'll think otherwise."

* * *

The trade was made where Travis had suggested, just past the bony remains of what once had been a very large spruce. Tipped into the water years earlier, all that remained of the once mighty evergreen was the trunk and few skeletal branches.

Jess got her wish. The river was again confined between narrow banks. And because the flow was steady and level, they decided she could take a turn rowing. Once underway she'd caught on quick, pulling one oar, then the other to keep the craft centered.

The boys hung back in the canoe, purposely keeping their distance. Seth sat in the front, trailing one hand, then the other, letting the blistered palms cool in cold water. Even without help, Travis barely stroked. Mainly he used the paddle as a rudder, sculling from side to side, keeping the canoe on course.

Tree lined and shaded, the river ran fairly straight. Other than an occasional windfall to steer around, the stream was free of debris. Even the bends were wide and tame, offering little challenge.

Neither said much for the first mile or two. Travis was having trouble accepting Seth's stupidity. He could forgive Seth for the damage done to the boat. That had been an accident. He was having a harder time coming to grips with the damage Seth did to his hands.

How Seth could not have realized what was happening was impossible to understand. He had to have felt the blisters coming on. Yet, when asked to swap, Seth had refused. So for the rest of the trip, other than to carry the canoe or duffels, his buddy's strong hands were a thing of the past.

Travis was paddling on auto-pilot, head in the clouds. He didn't notice Jess turning the boat toward the bank.

Seth interrupted Trav's reverie. "What's up with her?" he barked. "She can't be tired. We haven't gone that far."

Travis glanced downstream. Sure enough, the boat had pulled in. The Lund was parked alongside a windfall. Jess sat still, clutching onto a naked branch, anchoring the boat in place.

Travis's first thought was that something happened to Bob. He thrust hard, propelling the canoe forward with a burst of power. Feeling the urgency of the stroke, and disregarding blisters, Seth picked up his paddle and did the same.

Drawing close, Travis slowed the Wenonah by dragging his paddle. When the space narrowed to a few yards, he reversed direction, slowing the canoe to a standstill.

"What's wrong? Why did you stop?" Seth asked, reaching out to grab the boat.

"Look up ahead. Uncle Bob thinks we're about to join another river," Jess replied, clutching tight to the limb.

The boys studied waterway ahead. Bob was correct. Where the stream made a turn, it abruptly widened.

"So? What's the problem?" Seth asked. "We knew that was going to happen. It means that we're closer to the road than we thought. Besides, a wider channel should be easier to navigate."

Bob rubbed his stubbly chin before clearing his throat. "Harrumph. Well...I think you boys should go on ahead. Keep a close eye for rapids. At the first hint of whitewater, pull in and wait. We don't need more surprises. I don't think the boat can't take more abuse."

"You mean portage around any fast water?" Travis asked. "That could really slow us down."

Bob took several sharp breaths and then replied. "Not necessarily. But I'd want one of you to walk ahead and make sure we won't be taking a tumble through any chutes or rocky narrows. If it means we have to spend another night in the woods, so be it. There's always tomorrow."

Seth scowled, face pointed toward the sky. "Yeah, but we haven't got much left in the way of grub. And I'm half-starved. What are we gonna eat?"

"Not to worry. Jess tells me she secreted a package of cookies before the bear visit. And Trav, didn't you pack along some smoked fish...enough for a couple of meals?"

"Yeah, I did. Seth, if we read the map right, there's only one more lake to navigate. We don't have a rod, but I still have my pocket tackle box. There's a roll of leader material in it. We could try catching something with a drop-line."

Still frowning, Seth shrugged in agreement. "Well, one thing's for sure. We aren't gonna get anywhere chewin' the fat. We'll go on ahead like you want. If we see rough water, we'll pull over and wait, just like you said."

Two streams did connect where Bob predicted. But other than a wider channel, the landscape remained gentle, the flow smooth and rock free. Travis kept busy swiveling to check the boat's progress. They didn't want to get so far ahead that they couldn't see it.

After several lazy miles, the boys saw that the river ahead abruptly fell; creating a short set of rapids. But just as quick, beyond the last boil, the stream calmed. A short distance later a bubble-filled current poured into the rippled water of a lake.

"What d'ya think? See any reason not go right through?" Travis asked.

Seth studied the channel and then shook his head. "Naw. As long a Jess keeps the boat straight, it'll shoot through without a problem. But we better pull in and wait. She might get nervous. Maybe one of us will have to take it through."

Travis turned the canoe toward shore. Seth crouched, and then grasping tight to the bow, stepped into the water. He stood, clutching one side, keeping the canoe from surging off on its own.

The water was cold and soon his feet began to ache. "I'm gonna tie up. You can stay put until they pass," Seth declared, reaching for the line.

Moments later the Lund drew near enough to shout out instructions. Shaping his hands into a miniature mega-phone, Travis yelled, "Jess, There's a little whitewater ahead. But you can handle it. Just keep the boat straight and the current will take you right to the lake."

Jess let the oars dangle and then turned to face front. From where she was sitting it appeared that the river fell four or five feet in very short space. Boils of white frothed and galloped where the flow surged over hid-den boulders.

Jess wasn't certain she was up to the challenge. "But how do I make sure it stays straight? What if the boat turns sideways?"

Seth added instructions. "Stroke the oars as fast and hard as you can. Just make sure the boat's moving faster than the current and you'll be fine. If you get in trouble, your uncle can tell you which oar to pull. Are you okay with that, Bob?"

The old outdoorsman concurred. Although the channel dropped, the current was steady, the waterway open. He saw no real danger with the plan. Rather than yell out a reply, he lifted a hand and gave a thumbs up. Then he leaned forward and whispered something to his niece.

Nodding, Jess began pulling with everything she had. For a short moment the Lund seemed to wallow. But as paddles found purchase, the boat plunged forward.

Moments later the craft jerked and kicked as it bobbed through the chute. Just as swiftly, like a tired bucking bronco, it slowed before hobbling to calmer waters.

Chapter Twenty

C H A P T E R   T W E N T Y

"How far?" Travis asked, leaning over Seth's shoulder.

The boys were kneeling on a finger of granite that sloped gently into the lake. Their eyes were trained on the map. After regrouping with Bob and Jess, the senior had suggested a rest stop.

The stumpy point provided a perfect place to pull in. Once boats were beached, they got out and stretched.

"I don't think we have to go all the way to the far end. Best I can tell, the outlet's about halfway down the other side," Seth said, placing a finger on a tiny splotch of blue bordering the red-inked travel route.

"It looks like water flows out from a bay a couple miles from here."

Jess moseyed over from where she'd been conversing with her uncle. She knelt and peered over Seth's second shoulder. "What do you think? Can we make the road before sunset?"

Seth ran his finger on top of a curvy blue stripe. He stopped where the squiggle crossed a dotted line. "Here's where we think we are. And here's where we're headed. It looks like we've gone more than halfway."

Travis glanced at his watch. "It's past two now, but I think we can do it. This is the last open water. From here on it's all downhill. The question is; do we want to stop and fish for a while—fill our bellies—or push on? Risk having to eat the last bit of freeze dried and smoked fillets in the dark?"

Jess plunged a hand into a pocket of her sweatshirt. It emerged holding tight to three Tootsie Pops. "Here," she said, handing one of each to the boys. "There's at least a half dozen more in my duffel. But before deciding what to do, maybe you oughta check out those clouds."

She was pointing her sucker toward the distant shore. Looking much like the day the ordeal had begun, fat black-bottomed billows were building. Would they reach their destination before receiving a soaking? Or would they be forced to stop short and camp?

Travis turned his gaze from the cloud bank and refocused on his old friend. Bob was reclining near the Lund, half-sitting, half-lying on a mossy rise of rock. Unlike the morning the stroke occurred—when his skin had a yellowish pallor—his complexion now was more a bloodless gray.

Travis resolved that it was Jessie's call. "I can't speak for Seth, but I think you should be the one to make the decision. Bob's my friend, but he's your uncle. We've pushed him awfully hard today. He looks all-in, like death warmed over."

He broke the thought off, contemplating. After a short pause, he continued. "But Jess, we can't tell from this air map whether we'll have to make any more portages. It's not detailed enough to show stuff like that."

Travis's suggestion caught Jess off guard. She stood quiet with eyes darting back and forth, first at her uncle, and then at the haze on the horizon.

Seth grew impatient. "Remember, we only have a couple miles of lake rowing. Trav can take care of that. Once we get to the river, we won't have to paddle much—just float with the current if we want. And don't forget, we can always stop and camp along the way."

Jess closed her eyes as if viewing a mental preview of how it might go. After a time she said in a small voice, "Okay. Let's move on. I guess I agree with Seth. If my uncle gets too tired, we can always stop and stay over."

* * *

Travis returned to boat duty. It didn't take long to realize what his bud had already accomplished on this 'up and at 'em early' day. After an uninterrupted stretch of steady straining, his shoulders ached and arms felt like a pair of lead weighted logs.

Bob held down the bench in the back. The formally chatty fellow sat silent, often with eyes closed, letting the on-again, off-again sun kiss exposed skin. Facing the rear, as one does when rowing; Travis studied the man's features.

When opened, Bob's eyes were glazed, almost as if they were covered by a transparent film of thin plastic. And even with a week's worth of whiskers sprouting from chin and cheeks, the deep furrows etching the man's face looked as if they were carved by an artist sculpting age lines on a clay figure. Despite bursts of sunrays, his color remained ashen and dreary.

Seth and Jess had gone on ahead. Their immediate mission was to find the outlet, and then flag the boat into shore. Every minute or two Travis would pivot around front, hoping to see that happening. The sooner the better, he thought. He hadn't been pulling on the oars all that long, but muscles were already pleading for a recess.

As it turned out, it was Bob who spotted the canoe.

They had just rounded a peninsula when he caught sight of the Wenonah pulled up on shore.

"Over there," he said, aiming with a finger. "Your friends must be exploring on foot. Let's hope we don't have anymore Niagaras to get around. One a day is more than enough for this old codger's taste."

By the time Travis made land, Jess and Seth were ready with a report. The bad news, they said, like the first river entry, the outlet began with a stretch of whitewater. A portage was in their future. The good news being that the section was short, not more than fifty yards in length.

Another favorable tidbit; they weren't the first to walk the stream bank. A meandering path led along the rapids, possibly tramped by fishermen or animals treading close to the river's edge.

The portage went perfectly. The brief burst of rapids caused little delay. Less than fifteen minutes after the Lund was hauled out, the teens had it emptied of water, relocated, and ready to row.

Jess would take another turn at being the rowing master. Bob would be placed in his usual first-mate's station.

With a grunt and a heave, Seth shoved the boat into the channel. Then he bellowed to Jess, "Go on ahead! We'll catch up." Orders given, he spun on his heel to chase after Travis. The canoe and heavy duffel were still at the lake, waiting to play leapfrog.

"How far d'ya think they got by now?" Travis asked as he settled in the Wenonah and prepared to scoot downstream.

"What's it been? Ten minutes? They might've made a quarter mile. We should be able to close the distance in half that time, even if you have to do all the work," Seth replied, his paddle lying lifeless across the gunnels.

Travis plunked his paddle into the water and thrust, propelling the canoe midstream. Then he switched sides, sweeping rudder-like until the bow pointed with the flow. He took a big breath and began stroking, happy the lake work was at their backs. They were quiet for a spell, content just to watch the undergrowth slip by soundless as smoke.

After a time Travis spoke. "Bob's not looking well. I swear he's aged ten years. And did ya notice his color? It's worse than before. My gosh, his skin's as gray as a dirty sheet."

"'Course I noticed. And all that coughing is scary. The man must be in the first stage of pneumonia. Jess is right. He needs to see a doctor, pronto; or better yet, airlifted to a hospital."

The canoe had veered to one side. Travis stroked double-speed to get back on course. Once in center of the river again, he changed topics. "I feel sorry for Jess. She must think most of this is her fault."

"Well, I guess we really can't blame her for being blasted by that twister," Seth muttered over his shoulder.

"Yeah. But she probably thinks that if Bob hadn't detoured to drop her off, we woulda missed the storm altogether."

Seth twisted about in his seat, wiggling the watercraft from side-to-side. He considered his friend's facial expression.

"Hey! Knock it off! You know better than to turn around like that," Travis scolded.

"I wanted to see your face. You're serious, aren't ya? You really think Jess feels responsible?"

Travis flipped his paddle to the opposite side and made a couple of correcting strokes. "Yeah, I think she does. And if I remember right, the first couple of days you laid the blame on her too—thought it was all her fault."

Seth turned toward the front, gently this time as to not rock the boat. "I guess I did. I really acted like a jerk. Why didn't you hit me alongside the head with a big stick? I deserved it."

"Yeah, you did," Travis agreed with a chuckle. "I woulda hit you but I couldn't find a stick big enough for the job."

Travis concentrated on steering as the river made a sharp turn. Shortly after the bend the stream frolicked and laughed through a series of mild drops and dips. It wasn't until they made another sweeping turn that they could see the Lund ahead.

Seth was first to spot the boat. "There they are. Check out the way Jess is tuggin' away on the oars. No wonder it took so long to catch up. She must have a super-charged Hemi hidden under her hood."

Staring downstream, Travis could see his bud was right. Like Seth had done most of the morning, Jess was working the oars as if listening to a rock station—in, yank, up, back—in, yank, up, back—a steady, uninter-rupted rhythm.

"She better slow down or she's gonna get blisters, just like me," Seth mumbled, barely loud enough for Travis to interpret.

"Don't think so. Check out her hands. It's hard to tell from so far away, but it looks like she did something you shoulda done without being told."

Seth peered intently ahead, attempting to decipher what his friend was prattling about. "Okay, Hawkeye. I give up. What she'd do that I didn't?"

Lifting the paddle and pointing it like a shotgun, Travis said. "Check out her hands. From where I sit, I see brown—like in a pair of gloves or maybe Bob's socks. She isn't gonna get any blisters, just a sore back from lugging on those long sticks without taking a break."

"How'd ya like that little set of rapids?" Seth asked as the canoe came alongside.

Jess stopped pulling long enough to answer. "No big deal. Actually they were kind of fun. The boat didn't wobble at all. It zipped through with only a few little bumps. How 'bout you guys? Have any trouble?"

"Naw, it was sweet...like cookies, cake, and chocolate ice cream. I don't think Trav even had to paddle hard, just enough to keep us straight."

"Bob, you want Seth and me to lead the way? You know, like we did before crossing that last lake? Make certain you don't hit any fast water?" Travis asked.

The senior sat erect. He fidgeted for a moment, centering the belt on his khaki trousers so the buckle wouldn't cut into his stomach. Satisfied, he looked up. "Yup. That'd probably be best. Who knows? These wilderness rivers tend to be fickle—smooth and calm one minute, all jumbled up the next."

With a shove Seth pushed the Wenonah away, stuck his paddle in the water, and took a couple of pulls. Nothing extraordinary came into view as the canoe completed the curve. The channel was clear, the current flat, and similar forest foliage embraced the riverbank.

Seth kept to himself, dangling one arm, then the other in the water. It wasn't until they were finished floating a straight stretch did he speak. Peering over his shoulder, he studied the boat trailing some distance behind.

"You know, don't you?" he said, "Pretty soon you're gonna have to take a turn rowing. Jess won't be able to keep going like she is. She's gonna burn herself out."

Travis let the paddle drag and then carefully pivoted to look. What Seth said was true. From the way the oars dipped and rose, dipped and rose, Jess would be exhausted in no time flat.

"Probably. But we can let her decide when it's time to switch. Who knows, maybe she rests now and then when we aren't looking."

Travis had figured right. Jess knew she couldn't row without taking a break every few minutes. She'd have to pace herself. So she started counting strokes in her head, setting up a work rhythm.

After approximately fifty pulls, she'd lift the paddle end of the oars inside the gunnels. They caught a break while she rotated shoulders and arms, loosening aching joints. After a minute or two, she'd lean forward and jingle-jangle her hands.

With exercise completed, Jess would pick up the pot and bail. When satisfied enough water had been removed, she'd sit stone still, letting her body relax. Feeling better, she'd grab the oar handles and begin the cycle all over again.

"Uncle Bob," she said, snapping the man's eyes open. "This may be a dumb question, but how come sometimes the tree branches along shore look like they've been trimmed with a saw? You know, like they do with trees in a park."

Bob shook his head, shaking cobwebs clear. He didn't speak for a time, contented to gaze at the tree-lined river bank. Jazzi was right. The trees, mostly spruce, did appear to be pruned from the ground up.

For a few seconds Jess was worried that her uncle had lost his power of speech. But he hadn't. Instead he was trying to visualize the surroundings through a newcomer's eyes. Things he and the boys didn't think twice about were new to a city kid.

Jess was about to drop the oars and ask a how ya doin'

question when Bob cleared his throat.

"Well Jazzi," he drawled, "this far north, summer's a pretty short season. Couple of warm months under an eighteen-hour sun lamp, and wham, before you know it, Old Man Winter starts pushing down from the north. Come the end of August, first of September, most leafy trees change color. Soon after that, they drop their leaves."

He again cleared his throat, coughed, and then leaned over the side of the boat to spit.

"So what you're looking at is something we refer to as a browse line. Some winters—when the snow gets deep—moose and deer migrate to riverbanks or the shorelines of lakes. What you see there is how high they can reach with their teeth. Even if the needles aren't nourishing, they want to put something in their bellies."

When Bob finished all she said was, "Cool. It's been bugging me since the first day. And now I know."

As the sun peeked past a cloud, Bob closed his eyes and tipped his head to catch some rays. The sudden sun-burst lighted the waterway, reflecting off the dappled surface with the brilliance of a thousand stage lights.

In the middle seat, Jess clutched the oars and went back to work.

"What does that Mickey Mouse watch of yours say?" Seth asked. "My guess is it's about three-thirty."

Travis clutched the paddle in one hand and looked at his wrist. The birthday timepiece received a few days earlier already looked shabby. The band had been in the water so many times the leather had discolored. Rather than a new cowhide brown, it was closer to midnight black.

"Almost. It's twenty after," Travis announced.

Seth swiveled sideways and craned his neck toward the stern. For a moment he studied the straight stretch of river behind the canoe. "When's the last time you turned to look for the Lund? I don't see it."

Travis halted mid-stroke. Careful not cause the Wenonah to wiggle, he slowly rotated to check the view to the rear. Except for pot-bellied clouds, it appeared like the scene ahead—bluish-brown channel—numerous shades of green—nothing out of the ordinary.

"It's been a while. I've been doin' some wishful thinking about what I'd like to eat when we get to the resort, a California or a pizza with all the toppings."

Seth turned hastily to face front, waggling the canoe

from side to side. "I've been doin' some day-dreaming myself. Gotta wonder what's up with the wedding. I suspect it's been postponed."

Travis made several wide strokes, realigning the canoe with the flow. "Ya think we should pull in and wait, let 'em catch up?"

Seth's disheveled hair wiggled back and forth. "Naw, there's no reason to do that. For the past half hour the current's been as quiet as a country cemetery. Let's keep going until we get around that next bend. Then we'll beach the canoe and take a whiz without Jess seeing anything she shouldn't."

"Ha! In your case that probably wouldn't be very much. Umm...to change the topic—and I know it's only been a little while—how are the blisters? They hurt?"

Seth pulled in his arms to inspect his palms. "You know, they aren't as bad as I first thought. The swelling seems to have gone down some. I think if I were to wrap 'em up, I could probably lend you a hand."

Still smoldering from his pal's lack of common sense, Travis didn't comment.

"What? Did you swallow your tongue?" Seth asked after several minutes of silence. "Do you want my help or not?"

Travis yanked on the paddle. "There's really no reason for you to aggravate your sores. And we wouldn't be saving any time. We're already too far ahead. There's no need to hurry up and wait. Best to save your strength in case we hit rough water."

* * *

Jess was troubled. She sat sideways on the seat and stared ahead. Only trees and water for as far as she could see. The canoe had vanished. She turned back to the rear, worry increasing with every whoop. Her uncle had been coughing unchecked for over five minutes.

Letting the oars drag, Jess bent forward and squeezed his knee. "Uncle Bob, do you want me to row the boat to shore? You could get out and lie down, catch your breath."

Wheezing to grab a gulp of air, the senior shook his head. He pointed to an oar, coughed several more rasps, and whispered, "Keep going, Jazzi. As long as you have the oomph, keep going."

Jess grasped up the wooden handles and returned to pulling. Moments later, the boat jumping forward in oar induced spurts, they arrived at a wide sweeping curve. She swiveled to take another forward look.

Ahead lay a flat stretch of channel. After a moment of mental calculation, she estimated it to be at least a half-mile long. With exception of the marshy mini-lake, the longest straight section they'd encountered.

She almost missed seeing them. The canoe was closing in on the far curl, where the stream disappeared in a turn. Without a second thought, she stood and started flailing her arms, hoping to gain the boys' attention.

The effort went unrewarded. Both boys were facing front. And unfortunately, neither chanced a last glance before rounding the corner.

* * *

There was a very good reason the boys hadn't bothered looking back. Just as the canoe entered the curve, the river narrowed. Enough that Seth thought it prudent to clutch tight to his own paddle. With the stream squeezed between banks of bedrock, the speed doubled, jetting the Wenonah through the turn and into an even narrower chute.

By then it was too late to change course. They were

committed to riding out the whitewater or risk rolling over. Caught between rock-faced mini-cliffs, and with a dashing current, beaching wasn't an option.

"Look out! There's a big boulder dead ahead. Trav, quick! Go right! Go right!" Seth bellowed, coming to life with a rush of adrenaline.

Travis made three sweeping strokes and held his breath as the canoe grazed a sharp block of granite.

"Whoa! That was close!" He hollered, glancing downstream. But what lay ahead made his insides cartwheel.

Not only did the channel pinch between cliff-like walls, it started falling. So much drop that the water whipped and roiled, leapt and skipped —and as it did—the current churned out long chains of frothy suds.

"Holy cow! There's no end to it!" Seth yelled in a high-pitched tenor.

Travis wasn't listening. He could see for himself. The torrent of whitewater appeared to extend without end— to the next bend—more than a quarter mile distant.

He sucked in his breath, mentally crossed his fingers, and frantically increased his effort. If they were to stay alive through the series of drops, he'd have to keep the canoe on a forward moving course; one faster than the flow. Getting pushed sideways would be an instant calamity.

* * *

Jess was spent. She had to take a break. Letting the oars trail, she sat upright, rotating shoulders, grabbing air in bursts.

Bob had quelled the coughing attack. For several minutes he'd been bent over, arms crisscrossed on knees, face hidden in the bulk of the orange preserver, apparently resting.

When she regained her breath, and muscles stopped quivering, she made a suggestion. "Uncle Bob, maybe we should go in to shore and lie down for a few minutes. I'm pooped."

The man didn't respond.

She repeated the question using a loader voice. "Uncle Bob? Do you think we should take a timeout?"

Again, no answer—except for the gurgling stream, wind rustling leaves, and a bird cry far off in the background, all was quiet. Despite her overheated, sweaty state, a chilled quiver raced down her spine. She sat frozen in place—petrified—her mind conjuring up a terrible image. It had to have happened! The ordeal had been too much. Her uncle must have suffered a second life-ending stroke.

Unattended, the Lund continued floating with the current, closing in on the curve. After moments of silent shivering, a recently familiar sound reached Jess: the burble of gushing water.

She turned in her seat to get her bearings. They were closing in on the place where the canoe had vanished from view.

With tense willpower, and without looking at her uncle, Jess clutched the oars. Then she tugged with all her might, turning the Lund toward the riverbank. If her fear was reality, she wanted to be on land when learning for certain.

* * *

"Pull hard! Pull hard!" Seth screamed. "Left! Left! Stroke left! Now quick, pull on the other side!"

On the edge of terror, Travis was desperately trying to follow Seth's ever-changing commands. Twice the Wenonah clunked hard on boulders, nearly capsizing, so close to that water spilled over the sides.

But for some unexplainable reason, the canoe stayed afloat; over rocks, rapids, and boiling swirls of liquid. The canoe was closing in on the next blind curve. Although neither had a clue to what waited around the bend, their paddles remained a brownish blur as they thrust in and out. If either were to dawdle, the Wenonah would be the river's toy, something to roll, twirl, or swallow.

Then, just as abruptly as it had begun, the wild ride was over. Like the last leg of a roller coaster, the stream turned, leveled, and slowed. The rock-lined shore lost its hold as more and more evergreens sprouted along the edge. A little farther down the channel widened, the flow evened, and the surface steadied.

The only telltale sign of what the youths had endured were remnants of foam; small villages of bubbles floating serenely along the surface.

"Man! We caught a break! For a while I thought we were gonna be freakin' waterlogged bear bait," Seth bawled once Travis had the Wenonah targeted toward an opening on shore.

Seth scrambled out an instant before the bow bumped land. He stood calf-deep and held the canoe steady. "I owe you one. You probably saved my life."

Out of immediate danger, Travis suddenly felt weak, and for a time, too limp to do anything but slump in his seat. After a long moment, he squeaked, "What d'ya mean your life? I was tryin' to save my own skin. I'm not a cat, sure don't have nine of 'em. I thought we were gonna lose it."

He closed his eyes and sent up a silent thank you. That done, he added, "I wouldn't want to try going through there a second time. At least not without a life jacket strapped tight to my chest."

Seth busied himself with the line. He wrapped the cord around a tree, strung it back to the center thwart, and made a knot.

Satisfied the canoe would stay parallel to the bank, he asked, "Did you wanna get out and stretch? Or maybe we should start hiking upstream? Sure hope Jess had the sense to pull in before hitting the whitewater."

Travis thought for a time before he said, "Steady the canoe, would ya? I'm gonna get up on the bank."

Seth did as asked, and then repeated the question. "What's it going be? Wait here, or hike upstream?"

"Well, if Bob didn't recognize that there were rapids 'round that curve, the boat could be shooting through anytime. Maybe we should stay put for a while, see what happens."

Travis glanced at his watch. "Let's give 'em fifteen minutes. If they're not here by then, we can start walking. If Jess pulled in, one of us can put on the life jacket and row the boat through. If the canoe didn't swamp, the Lund isn't gonna tip. With its fat back and high sides, it should bump its way down here without too much worry."

"Maybe, if it doesn't get banged up on that rocky stretch; knock a hole where the rivets are loose." Seth added. "You know, don't you, that the one who brings it through will have to face front. Rowing with your back to the rapids would be real risky. You won't be able to see to steer around boulders."

"Hey!" Travis interrupted. "Why d'ya keep saying 'you'? You're the rowing expert."

Seth held out his hands. "Yeah, well maybe before I was. But it looks like picking up the paddle without wrapping 'em was the wrong thing to do. The blisters broke, all of 'em."

Travis winced. Seth's palms looked like uncooked ham-
burger, splotched with red, raw skin. And to add to the
grisly picture, blood was dripping from the week-old
cut, apparently ripped open from the hectic activity.
Seth's turns at rowing were null and void. If the Lund
had to be piloted through the rapids, there'd be only one
candidate for captain—Mr. and Mrs. Larsen's first born.

* * *

Jess managed to wedge the bow into a V-shaped opening between a windfall and a big boulder. Satisfied the
boat would stay put, and though her insides were a jan-
gle of nervous expectancy, she stayed glued to her seat,
uncertain what to do.

Bob hadn't moved so much as a muscle, not the slightest twitch. Even the abrupt stop as aluminum crunched
rock hadn't caused him to stir. He remained bent at the
waist, face buried in the sleeves of his shirt.

As she sat frozen with fear, lost in jumbled thought, it
dawned on Jess that her feet were wet. Preoccupied
with rowing, she'd neglected to tend the bailing pot.

Needing to do something—anything—she grabbed the
pan. Then she lifted her legs over the seat and faced front.
With a jerky motion, she started scooping and pouring,
scooping and pouring, oblivious to the tears streaking
down her cheeks. When there was nothing left to bail,
she dropped the pan with a clunk, and then sat motion-
less, a disturbed nest of wasps buzzing in her head.

What now?

Hesitantly, Jess chanced another look. No change. Her
uncle remained stooped and still, immobile as a depart-
ment store mannequin. A part of her mind said 'go
ahead, reach out and shake a knee.' Another part said
'leave well enough alone—there's not a thing you can do.'

Heart pounding like a runaway freight train, Jessie spun around to face her uncle. Leaning in close, she strained to hear if he was breathing. For a few horrible moments, she heard nothing, then a wheezy, rattling breath broke the silence.

Slightly giddy, Jessie gripped her uncle's knee. "Uncle Bob," she said, past the lump in her throat, "I'm going to walk ahead to see if the stream gets too rough. I'll be right back."

He gave no response, but Jessie felt a bit reassured by her words. A quick walk to scope out the stream was the break that she needed from rowing and then the paralyzing fear that had crept in when she thought her uncle was dead. Rummaging in her pack, she pulled out a Tootsie Pop to savor on her walk, then scrambled out of the boat and up the rocky bank. To her amazement, there was an animal trail meandering along the shore. With tingly nerves, she turned to take a last look. Bob still hadn't moved.

Chapter Twenty-Two

C H A P T E R T W E N T Y - T W O

Projects were completed. Tent sites had been cleared, fire rings constructed, boats rigged and waiting for the first flight of fishermen. The pilots were calling it a day.

The woman piloting the Beaver was first to notice the SOS. How in the world, she wondered, had they missed seeing the message when landing?

By radio, she communicated the find to her colleague. Then, after a circling approach, she set the floatplane near shore. With a burst of prop wash, the floats came to rest on the sandy section of cove. Minutes later, dangling from a tree next to a little blue tent, the woman discovered a plastic covered note.

Meanwhile her partner remained airborne, circling in wide arcs, waiting for a second broadcast. When the callback came, the two quickly developed a plan.

The Otter would fly directly to the survivors' destination, a not-so-distant fishing camp. By air the lodge was mere minutes away. He'd inform the outfitter of the predicament. They could throw a boat on a trailer, maybe even round up guests willing to give up an evening of fishing, and then all could scoot down the gravel lane to the wooden bridge.

If the teens hadn't yet arrived at the crossing, the boat could be used to go upriver, at least to Bear Paw Rapids. But that would be as far as the motor boat could travel. At that point the current plummeted over rocks, the flow too active for upstream passage. Bear Paw was 'expert only' whitewater, a dangerous section only experienced kayakers dare attempt.

The Beaver pilot would continue observing the channel—hoping to locate living treasure—three young adults and one senior—alive and well.

Within minutes of finding the note, the woman was airborne, winging toward the outlet end of the lake.

* * *

The boys heard the airplane long before they saw it. For a time it was fly speck in the distance; a vibration in the background. Moments later, it was a wide-winged bird roaring overhead in a display of color and noise.

"You think they saw us?" Seth yelled, staring off in the direction of the plane's passage.

"I doubt it, too many trees. But let's hope they spotted the boat. If Jess stopped before the rapids, they'd be at the end of that straight stretch. It'd be a lot easier to see the boat than us."

The boys were laboring along the faint trail bordering the river, not certain if it was the right thing to be doing. They'd waited the fifteen minutes without results. After pulling the Wenonah from the water, they started off on foot.

"Listen! Hear that? It sounds like the plane's coming back!" Seth yelled excitedly. "Let's go!"

Without waiting for a reply, he spun and started jogging in the direction they'd just come. Travis broke into trot and followed in his friend's footsteps. Reaching the canoe, and without missing a beat, they grabbed the gunnels. Then, almost as if they'd rehearsed the action, lifted and then plopped the craft into water without missing a beat.

Seth held the bow while Travis half-crawled, half-stumbled to the rear. The teen grabbed his paddle and began waving it in the air, hoping to catch the pilot's eye.

The boys had no way of knowing, but she'd already made a sighting—one small boat with a single passenger—free-floating toward Bear Paw. After putting the Beaver though a tight turn, her attention was focused farther upstream. Passing over the boys' heads, she hadn't a clue there was a paddle-waving adolescent directly under the wing.

"Shoot!" Travis spat disgustedly after the plane howled past. "There's no way on God's green earth they can see us if they keep flying directly over the channel. Not unless that old bird has a glass bottom."

"Yeah, but stay put. Maybe the pilot will take another run at it," Seth said, seemingly unaware that he was standing knee deep in icy water.

Travis's scowl suddenly broke into an inspirational smile. "Keep your pants on! We're a couple of block-heads. They had to have spotted the Lund. Why else would the pilot make such a quick one-eighty?"

Seth thumped his forehead for the umpteenth time that day. "You know, you're right. So how 'bout you gettin' out of the boat before my toes turn blue."

* * *

Jess also heard the plane as she approached the bend where the river started to drop. She paused to wipe away tears and was just about to start off again when the distant growl of an airplane engine put her on full alert.

Suddenly recognizing what she heard, Jessie scurried

out of the woods and scampered to the river's edge. Moments later a low-flying floatplane roared past, vanishing over the forest in a blink of an eye.

Although she had waved, screamed, and jumped up and down, Jess reached the same conclusion as the boys. Veiled by leaves and needles, there was no way a pilot or passengers could have seen anything but river, rocks, and tree tops. Sucking in a deep gasp to calm jittery nerves, she turned her back to the water.

Had she not been so quick be on her way, Jess would have witnessed what the pilot had seen; one old aluminum boat floating with the current with an elderly male occupant, slumped as if sleeping.

* * *

Twenty minutes after the radio reply, the second pilot had his aircraft secured to the outfitter's pier. Once on land he had a bit of good fortune. A husband and wife fishing duo were about to head for home and their modern wide-hulled boat was strapped tight to a heavy duty trailer, hitched to their pickup and ready to roll.

Moments later the pilot, outfitter, and the boat's owners bustled into the crew cab. The Ford's big engine came to life with the first turn of the key. After spitting out a spray of gravel, the rear tires found purchase and rocketed the rig across the open parking area. The pickup slowed before turning onto a dirt road, trailing a brown haze to mark its sudden passage.

After overhearing the pilot's account, the lodge's four other guests abandoned fishing plans. Leaving an early supper untouched, the group jumped into their SUV. Escaping from the parking lot dust cloud, the Chevy slid around the corner, and with a heavy foot on the pedal, pursued the pickup down the primitive road.

The fishermen had stopped on the trestle on their way

to the lodge. So all were aware the site lacked a landing ramp. For a boat to be launched, the rig would have to be slid down a rock-strewn grade, and then—trees and other vegetation permitting—man-handled to the river's edge. The more hands to help, the sooner the boat would be in the water.

* * *

"So now what?" Seth muttered.

The boys were standing idle near the canoe. They'd pulled the Wenonah partially out of the water and had tied it to a tree. Seth was jiggling his feet up and down, trying to warm toes.

"Don't know. Maybe we should stay put, see what happens next."

Seth put a halt to his foot shuffling to peer at the river. Except for scattered chains of foam, the channel was a blank sheet. "Or, maybe we should split up. One of us stay here, see if the Lund comes along. The other head upstream, see if Jess pulled in and is waitin' for us."

Travis reached up and broke a dead branch off an overhanging limb. He started peeling the bark off, considering the idea. After a spell, he said, "Yeah. Let's do that. You want to stay here while I go look?"

"Naw, I'll go. My toes are cold. Walking will warm 'em up."

Travis went quiet again, his head cocked to the side, listening. "Hear that? It sounds like that floatplane's flying in circles. What d'ya suppose that means?"

Seth cupped a raw hand to an ear. After a moment he twitched his head in accord. "It means for certain they've spotted the Lund. Bob probably saw the whitewater and had Jess pull over."

"If that's true, do you really want to be the one to take

the Lund through the rapids? What about your blisters?"

Seth thought about that for only a short second. "Ah, remember earlier? It looked like Jess was wearing gloves, or at least covered her hands with socks. I can borrow 'em. With the way the river drops, I'll be mostly steering anyway. I'll manage somehow."

He turned to leave. Then, just as he was about to slip behind a screen of leaves and needles, Travis yelled a bit of advice. "Hey! Remember to wear the life jacket. I know you swim like a fish, but better safe than sorry."

Seth paused to look over his shoulder. "Okay, Mother. I won't forget. Just be here when I get back."

When she'd started off, the path roamed but never strayed far from the river. Not now. Now the path angled inland and the only clue she was near the stream was an occasional murmur from water burbling over boulders. But the babbles were whisper soft, filtered by an ever-widening barrier of evergreens. Jess pushed on, hoping that sooner or later the trail would wind its way back to the channel.

Instead, the trail all but vanished. Jess never felt so isolated. Not even the bear scare had been this frightening. At least then she knew company was nearby. She stopped short. But what was she hearing now? A rustling sound, and the snap of a twig reached her. The boys must be walking back; maybe the stream was too rough and they were trying to find her to warn her.

"Travis?" she called. "Seth?" No answer. "No jokes, you guys. I think Bob needs help."

Still no answer. Becoming annoyed, she pushed through a thick tangle of undergrowth, right where she heard the sounds. As the bear looked up, startled, Jessie screamed and ran for her life.

* * *

245

Travis was in a state of nervous anticipation, relieved that the wild adventure was almost over. Needing something to pass the time, he pulled his survival tool from its belt holster. For a few seconds he cradled the shiny device in his hand, checking for rust. Finding the stainless steel good as new, he unfolded the knife blade and then started whittling on the now bare branch.

With the floatplane's return passage, and continued circling, Travis felt confident this unplanned chapter was about to close. In a matter of hours they'd be gnawing away on a gut-busting meal.

A distant clunking caught his ear. Travis dropped the branch and stepped to the river's edge. Peering upstream through limbs and leaves, he was stunned to see the Lund.

Though it was still some distance off, he could see that it was riding low; the hull looking even more bent and bruised than before. Travis glanced down at his watch. It wasn't possible. No way could Seth have covered the half mile or more in such a short time. He had only been gone a matter of minutes.

Both curious and concerned, Travis stepped into the current. Without overhanging branches obscuring his line of sight, he was able to focus clearly on the boat. He stared in disbelief. He saw only one passenger, unmoving, and it appeared to be Bob.

Travis suddenly felt queasy, and some of his confidence drained away. Maybe his daydreams of a happy ending had been premature.

Chapter Twenty-Three

C H A P T E R   T W E N T Y - T H R E E

The man awoke groggy, wet, and befuddled. It took some time to grasp what was happening. He was sitting in the back of a boat bouncing and banging over rocks and boulders. And he was alone.

The last thing he recalled was being in the midst of a coughing spasm. One so long and severe he couldn't catch his breath. Then, like theater lights before the movie starts, everything had faded to black.

But he hadn't been alone then. His niece had been manning the oars. His pulse raced into overdrive. Oh God! No! Jazzi must have fallen overboard to flounder through the rapids without a preserver.

A jarring crunch of metal on rock, accompanied by a drenching spray, completed the wake up call, jolting the man to life. Though stiff and shaky, he bent forward and grasped an oar.

Then, as he pulled with all his might, righting the boat to the flow, he had a second thought. His niece could swim like an otter. Maybe there was a chance, maybe she'd made it safely to shore. But he'd never know unless he saved himself first.

Struggling to lean forward, he clutched the second handle with his weakened hand. Then sitting rigid, he braced himself for the ride of his life.

* * *

Like a sports replay in slow motion, time seemed to slog for Travis. After a bumpy voyage through fast water, the boat appeared to have stopped mid-stream, almost as if pausing to ask the river 'Is that the best you can do?'

Travis stayed on the bank, eyes riveted on the small craft. The question was printed in bold type—why? Why was Bob alone? He stood trembling, uncertain if the shakes were from wet feet or the horrible image spinning about in his brain.

As he stood there gaping, Travis became aware of engine noise coming from the sky. The aircraft had gained altitude and was circling high overhead.

Travis took his eyes from the river and looked up. He recognized the model. He'd seen one like it at Devil Track. His father called it a Beaver, the workhorse of the wilderness. As he looked on, the aircraft slipped farther to the north, almost out of sight. Before refocusing on the Lund, Travis saw the wings waggle.

He returned his attention to the water. Like an unwatched pot, the boat had made progress. It had picked up speed and was closing the gap. Fast enough, Travis thought, that it'd pass by in minutes.

Should he use the Wenonah? Paddle mid-stream and wait to make an intercept? But what would he do then? Could he manage two boats in the current? He wasn't certain but he could try.

Just as he was about to untie the canoe's cord, the boat's passenger sat tall in the rear seat.

"Over here! Over here!" Travis roared. "If you can do it, bring the boat over here!"

It proved to be a battle, but with Bob sculling, and with Travis wading hip high to grab a gunnel, the Lund had been brought to shore. Once the boat was secured, Travis helped the old man escape to dry land.

Only then did he dare ask. "Jessie? What about Jessie? Where is she?"

Perched on the Lund's bow plate, Bob slowly shook his head. He hacked, made a series of grunting sounds, and then spit into the river.

"I don't know, Trav. I don't know. I must have passed out. All I remember is we were floating that long spell of smooth water. That's when I had a coughing jag."

He stopped, stared at Travis, and then brought up a hand to cover his eyes. Bob snuffled as if to stifle a sob, pinched his nose, and then went on. "All I can tell you... that when I came to...I was alone. Jazzi was gone."

Travis was about to say something when Seth suddenly bounced out of the brush. "Came back after I caught a glimpse of the boat passing downstream. Good deal. You guys made it through the—"

But then, reading Bob's face, the unfinished sentence hung in the air like the stench of dead fish. Seth eyes darted around the opening but came up empty. "No! No way! She swims too good."

Travis locked on to his friend's eyes. "Did you see any sign of her along the path?"

Seth broke off the stare, choosing instead to focus on the river. "No," he said so softly Travis had to strain to hear. "No. I didn't see a thing."

All three went quiet. Finally Travis spoke. "Look. That floatplane had to have spotted the boat. I saw it tip its wings back and forth, over that way, where the bridge should be," he said, pointing north.

"We're gonna have company soon. I'm sure of it. Seth, I want you to start a smoky fire. It'll let the pilot know exactly where we are. Besides, Bob needs to warm up and dry off."

Seth shot his buddy a bewildered look. "What's up with that? You're the expert at starting fires."

"Just do it, okay? I'm gonna go look for Jess. Maybe she's stranded upriver. In the meantime, if the airplane has radioed for a rescue boat, and it arrives before I return, you and Bob go ahead. Let them haul the two of you out of here."

For a moment Seth was dumfounded. Travis never gave orders, only suggestions. "Hey! No way. If somebody should come for us, they can take Bob first. Okay with you, Bob?"

Bob had been only half-listening. He was trying to piece together possible explanations for his solo whitewater run. His teary pupils went first to Seth, then to Travis. "You know, I am cold. A fire would be nice. As for that help coming, we'll just have to wait and see."

The man's gaze sank to the needle dappled earth. When he looked up again, his wet eyes seem to hold a slight sliver of hope.

"Go find her, Travis. Go find my Jazzi girl."

* * *

Jess didn't pause until she was well past the rocky bend. She had been running fast as legs would allow. But like any engine pushed full throttle, her fuel gauge was rapidly tilting toward the empty mark.

First slowing to a jog, then a walk, she finally stopped, uncertain how far she'd traveled. For a time she stood bent, hands on her knees, winded. When her breathing slacked enough to allow her to look around, she did.

The river was to her right. That fact offered a morsel of comfort. At least she wasn't lost. Moments earlier she'd recognized the bend where she'd waved at the airplane. So, if she had things straight in her head, the Lund should be a little further upstream. She would just go back that far. She'd rather wait in the boat than take her chances with the bear.

* * *

Travis never ran so far, so fast. Twice he was victim of nasty spills, tripped by unseen roots rising to snag the toe of a tennis shoe. Both times he bounced back to his feet and trotted on, seemingly unaware of overhead limbs slapping cheeks or branches scratching and clawing unprotected skin.

He had to find her. Had to! This last chapter had to close with a joyful ending. If not, he'd have to share the blame.

This trip had been his idea in the first place. A small seed he'd planted months ago in his parents' heads. And they'd gone along with it. Even after his close calls. He was blessed to have such understanding folks. Parents that trusted him to make wise decisions, safe decisions—smart choices.

Travis paused for a breather and then listened with both ears. Although surrounded by thick foliage, he could make out the sound of the river. Its laughs and gurgles, though softened by forest growth, were unmistakable just yards away through the woods.

He studied the faint animal path. To him, the trail was as bold as headlines. But he knew what to look for; all the little clues—the easiest route through trees and around windfalls—packed needles and leaves—exposed earth—broken twigs and branches.

But would Jess be able to read these subtle signs? Not likely. So maybe she panicked. Maybe, like she'd said that very first day, she gotten lost as soon as she couldn't see water.

No. Travis didn't think that held true. Jess was smart. She'd learned to take one small step at a time. He didn't think running off in any and all directions would be something she'd do.

As he stood there, catching his breath, a slight bit of worry weight sloughed from his shoulders. At least now he was certain Jess couldn't have been in the boat. For lying on the faint trail was an orange Tootsie Pop, half-covered in dirt.

Travis dropped to his knees. Maybe he could find footprints, see which way she went. He could make out his own running tracks; scuff marks with bits of overturned forest debris. There were similar markings farther upstream. That didn't make sense. Jess should have been moving downstream, around the rapids.

He was kneeling when he saw the final clue. Just off the trail, in the middle of a low soft depression, was a very fresh, very large paw print. And he had the answer.

Jess must have startled a bear, and in return, the big bruin had no doubt startled her. Jess must've run for her life.

Travis hoped the bear had done the same, only in the opposite direction.

* * *

With six backs and twelve hands, the boat slid into the river without delay. The outfitter, along with the boat's owner, would be the only ones making the voyage. In case there was a need for immediate medical attention, they wanted space for passengers.

With a wave of crossed fingers from the riverbank gallery, the boat motored upstream. Seth and Bob would be getting visitors very soon. The outfitter knew they had to go four and half miles. He'd gleaned that info from the floatplane pilot. Because before securing the Otter, the aviator had grabbed a hand-held radio. At first sighting of smoke, the Beaver pilot had circled back, and after seeing Seth's waving arms, radioed her partner.

Chapter Twenty-Four

C H A P T E R   T W E N T Y - F O U R

Jess was perplexed. It looked like the spot where she'd parked the boat. But the Lund was gone. Could there be two such places that looked so much alike? Each with a fallen tree and a large boulder nestled V-like along the bank? She didn't think so.

Would this nightmare never end? Like a poorly written paperback, this story got worse page by page. Had her uncle taken the boat, or had she missed the boys in the woods? Maybe even now one of them was on his way back here, to walk with her down the stream. Jessie certainly didn't want to go back into the thick woods alone. Best to wait right here, she decided, settling against a sun-warmed boulder. It felt good to lean her head back and close her eyes.

* * *

The first part of Jessie's path was a walk in the park, as easy as following a fresh bread crumb trail. Because Jess had been running full speed, her Nikes had kicked up bits of forest duff. Travis never had to slow.

But things changed when he arrived at the big bend. There the forest thinned and the ground became rocky. He made an abrupt stop, eyes scanning the hard earth for any hint she'd passed this point.

Maybe the first thing to do was to try a little shouting. He sucked in a lungful of air, cupped his hands to his mouth and bellowed. "Jessie! Jessie, where are you? If you can hear me, holler!"

He placed the bill of his cap up to an ear to act as a hearing aid. Mostly silence, only the river's babble and the cawing of a raven reached his eardrum.

Travis noted what could be a hint of a trail at the far end of the opening. Lacking other options, he trudged in that direction. Once the ground softened again, he began crawling along on all fours. He hadn't gone far when he found what he was searching for—shoe prints.

One was soft and shallow, heading downstream. The other, much deeper, was aiming in the opposite direction.

* * *

Seth waved the boat to shore. After a briefing from Bob, the outfitter was forced to make a decision. Years earlier he had worked as a medic in the service. He recognized the elderly man's need for an immediate health check.

And he'd also heard the forecast. A large low was sliding over the region, dragging with it low clouds and heavy showers. He wanted to get the gentleman to a doctor as soon as possible. An overnight delay might mean being hemmed in by foul weather for days on end.

Plans were quickly made. Seth, healthy except for blistered hands, would remain at the site. He was to keep the fire burning until the boat returned, with luck, within the hour, two at the most.

If or when the Larsen youngster returned, he too, was to stay put. And because it sounded like the girl in question had fallen victim to whitewater, Search and Rescue would be notified.

Until the boat came back, Seth was to keep a close eye on the river. Because at this point, who knew what might come floating by.

* * *

Jess woke to the relentless hum of mosquitoes. Hundreds of the pesky little buggers hovered over the hood of her sweatshirt. She sat up, swiping a hand to clear her cheeks of biters. How long had she dozed? She hadn't meant to conk out. She gazed straight up. From the murky cast of the sky, nightfall appeared to be just around the corner.

No! She did not want to be in the woods at night alone!

That thought caused a shudder to rattle her bones. Quickly squashing that thought, she wondered instead why neither of the boys had made his way to this spot yet. Had she slept as Travis or Seth walked right past? There must be something slowing them down. Her heart skipped a beat: something must have happened to Uncle Bob.

Through a small opening, Jess caught a glimpse of movement. A second spine tingling image flashed—the bear. Dang! The bear had pursued her. But what could she do about it?

Seth's words came to the front; "More afraid of you than you are of them." The bear that had raided the cooler acted that way. One long shriek and the food-stealing furball took off like it had been blasted with buckshot. And this second bear had also turned tail when they'd almost collided. Maybe there was a slice of truth to what Seth had said.

But for some reason, this bear must have had a change of heart. And with its big nose, it obviously knew where she was. Jess searched the ground for something firm and stout. She needed a rock or limb. She didn't want to get that close, but if she had to, she'd slam a stick across the old fellow's snout.

* * *

Travis had called her name so often he was becoming hoarse. If she was in the area, Jess would have to be under a rock not to have heard. The rumble of the rapids was no longer a huge factor. He'd trekked a good quarter mile beyond that sound maker.

Search as he might, he hadn't seen any more shoe prints pointing upstream. He'd spotted two or three going the other way and that was confusing. If Jess had done a one-eighty, he should have run into her by now. He hadn't, and the afternoon was getting darker.

Thinking of nightfall, Travis looked up. Clouds were congregating. Chances were he'd be getting soaked later. But right now he needed a drink. The walking had warmed him, but running had made him thirsty.

* * *

Jess found the perfect club; a stout limb with a thick bulb of wood on one end that was shaped like an axe blade. Grasping the crude instrument in both hands, she hefted it over her head. Pretending that the bear was only feet away, she slashed the air in a downward sweep.

Satisfied, Jessie snuck into the woods. She'd come at him from downstream and scare him away from where she knew she had to go. Hefting the club once more, she crashed through the woods toward the bear, yelling as loud as she could.

* * *

Although sprawled flat on his stomach, Travis's outstretched hand couldn't quite reach water. If he wanted a drink, he'd have to step down to the river and balance on a rock.

He was in the process of doing just that when a hellish shriek shattered the afternoon air. The noise was so unexpected, so alien that Travis lost his footing. With arms wind-milling uselessly, he tumbled head over heels into the stream.

Unsure what had created the cry, he scrambled to his feet and stumbled deeper into the current; a wail of panic rising in his own throat.

And then he saw her—a crude club raised overhead, her face wild. Yet at that instant, though smeared by bug lotion, dirt, and tears, Travis thought that her face was the loveliest he'd ever seen. When his mind recoiled from the initial shock, he started laughing.

Then Travis did something so impulsive that he even surprised himself. Without another moment's hesitation, he staggered from the river, scampered up the bank, and wrapped his arms around his new friend. Embracing her in a bear hug, he lifted Jess off the ground and spun in a circle.

Once he set her down, it was Jessie's turn to squeeze. She flung her arms around Travis's neck, burrowed her face into his wet shirt, and began to laugh and cry at the same time. Travis was mildly surprised. With her spunk and grit, he hadn't expected a tearful reception. For a few moments Travis just hugged her. He'd never been this way with a girl before. Especially one, that up to a few hours ago, he didn't even know he cared about.

As Travis released her and gripped her shoulders, he smiled even more broadly. This chapter was going to have a happy ending after all. And maybe in the future, he'd be doing some writing of his own—pen pals with a very special new friend.

* * *

Once she calmed down, Jess could hardly believe the

words; that her uncle had awakened alone in the boat in the middle of the rapids; that he was alive and doing okay. As they arrived where the Lund was beached, Jessie's heart sang with joy. Not to leave any stone unturned, Jess also hugged Seth. But, as Travis respectfully observed, it wasn't nearly as long and tight as the one he'd been given.

Prodded on by the ever-darkening sky, the trio took a vote. They wouldn't wait for the boat to return. Leaving the duffels near the Lund where the rescue crew could retrieve them, they piled into the canoe and headed for the bridge.

'Sore-hand Seth' sat in the middle on the floor. But he didn't seem to mind. Jess handled the paddle like a pro, and he told her so.

The rescue boat's engine was about to be fired up when the canoe skimmed into sight. Onlookers were surprised but delighted to count three passengers. The skills of a professional search team wouldn't be needed after all.

* * *

After arriving at the lodge, Bob had refused to be airlifted out until he knew the fate of his young companions. He didn't have a long wait.

The senior had just finished sipping a bowl of chicken soup when the Chevy pulled in. With two long toots of its horn, a trio of smiling faces spilled out the passenger doors. Without delay, the jubilant teens tumbled through the lodge's wide entrance and into the large open dining area. There they smothered Bob in a sea of gentle back slaps, high fives, and in Jessie's case, a kiss on the cheek.

Once celebrating ebbed, and after making arrangements for the camping gear to be picked up and shipped home, Bob played the sympathy card. After promising to seek immediate medical attention in the states, he was able to convince the pilot to fly everyone back to Devil Track in one long leap. If they took off right away they could beat both the weather and sunset.

After a bit of good-natured haggling, the pilot relented, providing that the old man had a credit card they could use to refuel the big Otter. Bob did and the deal was done.

Several hours later the castaways witnessed a breathtaking sunset near the floatplane pier on Devil Track where their saga had its start.

Apparently the forecasters had gotten it right all along. The Boundary Waters Canoe Area Wilderness had basked under blue skies and light winds for an entire week—a string of perfectly delightful days. The only foul weather reported had been far to the north, up in the area of a spidery-looking lake.

about the author

Minnesota native Ron Gamer has held a passion
for woods and waters since early childhood days.
Now retired after thirty-four years of teaching in the
Robbinsdale School District, he continues to be active
in the outdoors. When not out fishing, bow hunting,
or piloting small aircraft around the state, Ron can be
found at his computer—creating realistic adventure
he hopes will be enjoyed by readers of all ages. To
read more about the Chance trilogy and Ron's school
presentations, visit www.RonGamer.com.

1949